THE CONSTANT RUMORS...

"Rumors? Don't tell me you're here because of some rumors." Was that why she seemed so eager to accompany him?

"Hell, no. I'm here because you asked me along to the wedding. Remember?"

"Well, yeah, but what's this about rumors?"

She rolled her eyes at him, at his patently stubborn refusal to understand what she was implying. "Oh, come on now, don't tell me you don't know what's being said about you?"

"Like what?" he grinned, truly wanting to know. He'd heard some rumors himself. Were they the same?

"Let's just say that you never miss an opportunity and you never leave a lady hanging."

"Oh. Those rumors." He laughed...

Lumau Publishing
Double Take © 2017 by Sonia Gay
Cover image © Coka / Shutterstock
Book and cover design © 2017 by Sonia Gay
and Lumau Publishing

ISBN: 978-0-9958376-6-9

Lumau Publishing
lumaupublishing@gmail.com

DOUBLE TAKE

Book Two of
the O'Farrell Legacy

S. M. Cross

BOOKS BY THE AUTHOR

The O'Farrell Legacy Series:
Mulligan's Dream
Double Take
Brandon: Bad Boy of Kinsale
A Winter Sky
C'Mere to Me

Celtic Dreams
By S M. Gay

I'll tell a tale of Ireland's blood
Where love and turmoil grow,
Where cupid's bow hath touch the hearts
And vanquished every foe.
***

A tale of Hank, so strong and true
And of his love, fair Laura.
Of broken hearts and broken dreams,
Of mending lives with honor.
***

Of Niall, whose love for Michael
Was censured and love forbidden
But in the dark and in their hearts
That love was never hidden.
***

So hark ye now and learn the tale
Of Ireland's children, free.
Of lives and loves, of romance sure
And O'Farrell's Legacy.
***

DOUBLE TAKE

A 'Guide to Irish Slang and Pronunciation'
can be found at the end of the book.

Chapter One

Niall felt Michael's hand on his arse, soft, caressing. Even through his dress pants, the warmth soothed and comforted. Or should have. But they were out in public, in a field before a great ruin of a castle in County Kerry, just west of Killarney, there to witness the joining of Niall's half-brother, Hank Mulligan, and his Canadian bride-to-be, Laura Foster, in holy matrimony.

The weather held fair, and was expected to according to Ciara, his younger sister who had, as many old people used to call it, 'the sight'. These days, people just said she was psychic. And she was. She'd predicted this wedding, this day, and said that if they all got together and had an early wedding, the rain wouldn't spoil it at all. So far, so good.

His identical twin brother was in attendance as well, as were all the O'Farrell siblings. Liam, the outgoing twin, the one who laughed and joked and dangled life from his little finger the way local fishermen played with a fish on a line. Nothing was too good for Liam. He had the world by the tail. An actor and a lady's man, he was the one who didn't care what people said, who thrived on rumor and innuendo. His photo was front page news, his antics made headlines. He was Ireland's hero, and he knew it. And loved it.

Not so Niall. The less people knew of him, the better. He was uncomfortable to the extreme in public, and having his brother's picture plastered in the news was bothersome to him. He neither wanted nor looked for attention from anyone, and so he stood, uncomfortable and edgy, feeling Michael's hand on his arse.

Michael pulled Niall close and kissed him quickly, fully on the lips.

"Change of heart?" Niall asked.

"Talk later. There's a wedding trying to take place," said Michael, his hand possessively resting on Niall's very delectable rear end.

"I thought you said ye'd never attend," he whispered hoarsely to Michael, ignoring the circular massage of Michael's fingers through the fabric.

"I had second thoughts," said Michael, his cultured English accent pouring into Niall's ears like a good whiskey. Smooth, intoxicatingly deadly. "Let's go inside."

They followed the family into the castle, to the one room that still remained with four walls and a ceiling. Hank was already standing at the altar they'd built, waiting for his bride.

Michael bent to say something in Niall's ear but was quickly shushed. "They're about to begin," Niall said.

Michael straightened, his hand once more straying to Niall's arse, his thumb hooked into the back pocket, almost, but not quite, concealed beneath the edge of Niall's jacket.

Niall shifted, felt Michael's hand cup the globe of his arse, and shifted again. The hand stayed. A look was exchanged; Michael winked. And so Niall stood with Michael's hand caressing his arse and the multitude of folk, there to witness Hank and Laura's wedding, also witnessing the possessiveness with which Michael claimed Niall. The only blessing was that everyone was standing in very close quarters because no one had thought to bring any chairs. It was an old castle, and they were in the only complete room—a room with a dirt floor and stone walls with niches where candles were lit and mirrors had been placed to reflect the candles' glow a hundred-fold. The effect had been staggeringly romantic and the old ruin seemed to glow with new life.

The room being small, any folk who could not squeeze in looked in from windows vacant of any coverings, or from the doors at either side of the room where entrance and egress to other parts of the castle lay. Niall felt lucky that only a few people would see the familiarity with which Michael possessed him in public.

Michael Johnson. A truly different sort. They had met at a conference in Amsterdam a few years back; they had been working for the same computer software company, Michael in London and Niall in Cork. Over the past year, though, Michael had relocated to Ireland to be closer to Niall and was prized enough to be re-hired in Cork to work alongside him. Neither of them worried too much about working in the same office, they just wanted to be together outside of work.

At least Niall thought they did. He was never sure where Michael was concerned. Michael, who was much more confident than Niall in his body, his looks, his sexuality. He was used to standing out in a crowd, him with his mixed Middle Eastern/English background. His swarthy good looks turned many heads, usually female. But those in the know would never mistake his masculinity as a tidbit for feminine wiles. Michael was as gay as they came.

Niall, also gay, was not so comfortable. Raised in a staunch Catholic family of four boys and one girl, he remembered always identifying with his younger sister, wishing he could play with her toys, and later on, watching the boys she went out with as she got older. He didn't care what they wanted of her. He only thought they might be interested in him.

Ciara was now a young woman, and he and Liam young men. Liam could get any woman he wanted. All four brothers possessed the full head of black, wavy hair and midnight blue eyes that seemed to be a trait within the family, inherited from their father. The only one who'd missed those attributes was Ciara. She had taken their mother's coloring, the blonde hair and clear emerald eyes of the fey folk. Even though their mam had no psychic ability beyond a mother's intuition, it was said that in generations past there had been a few that were that way, and Ciara was one of them.

The priest had concluded the ceremony, the bride and groom had kissed, and Michael turned Niall's face toward him with a firm grip on his jaw and planted one full on his mouth.

Niall pushed him off. "Cop on," he scolded.

But Michael only grinned. "You're the finest looking

man here," he said, his fine English accent so different from the chatter around them. Hank and Laura were walking out of the room and its makeshift altar that Liam had contrived with help from the design crew of the set of his latest film. His brother had connections, and no mistake, thought Niall.

Brandon, another brother, second oldest only to Henry, had pitched in to help. Brandon had been offered work by the men that delivered the altar and helped set up, but Brandon had only grinned and declined. It seemed he had a better gig going on down Kinsale way, with surfing, women, and something about taking tourists around. It was a craic gig, he'd said, and too good to give up in order to work for someone else where the women were maybe scarce.

* * *

Liam watched the crowds go off to enjoy the luncheon after the wedding. He was proud of himself and of his brothers for helping to get the altar set up and turn the castle's one complete room into a makeshift chapel, ready for the wedding. He'd cajoled and bugged the design team to help him out by building an altar out of scrap materials. It looked like stone but was mostly plywood, Styrofoam, and a lot of paint. Hank and Laura hadn't wanted a wedding at any of the churches in Killarney; they'd almost refused a Catholic wedding at all. Hank had wanted a pagan wedding. Laura hadn't cared. She was carrying their child and stated that, really, she just wanted it over and done with and legal in two countries: Ireland and Canada.

Liam had wanted to do it just for fun; to have the old

castle look like something out of a medieval movie, with knights and damsels and all the trimmings.

And so he had. They'd "borrowed" more than one piece from the film's properties house and re-created a religious sanctum for Hank and Laura. Liam couldn't have been more pleased. The best part was that his brothers had been involved. Niall had hung back but even he had come up with his own touch at the end. The mirrors behind the candles reflected light from the deep niches in the stone walls, niches that were once used as storage cupboards, likely for dishes, hundreds of years ago. It was a magical effect and Liam was happy with his brother's contribution. Niall didn't often think of such things. He was entirely unemotional, in Liam's eyes.

The woman on his arm, a supporting actress with a substantial role in the film, put her arm around him. "Let's go," she whispered huskily, and Liam was inclined to agree. He'd hired some buddies from the set to stop by before nightfall to gather up the bits and pieces that belonged to the company and, since it was now midafternoon, he knew they would be there within the next hour or two. In the meantime, his little actress would provide plenty of entertainment. He'd teased her when they first met, calling her Sine of the Jungle. But Miss Sine Maguire was no joke. She was as foxy as they came, a tall, copper-haired woman with luscious curves that Liam was curious to find out if they were all hers or not. He was pretty sure they were.

Sine had giggled at the jungle joke when he met her, telling him she'd heard it before and rolling her eyes in a tolerant fashion. Liam didn't care; rarely a phrase came out of his mouth these days that wasn't a quote from some film or play he'd been in.

His success as an actor was ramping up. Over the past month he'd been seen, and photographed, with no fewer than five women. Intimacy hadn't been a part of any of those relationships but one read through the tabloids would provide the reader with enough innuendo to draw an entirely different conclusion.

Instead, Liam had been watching Sine Maguire, and had been doing so for a long time now. He'd first come across her in an American film, but then she'd dropped off the radar for a while and suddenly shown up in Ireland. He didn't care how she got there; had in fact been quite impatient to get to know her and so had followed her around once she arrived on set, waiting for an opportunity to ask her out. While outwardly chasing the previous five females, he had set his sights on her alone. He could have asked the leading lady to be his date at his half-brother's wedding, and very nearly did. But Sine's arrival changed all that.

After the ceremony, everyone filed out of the castle to linger on the grounds and partake of the food and beverages that had been brought in, picnic style, for the event. Liam led Sine to the tables and grabbed two plates, then soon had them filled. While Sine carried two mugs of ale, he led her round to where some blankets had been spread and chose one in the shelter of the castle walls, away from the wind coming in from the sea.

He fed her, let her take food from his fingers, and was surprised when she held on to one lean digit, sucked the juices off, and let him slide it from her mouth to watch her lick her lips afterward. He was suddenly very glad she'd consented to spend the night with him.

And then it was time to toast the bride and groom and cut the wedding cake, and so they all stood around while Henry, as best man, and Sarah, Laura's best friend from home and maid of honor, said their speeches, encouraging the couple to kiss each time the gathering urged them to do so.

Liam wasted no time during such episodes, turning Sine's heart-shaped face to his to kiss the lips that seemed to cry out for it.

Niall, feeling Michael pull him into a hug, shrugged off his lover's touch. He was not an exhibitionist like his famous brother, and the fact that they were twins, which made his life more observable to the masses, convinced an introverted personality such as his to vigorously shun public displays of affection. Michael was not put off, he knew. There would be all the time they needed, later.

The crowd began to file out of the castle and down to the small parking lot at the base of the hill after the cake cutting ceremony. Friends helped load the excess into Henry's large van and soon Hank and Laura were on their way, leaving the revelers to party or go home as they chose.

The rest of the family all met up at a pub in Cahersiveen that boasted a large taproom with plenty of room to dance, if a band was in attendance, or just to gather round the tables in the center or the trestles at the room's edge. The place was hopping when they got there, and Liam noticed his twin, gaining more than his fair share of attention. He was used to that. Used to having himself and Niall confused by the masses who wanted an autograph and sometimes more, although right now, Liam's head had been shaved for the production they were still shooting. His normal locks might be absent but that didn't throw off the crowds completely. They simply gathered around Niall instead.

Niall seemed to be handling it well enough, although one keen look told Liam that his brother was well onto becoming paralytic. He was flaming, no doubt about it. And Michael, Niall's love interest, wasn't far behind.

They were kind of cute to watch, thought Liam. Michael was all over Niall like a sailor on shore duty and Niall, for once, was letting himself go, acting as if it was an everyday occurrence. They held their heads together when talking, seated at the bar. Michael would slide his hand down Niall's arm in a possessive manner and Niall had his hand on Michael's knee. He expected them to kiss, any moment now.

Sine sidled up to him. "Let's get a drink," she said, and then thrust her breasts out in front of her like spotlights on a stage and waltzed over to the bar to order. She noticed Michael first and did a double take. How could she help it? thought Liam. Michael was a looker whether you knew he was gay or not. But then she spotted Niall and the double take doubled. He really hadn't had time to introduce her to anyone before the wedding, and afterward…well…

9

Liam only shrugged. What could he say? He didn't feckin' care. She was with him, and Niall was certainly no threat, nor Michael. He followed her to the bar and ordered their drinks. Before long, a trio of fellas came in and set up lights, mics, amps, the whole bit. The pub would soon be rocking!

* * *

The hotel room was dark and unfamiliar. Niall held his head to stem the solid thumping of his brain against his skull. Any minute now, his stomach contents would decide to leave. Maybe if he just lay there and didn't move…

"What's the matter?" came the voice at his side.

"Shhh," hushed Niall. "M'head's about to blow off."

A chuckle came from the darkness. "Hm, had a bit too much, did you?"

"Don't tell me ye don't feel a thing," Niall replied through gritted teeth.

The chuckle repeated itself. "Well," said Michael, "let's just say that I can hold my liquor better than you."

"I don't bloody drink," exclaimed Niall, then wished he hadn't; hadn't drunk nor spoken. His head hurt when he moved and, unfortunately, talking meant you had to move something.

"Tell me something I don't know, boyo." Michael laughed.

"Don't 'boyo' me," Niall snarled, regretting his action. "Just shut up. Just feckin' shut up."

Michael's hand ran along his thigh. "Let me give you a

massage," he offered. "It'll help. Trust me. You'll soon forget all about your aching head."

"Mmm," was Niall's answer.

The bed shifted and Michael turned sideways to begin his ministrations of his lover's body. Niall lay still, letting Michael have his way.

Warm hands kneaded the tense muscles at his shoulders until they finally began to relax against Michael's ministrations. Niall was on his side, Michael half astride him, just below his arse. He could feel his lover's lad, settled between his legs, touching his own; felt the erection that he knew he'd soon enjoy. The insides of his thighs tingled in expectation.

Niall shifted and Michael's strong hand slid down his side, caressing Niall's buttocks, cupping his nads, rolling them around in those lean fingers like dice in a game. Niall felt his lover's kisses, warm and tender, down the length of his body, seeking out all those sensitive spots, just like Michael knew he craved. Michael's hand was splayed across Niall's belly, taut with desire, sliding upward across the bare skin of his pecs, tweaking nipples ripe for rolling between strong fingers.

Niall felt his hips begin to move; his own erection was primed and ready. Michael's hands shifted, stroked his lad as Niall pressed into Michael's palm, hearing his lover's words, breathing warm and tender into his ear. "Soon, luv. Soon."

Fingers traced a line between the globes of Niall's arse, worked his anus, allowed it to soften beneath his touch.

Headache or not, Niall knew he wanted Michael just then, just that way.

A towel appeared out of nowhere and Niall realized that Michael must have planned this interlude while he, himself, was still passed out. Then a touch of lubricant, cold, then suddenly warm. And then pressure as Michael entered him, slowly, deliberately, filling him. Hands engulfed Niall's flute, stroking, gripping. Niall lay beneath Michael, feeling the passion engulf him, taking over his being so that everything disappeared except for the dark man who rode him and the delicious sensations he was feeling.

Michael's thrusts became intense and Niall grabbed a fistful of sheet, gritting his teeth in pleasure. Very soon, he knew, they would both be fulfilled.

A moment more, then Michael's breathing hitched, his gasps sounding like someone in pain; but it wasn't pain, Niall knew, it was the way Michael sounded just before he came. Then suddenly the room and everything in it disappeared and all Niall saw was the blackness and the stars exploding like fireworks behind his eyes. Awareness of every nerve in his body intensified, coalesced in his nads as the twin balls tightened, then let loose in the heat of a climax, both men panting their completion in each other's arms.

Michael had been right. Niall hadn't thought about his headache the whole time.

* * *

In another room, Liam and his starlet were having their own tête-à-tête. Liam had just spent the last hour stroking, teasing, biting, and suckling his little starlet's womanly parts with only minimal success. It seemed his little lovebird was too inebriated to enjoy his offerings, and so, never one to take from someone who was completely unaware, Liam gave up and tried to sleep. In the morning, he'd tell her she'd had a wonderful time, that he'd never had such a night in his life. He'd say how sexy she was, how responsive, and then he'd tell her how he'd made her come twice, and how was it that she didn't remember that particular little item?

And if she looked completely confused, he'd just brush it off and tell her that she had been very tired, after all. Yeah. He could do it that way. In the meantime, he'd just go into the toilet and…yeah. He'd just do that. At least then, he could fall asleep himself.

* * *

They met in the breakfast room in the morning. Unintentionally. It was awkward. Michael knew, of course, that Niall had a twin brother. He'd seen him on screen and knew intimate details of the brothers, thanks to Niall's stories of growing up in Inishannon and of spending summers in Garrettstown at their grandparents' home; of surfing, of swimming, of other, much more titillating things. Plus, they'd all met yesterday, brief though that meeting had been.

Never one to miss an opportunity, Liam sat down on the opposite side of the table from his brother, next to Michael, forcing his little starlet to take the only other seat, next to Niall. Niall felt uncomfortable and, clearly, Michael didn't care. Liam was having the time of his life. Of Sine, Liam had no concerns. She was being fed. She'd had a good sleep. And as far as she knew, she'd had the time of her life with him. No complaints.

They ordered the Irish breakfast, the kind of meal that you had when you came home from church with the entire family. There were black and white puddings, rashers, sausages, eggs, potatoes, everything you could possibly name. The four ordered it and out it came. The coffee was fresh, the juice sweet, and if the conversation at the table was stilted, no one knew except Niall.

"Good night?" asked Liam with a twinkle in his eye.

"Oh, of course," said Niall. Michael began to chuckle but Niall's noticeable kick under the table soon put paid to that nonsense.

"Yours?" asked Niall politely, ignoring the fact that he'd done anything at all.

The little starlet looked worse for wear and wasn't answering. She wasn't Irish, at least, not raised in Ireland. Wasn't even British, and so when the black and white puddings arrived, clearly not what she was expecting, her pallor grew substantially and she decided to stick with just coffee.

"Have some cereal or yogurt," offered Liam, knowing he wasn't helping in the least.

Michael seemed to take pity on her state and offered a suggestion. "It's better if you eat something. Try the potatoes and the bacon. Or maybe just the potatoes. You can have some toast, too."

14

"You're not Irish," she said, looking at him and sounding surprised.

"And thank God for that," exclaimed Michael. "These two at the table are more than enough for anyone," which brought a smile to her wan face.

"I'm from Chicago. It's a bit different there," she said, eyeing the food on the table.

"How so?"

"Well, for one, the bacon is different. And whatever this black pudding is, and the white stuff, too, it isn't pudding. Pudding is a dessert."

"Ah, she's homesick, she is," said Liam, winking at her and smiling.

"No," she stated, sounding a bit more together after sipping her coffee, "just making comparisons."

"Well, the pudding may not be to everyone's taste but ye should give it a try so at least ye know what not to order next time," he advised.

She must have taken his words to heart because she cut off a small piece of the black pudding and chewed thoughtfully before doing the same with the white. The slices were not large and she'd only taken a very little bit, but Liam was pleased that she was at least that adventurous, especially since he was certain she was still flaming from all the drink last night. After the black stuff, they'd moved on to whiskey. Not a good combination at any time and especially not for someone unused to Irish whiskey. So far, other than looking a little pale, which could be from not having enough sleep, she

15

was holding her own.

"Well?" asked Liam, when she'd swallowed.

She turned her nose up, wrinkling the sprinkle of freckles across it and making a moue with her mouth. "It's okay, but I wouldn't be crossing the street to get more any time soon. I like the white better than the black, but they're awfully dry. What are they made of, anyway?"

Before anyone else could say anything, Niall informed her in his cut-and-dried way, "The black pudding is made from blood and the white isn't," as if that explained everything.

"Blood? Eeew," she said, and her grimace intensified.

"Ah, it's alright, ye won't die from the wee bit ye had," laughed Liam. "Try the rashers. They taste the same as American bacon, I can assure ye. Just meatier, less fat."

She gave him a dubious look but did as he suggested. Seeming to find the bacon more palatable than the pudding, she had another bite and before long was tucking into the eggs and potatoes before picking up some toast and spreading it with marmalade.

By the time she'd finished and was helping herself to a final cup of coffee, the rest were done and Niall stood to go. "Michael and I have to get back to Cork. It's been fun but I'd like to catch up on some stuff before we're back to work tomorrow."

"Work? I thought ye were takin' some time off," said his twin. "Ye were goin' to come rock climbin' with us."

"Deadlines. They moved up the start date to push out the new software so we're doin' a bit of overtime. Once it's done, we'll take some time."

"Ah, that's no good. We'll be off to a tropical island by then for the next bit of filmin'."

"Sucks to be you," blurted out Michael, and they all laughed.

"Right, then, we're off," said Niall, and if he noticed anyone watching, chose to ignore them as Michael followed him out the door.

"They make a cute couple," said Sine.

"Yeah, but it causes all kinds of trouble for me, sometimes."

"I can see how it might," acknowledging their unmistakeable likeness, the differences in their current hairstyles notwithstanding. And then, "Hey, you got any aspirin? This headache is trying really hard to come back."

"C'mon, let's go back to the room and I'll find somethin' for ye."

He led her off and noted the time. It was just half nine. They'd been up much earlier than he thought and an idea came into his head that they'd have time for a quick one and maybe even a shower if they hurried. They didn't have to be out of the room until eleven.

Chapter Two

Hooking the "Do Not Disturb" sign on the door handle, Liam then closed it and heard the satisfactory click of the lock. They'd passed a couple of rooms already vacated and being cleaned, while a vacuum cleaner was standing, unused but ready, in the hall.

He was used to working under pressure. A fling in the bed and a post-coital shower could be easily done within the hour and a half time limit. Just like on set. Well, not quite, he amended. They wouldn't be doing exactly all that on set. Nudity? Yes. Actual sex? No.

Remembering her request for aspirin, he checked his bag and pulled out some acetaminophen tablets. "Will these do?" he asked, and at her nod, shook two from the bottle and put them in her hand. He heard the water run in the bathroom, and was waiting for her when she emerged.

"C'mere to me," he said, pulling her arm as she went to walk past him.

"Huh?"

"I'd like to make this memorable for ye, and, well, I don't think ye remember too much of last night. We have time now, if ye want?"

Her hazel eyes met his and a smile spread slowly across her face. "Well, seeing as we didn't actually do anything last night," she began.

"Oh, but we did. Ye just don't remember," he laughed.

"Liar. I remember you doing all kinds of nice things to me but I fell asleep before you could finish."

So much for spinning her a tale, thought Liam. "We could finish up now, though. We've time," he coaxed. He'd pulled her close, began rubbing her lovely arse and slid his hand up the back of her top to undo the clasp of her bra. He felt her large breasts flatten against his shirt with their release and pulled her closer.

"What do ye say," he breathed as he kissed her neck, worked his way down as he raised her top above her soft mounds. They were all hers, he now knew, no artificial implants there.

"Mmm, I could be persuaded," she sighed.

He felt her hands pop the clasp of his jeans open before pulling at the zipper. He was uncomfortable, straining against the fabric. "Careful, I don't want my flute to get caught," he said, sucking in his abdomen as well as he could.

"Your what?" She'd stopped the downward motion of the zipper, so he, thankful that she'd stopped, took over.

"Flute. Sometimes also called a 'langer'."

"Doesn't 'cock' work for you?"

He could tell she thought Irish vernaculars strange. "Ah, but it's not poetic at all, is it now?"

"Not really, but everyone understands what it is."

19

"So, take my cock, flute, or whatever else ye'd like to call it, and do what ye will with it. I'm fair chubbed and wantin' yer fanny." He'd sprung himself free and kicked himself clear of both jeans and shorts.

"Fanny? Okay, I think I get that."

"Coulda called it yer flange, but we should hurry. I'm fair horned up."

"You mean horny?"

"Christ, are we goin' to argue what's what all day or just get down to havin' a good time?"

"Mmm, a good time works for me, whatever it's called."

Without another word, he slipped her shirt off over her head, flung her bra across the room, and followed her down to the bed. He'd just tossed his own shirt aside, was blessedly nude, and happily pulling her jeans and panties off.

"You know, this is nothing like those nude scenes we've done together, even if I'm not the leading lady," she said, looking up at him from her prone position on the bed.

Nudity didn't seem to bother her. A good sign, thought Liam, very good. "Well then, ye'll have a much more natural way of movin' should the need ever arise to do it for real."

"Do you think it ever will? I don't mean actual sex," she amended, "just, well, do you think I'm destined to be a supporting actress forever?"

"Can't say. Don't care…at least, not right now. My mind is on other things, eh?" And they should hurry. He heard the unmistakeable sound of the vacuum cleaner start up.

"Mmm," was her answer as she reached for him.

He took only enough time as was needed to roll on a rubber before sliding into her moist depths. She was wet and willing, spreading her thighs wide for him as if she, too, had been feeling unfulfilled since last night. Rubber in place, he wasted no time in pressing home his advantage.

She voiced her appreciation with a long, drawn out sigh, "Aaah. Oh yeah, more." Her pelvis rose to meet his thrusts, spurring him on. She must have really wanted it because she was running rivers of juice, so much that he almost slipped out of her in his thrusting. Her legs lifted of their own accord, encircled his waist, holding him tightly to her, effectively preventing another accidental slip. But that wasn't enough for this woman; she grabbed his arse with deceptively strong fingers, spread his cheeks as she gripped him, and met him thrust for thrust.

Liam gave it all he had, felt his buttocks tighten in response to her body closing about him; felt the base of his spine tingle when the prelude to climax began to overtake him. He held off, wanting to make sure she came, too. His reputation was riding on it.

He slowed his thrusts, bent his head to take a puckered nipple, lapping at the tip like a cat drinking milk, and felt, rather than heard, the giggle that erupted. Then taking one into his mouth, drew on it, suckled, felt her insides grip him. In some other part of his brain, he could hear and recognize the vacuum cleaner coming down the hall, making him aware that time was ticking. But he wouldn't let her go until he knew she'd climaxed.

21

Renewing his assault on her breasts with his teeth, he slipped his hand between their bodies to the apex of her legs, felt the sweet spot awash in moisture, and took hold of her bud. Minutes later, he heard her breath quicken and felt her muscles tighten. And then he couldn't stop the feeling, couldn't hold back any longer. His nads tightened, his muscles contracted, and of its own accord, his body pumped, even as he felt her body contract around him. Her spasms were intense and he became rigid in her arms as she coaxed every last drop from him. Sweat lined his shoulders and trickled down his chest and the length of his spine as he puffed his final thrusts, noted her eyes, shut tight in what could only be ecstasy.

"Oh, my God," she breathed at last, when he'd thought she'd somehow died in his arms, "the rumors are true."

"Rumors? Don't tell me you're here because of some rumors." Was that why she seemed so eager to accompany him?

"Hell, no. I'm here because you asked me along to the wedding. Remember?"

"Well, yeah, but what's this about rumors?"

She rolled her eyes at him, at his patently stubborn refusal to understand what she was implying. "Oh, come on now, don't tell me you don't know what's being said about you?"

"Like what?" he grinned, truly wanting to know. He'd heard some rumors himself. Were they the same?

"Let's just say that you never miss an opportunity and you never leave a lady hanging."

"Oh. Those rumors." He laughed, which wasn't necessarily

22

a good thing right then because he began to slide from her body. If he'd thought her wet before, it was nothing like now.

"Jaysus, grab me a tissue, will ye?" She handed him the box and he took a handful. "I'm glad ye enjoyed that, luv. So let's have a shower and try to look presentable, eh?"

"Never mind a shower, I could stay here all day," she said, clearly wanting to be a bedbug.

"We have exactly forty minutes to shower and be out of here, or else they'll want money for another night, but that's only if they haven't already filled the room. I think we may be out of luck. It's tourist season."

"Shit. Okay. I'll get up." She pulled herself off the bed, all tousled copper hair and the pale skin that accompanies such redheads, pale with the final blush of a climax just fading.

"C'mon into the shower. I'll wash ye."

Her answer was to smile and walk, weak-legged, Liam noted, into the ample shower stall before him.

He washed her hair first, then finger-combed the tangles out with the conditioner the B&B had provided. It wasn't bad stuff, he thought, giving his own nearly bald pate a quick wash. He then took the soap and soaped her all over, massaging her breasts and the cleft between her legs. She opened once again for him and he slid a finger inside, working her until he felt her walls begin to tighten around him. Before she had completely recovered herself, he hoisted her up against the shower stall and slid into her. His own climax came quickly; he realized only later that he hadn't used a rubber. It was the first slipup he'd ever made and he hoped to hell it hadn't

23

left any lingering problems. He'd have to ask her to get the "morning-after-the-night-before" pill, but most actresses knew about that stuff anyway. None of them wanted to have their career either halted or ruined because some plonker forgot his rubber.

He mentioned it when they were drying off.

"Don't worry about it," she said, giving his back a good rub with the towel. "I'm on the pill."

The only thing that came into Liam's head at that moment was his half-brother's pregnant wife saying, "Oh, I was on the pill but then forgot to take it for a day or two, and bingo, here we are." No, he didn't have a whole lot of faith in pills.

"Right, then. But ye'll tell me, if things go wrong?"

She nodded. Confident. "Oh, yeah, but things will be fine."

* * *

Sine replayed the scenes in both bed and shower while Liam drove. She got horny again, just thinking about it. Sensations wrapped around her, pierced her so that she wriggled in the seat, not certain if she was looking to get more comfortable or trying to satisfy the desire to jump his bones yet again.

When he'd first said he didn't care about her becoming a leading lady, she'd been angry, or had tried to be. But then she remembered her own response after that, how quickly she hadn't cared either, at least, not at that moment. She tried to suppress the notion that he hadn't cared; that he'd said it because his mind was clearly on having sex with her. Perhaps

24

he wouldn't have cared if the world had come to an end just then?

"Liam?"

"Yeah?"

"Did you mean it when you said you didn't care if I never became a leading lady?" She bit her lip in worry.

"What? When did I say that?"

"When we, you know…when we were making love." She took a sideways glance at him while he drove. The strong features of his face, the straight nose and perfect jaw that provided such a delicious profile, were unreadable from this angle.

He began to chuckle. "I say a lot of things that don't make sense when I'm in that position."

It was true, he'd been doing wonderful things to her.

"Never mind. Just my insecurities showing."

"If it's any consolation, I think ye'd make a great leading lady."

Sine smiled her response, loving the way he said "great," as if it was "gree-ate," in a drawn out slur. She glanced at his hands on the steering wheel, capable, strong fingers, squared ends with finely kept nails. She remembered those hands, those fingers, working like magic to satisfy her and inhaled audibly with the memory.

"Alright?" asked Liam as he shifted easily round a turn.

"Huh? Oh, yeah, just breathing in some good, clean air."

That got a glance from Liam and a smirk. He wasn't fooled, she was certain. He was grinning but kept his eyes on

25

the narrow road, the tended fields on both sides, sometimes behind stone walls, and sometimes along the railed wooden fences so commonly seen here. Cattle grazed: the black dairy herds of Kerry cattle, virtually unknown anywhere else in the world, or so she'd been told.

"Would ye mind much if we stayed at my brother's place tonight?" he asked when the silence had stretched and she'd begun to daydream.

The subject wasn't too far off from what she was thinking. "No, I guess that would be okay. Does he have room for us?"

"He's a spare room with a double bed. But maybe that's too small for ye. I could take the sofa downstairs. O' course, ye could bunk in with Emily, she'd love a sleepover with someone like you."

That didn't make sense. "What?"

He laughed outright, and she realized he'd been teasing her. "Don't fash yerself. I've got us a room at a proper hotel tonight, right in town off Kenmare Place. It's high-end, lots of tourists there. Ye'll love it."

Sine wondered about that. The B&B was great. If anyone knew who they were, no one said anything and treated them like everyone else. But at a big, fancy hotel, the tourists might be different. His brother's spare bedroom almost sounded better.

"Sure, I guess that'll be okay," she said, wondering if it would.

"There's a downside, though." He paused, as if to give her time to think about what he'd said, or maybe tease her into thinking something else.

"And what is the downside?"

"They didn't have a room with a double bed."

"But doubles are pretty small. Did they have something bigger?"

Liam kept staring straight ahead. "A bit," he said, inclining his head to indicate it likely wasn't too much bigger. She didn't think there was anything between a double and a queen.

"It's a king," he said, his lips spreading wide to meet his ear lobes.

"You asshole," she laughed, "you had me thinking we were going to be in a broom closet or something."

"Ah, no broom closet, my fine little witch. Ye'll have to store yer broom somewhere else. They gave us a suite, since the rest of the place was full and I was very persuasive. We got a deal," he exclaimed, and then faced her with his grin, and a high five with his hand.

Sine settled in for the rest of the drive, thinking that they likely gave him a deal because of who he was. Regardless, she couldn't wait for nightfall.

They drove in an easterly direction from Cahersiveen to the Black Valley, where jaunting carts were lined up—those small, covered carts pulled by a horse that took tourists for ride. The horses were patient, standing idly by with tales swishing in the breeze while drivers were warning folks in cars away, pointing to a sign that looked official.

"Local traffic only, the horses have the right of way,"

they were saying, and disallowing anyone with a vehicle the ability to drive through.

"That's a lot of shite, that is," observed Liam. "It's a feckin' public road and there's no 'Failte' insignia on the sign, vouching for its legitimacy. That's bollocks." He moved the car forward as a driver made to stop him.

"Off, mate," Liam said through the opened window, "we're to be halfway between here and Moll's Gap in ten minutes and I'll not be walkin' it."

The man seemed to recognize him and hesitated, and that's when Liam stepped on the gas. He didn't blaze through in a hail of glory though, because he knew he could very well run into one of those jaunting carts, the same as those who plied their trade in Killarney every day, so he continued on at a moderate pace, aware of every turn and mindful of pedestrians and equestrians both.

A few minutes later they came to a small waterfall and pulled off the road as well as they were able, tucking the car next to a gap in the rocky landscape. "This is the place," he said, getting out of the car and pointing to what seemed to be a short climb away.

"That's it?" Sine asked, undoubtedly wondering if it really was going to take them two hours to do it.

"Yeah. Looks are deceiving. Ye've climbed before?"

She was still trying to imagine them taking a long time to do it, he could tell. Her gaze went up the mountain and back down before going back up once again.

"It doesn't look that hard," she remarked.

"Mmf." She'd soon find out.

An hour later, they were halfway up the slope, having dodged loose rocks, moss, and dung-strewn grasses making the way slippery at times. They'd obviously had a healthy rain the night before and that only added to the conditions.

Not to mention dodging sheep. A couple of the males eyed them closely, edging toward them, heads in butting position until Liam moved both Sine and himself out of range. They were protecting their womenfolk, he knew, and he wasn't about to upset the force of nature.

Finally, after two hours of slogging their way upward, they stood atop the mountain and, with laboured breathing, observed the land below them with awe. It was wild, as wild as the day God had placed it there, thought Liam. He never tired of the view, never worried that it would ever change because who would want to change it? There was nothing on that hilltop that anyone would want; not even the sheep and goats that ranged the hillside down below wanted to be up there. The grazing stopped a good hundred feet before the top, leaving only scrub, a bit of furze, and rocks to color the landscape.

And the waterfall. It was just a trickle at the top but it widened slightly before heading into the nature preserve at the bottom, increasing the falls to more than just a bubbling brook. It was truly a wild land and Sine was, apparently, in awe of what she saw.

"I never would have believed it," she said, finally getting her breath again. "That climb looked so easy from down below but it's obviously, as you said, deceiving."

"Look," he said, pointing. She was standing beside him in the shelter of his arm about her shoulder. "That's Killarney over there."

Breathing in audibly and then exhaling in a sound of wonderment, Sine couldn't contain her awe. Killarney lay amidst a myriad of shimmering lakes, reflecting the sky above. The sun warred with clouds for a bit of exposure and flocks of birds augmented the view. "It really is amazing. I didn't think we were so close."

"As the crow flies, we're close, and really, it isn't a great distance but it takes a while to get there from here. We may have to fight yon jarveys again."

"Hm, they weren't too impressed with you, that's for sure."

"I don't think they expected me to be Irish. I think they expected another ignorant tourist."

"Well, I can't blame them," she said, turning to take in the view on the other side. "After all, they're afraid for their horses, they need the tourists' money and…"

"And stop right there. That's what it's all about is the tourists and their money."

"They care about the horses, too," she argued.

"They do," he allowed, "most, anyways." No one wanted to see the animals hurt by crazy drivers.

"What's over there?" she shifted her feet, changing the subject.

His arms encircle her in his embrace as she indicated

with a nod what she was looking at.

"Across the Macgillycuddy's Reeks lies the ocean, a few miles away in that direction, toward Dingle Bay. That peak ye're lookin' at is Carrauntoohil, the tallest peak in Ireland." He was watching her face, the play of emotion on her mouth as it spread into a broad smile of appreciation. He couldn't resist, and taking her chin in his fingers, tilted it up for her mouth to meet his, for their lips to touch, and when she opened to him, for tongues to play.

"Ah, but I could take ye here," he smiled, feeling that he could, right on top of the mountain, with no witnesses but the sun and the clouds and the birds.

"Might be a bit rocky," she observed, kicking at a rock with her booted toe.

"Hm, ye could be right," he agreed, cupping her arse with his hand. "Later?"

"Don't you know it," she replied, sliding her hand between their bodies, taking the bulge in his pants and squeezing gently.

He grinned, couldn't help it, and kissed her again. "C'mon, let's head down. The sooner we get down, the sooner we can indulge ourselves."

He led the way, picking their way gingerly down the path they'd forged on their way up. They'd been chatting, exclaiming over the scenery, the view of the ducks down by the old bridge, visible as small specks on the water from this distance, and all manner of things, including the sight of yet another jaunting cart making its way down the narrow road.

Passengers waved; they waved back and Sine called out a hello. They were, by this time, only a few meters from the bottom, when Liam turned, his foot shifted, and he slipped on a mossy rock, his foot going out from under him. His other foot slammed into a hole and he gave a yelp of pain. "Fucking hell!"

"Liam, Liam, are you okay?" Sine raced to his side, helpless and panicking.

He howled in pain and frustration, felt the tears start in his eyes and didn't want to be seen that way. It wasn't the hero image he was used to portraying. But this wasn't a movie, it was real life, and he was in excruciating pain.

Sine scrambled to his side. She'd been following him down, over moss-strewn rocks and moist crevices, perfect for catching an unwary foot. As she got to his side, she paled, turned away, and stood for a moment.

It gave Liam a chance to catch his breath and his dignity, until he heard what sounded like retching. "Sine?" he called.

She seemed to have got herself together, wiping her face with a tissue from her pocket. "It's…I'm okay," she said, still looking pale and shaken. No, not shaken, he realized, but shaking. She was trembling like a leaf.

"Your foot," she said, pointing, and as Liam looked down, he noticed that something didn't look right. He had incredible pain lancing up and down his leg with every twitch of his nerves. His body was awash with agony, causing his breath to come in hitches. He tried to move his foot, to dislodge it from the boulders it was caught between, but he couldn't do it, just couldn't endure the pain that any movement, even the slightest, caused. His ankle was wedged tightly between the rocks and if he didn't get it out soon, it would be swollen in there for good.

He let out a primordial yell, didn't care who heard, and hoped to God someone had. They needed help. He needed help.

"We have to get your foot out of there," she said, tears streaming down her face. Clearly, seeing his ankle bent in such an unnatural position was not the most pleasant sight for anyone, let alone her.

Liam lay back on the rocks, tried to calm himself with deep breathing, and reached into his fanny pack for his mobile phone. He wasn't sure if he could get reception here but one thing was certain: they sure as hell weren't going to get out without help. He thought of Sine going for help but quickly squashed that notion. Not being raised in Ireland and only having been there for a few weeks, he doubted she'd even had the chance to drive a car yet. And could she drive a manual shift? He didn't know. But how else would they ever get out of here?

His phone beeped stubbornly and he put it back in his pack with grunt of finality. "Grand. Just feckin' grand." He wouldn't be finishing the film. He wouldn't be traveling to a tropical island and have his little starlet with him. Or his leading lady, either.

Sine stood helplessly by. "What'll we do? Maybe we can get one of those carts to haul you out?"

"No. No feckin' way in hell I'm lettin' them see me like this. I can just see their faces, callin' me all kinds of a fool for not listenin' to them."

"We should have just told them we were hiking and had all our gear in here."

"Grand. Now ye think of what to say."

"You didn't give me a chance, did you," she exclaimed, rounding on him and pointing to his foot. "So if you want help to get that out of there, we'd better call on them because I don't see a phone booth anywhere close by."

The incongruity of the situation hit him and he laughed. He was in so much pain he couldn't believe it and here they were, arguing. "Right," he said, when his chuckles had slowed. "Right ye are. Go to the road," he instructed, "and wait for one to drive by going back to the parking area. Hitch a ride, tell him ye'll give him a fiver if he takes ye back. Tell him anythin' ye want, just don't tell him I'm hurt. Got it?"

She nodded yes and asked, "Why not say you're hurt?"

"Because he'll spread the word and we can't have that. Got any paper? Somethin' to write with?"

"In the car." She seemed to quickly gauge the distance to where the vehicle was parked and said, "I'll be back in a jiffy."

"Mind yer step," he said shakily, and realized that he was going into shock. Mam, a nurse for many years, had taught them many things. Raising four boys and a girl almost single-handedly, her nursing skills were often put to use. He'd been through shock before, and seen it in each of his brothers at least once. They'd been a rowdy lot.

"Okay," she said, huffing and puffing her way back to where Liam was stuck and offering him the pen and a scrap of paper.

"No. Ye'll have to do it. I can't hold a pen just now." He was vibrating like a dildo on high, as if every inch of him was hooked up to some electrical current, just like on the early morning cartoon shows. He then gave her Henry's phone number and a couple of other options. "And when ye get in mobile range, make sure ye call where no one can hear ye. It's too important."

"Why can't anyone know? Help might come faster if they know who you are."

"No one must know, especially not anyone on the film. We have to keep a lid on this or the whole project could go down the drain."

"Well, what are you going to do? You can't even move your foot, let alone go running down the beach on some tropical island."

"I know. Just let me think," he ground out. The pain was still pounding through his leg and he could feel the sweat trickling down his body, moistening crevices, itching. He wanted badly to wipe the sensations away but the pain from any kind of movement was too great.

"Hey, I've got an idea," Sine said, brightening. "What if you asked Niall to take your place? He's identical to you. No one would know the difference."

"Niall?" He fairly shrieked his brother's name. "Are ye daft? Niall would no more run along a beach with a buxom woman on his arm than he would with a female of any kind. He's an arse bandit."

"So? It's just an act, right? He doesn't have to believe it; he just has to pretend he's you for a few days. Didn't you ever do that at school?"

Liam had to laugh at that. "We tried," he admitted. "The only success we had was switchin' classes so I could pass the mathematics exam. He's the brains. Always has been."

"Then he'll be good at switching spots with you for a while. No one needs to know," she reiterated.

"No one, except Felicia McKay, one of the most well-known actresses of our generation, a looker, and one who'll be all over Niall like shite to a blanket, thinkin' it's me. He won't stand for it."

"But I'll be there. I can help him through it," she argued.

She had a point. And though the pain was throbbing through his system, he felt numb. It was getting difficult to think.

"Just call Henry. Tell him where we are. He'll know what to do."

"What'll I tell the jarvey?"

"Just tell him ye're tired of walkin' and would he give ye a lift on the way back. Ye've got a fiver on ye?"

She checked her pocket and nodded. "I'll come back after I talk to Henry," she promised.

"Okay," said Liam. He was feeling very sleepy. "I'll be okay…"

Chapter Three

Even though an ambulance had been sent to retrieve Liam from the hillside, causing all kinds of interest from passersby, they'd managed to keep the identity of the hiker relatively unknown. Henry purposely did not tell Niall, wanting to keep him away for as long as possible. No one wanted anyone putting two and two together and getting five.

When the ambulance left, Henry handed Liam's car keys to Sine, saying, "Just follow me. I promise I won't drive too fast so's not to lose ye, and we'll get the car to where Niall can pick it up. Then I'll take ye with me to the hospital."

"Drive? Me?" She was as white as a sheet, paler than she was when Henry first saw her next to Liam, trying to make him as comfortable as possible. She'd been frightened half to death, especially when she said she'd returned and seen Liam passed out. She'd thought he was dead.

"It's alright. Ye just have to follow me," he said, clearly not understanding what was frightening her and doing his best to calm her.

"But I've never driven a standard before, let alone driven on the other side of the road," she said, almost in tears.

"Oh, for fuck's sake, are ye jokin'?" It was so easy. Everyone in Ireland drove a manual shift. Automatics were for the rich and the "greenies," as Henry liked to call them. But a shake of her shiny copper head and he knew she was telling him the truth.

He swallowed his annoyance, saying, "Right. Come with me, then, and we'll try to get some help to move the car."

In the end, he'd taken her to the pub at the valley's entrance, sat her down, and bought her a pint and some food to go with it. He then hired a jaunting car to take him as far as the vehicle, and when the man remarked that he'd seen the bollocks drive through the roadblock, Henry turned on him.

"I'll thank ye for the ride but you and I both know that yon sign is only for the tourists who know no better. Ye've no legal right to keep them off a public road. So here's yer money, now take yer cart and horse off and leave me to me own business."

The jarvey opened his mouth to say more but one look from Henry's furrowed black brows and steely hardened gaze, and the man took his horse and went back up the road. Soon after, Henry followed with Liam's car, realizing that the jarvey hadn't recognized Liam, after all. Small mercies, thought Henry with a thankful sigh.

***

They'd been driving for ten minutes before Sine finally got up the courage to speak. Henry's visage was dark, like a hundred storms gathering, getting ready to let loose their fury. "Is everything okay?" she asked.

"Hmmf," said Henry, navigating the narrow roads as fast as was permitted. "Oh, yeah, just grand," he said.

"I'm sorry I can't drive a standard. I never learned…"

"Don't blame yerself," he said. "It's no bother. The car is fine where it is. 'Tisn't that at all, really. It's just…it's hard to hear a man scream like that. You know, when they pulled his foot out from between the rocks and straightened it?"

"I thought they would have given him a painkiller," she said, remembering just how badly it had been broken, and how the foot was turned at an unnatural angle, and…she thought she might get sick again, just thinking about it.

"They gave him somethin'. He felt it anyway."

"Well, I'm sure they'll have him better sedated by the time we get to the hospital." And then, "You don't think he'll lose his foot, do you?"

"I doubt it, it's just broken, more a nuisance than anythin'. Feckit, he's got a career on the line. What else would he do?"

Sine only shrugged. She had always acted, from grade school plays to high school auditoriums and then the big stages in New York. She'd even played on Broadway in some lesser roles, but never the leading lady. Always close but never the star. Still, if something happened to prevent her from ever acting again, she wouldn't know what she'd do, either.

Finally, the hospital came into view and they pulled into the parking lot. Inside the waiting room they saw Siobhan, Henry's wife, and Emily, their ward. Emily was technically Henry's niece through his half sister, Meara, who had died

39

from a drug overdose.

"He's into surgery," said Siobhan after she and Henry kissed hello.

Henry nodded. "Good," and then, "Ye'll remember Liam's date at the weddin', Sine Maguire?" Not waiting for a response, he said, "Sine, this is me wife, Siobhan, and our daughter, Emily."

"Hi," said Sine. "I remember you. Such a lovely, fantastical wedding, taking place in a stone castle. The stuff of dreams," she said. It was awkward and a bit stilted, but then, they were all a little worried and it wasn't the time for idle conversation.

They walked to the lounge to sit together through the long wait. "How did it happen?" asked Siobhan, a concerned look on her round face. She had the ruddy cheeks Sine had seen on so many people, and since Siobhan was slightly heavy, her cheeks were full, intensifying the roundness and adding half a chin.

"We were hiking. Halfway to Moll's Gap, I think Liam said."

"Up there? I remember it. We did that hike a few times, did we not, Henry?"

Henry only nodded. "When we were younger," he said, with a twinkle in his eye.

"Where is he?" came a voice they all seemed to know so well. Except for Sine. She turned at the sound and saw who she thought might be their mother, if she remembered correctly.

"He's into surgery. They'll get him right in no time," said Henry as he stood and hugged his mam, he, over six feet tall, and she, five foot if an inch, and almost as big around. She was all strength and fortitude, thought Sine, but the lines of worry creased across her forehead could not be denied.

"Right, then, I'll go talk to the staff and see what I can learn."

Before anyone could say anything more, she was off.

"I don't know if there is more to learn," observed Sine quietly.

"Ah, but it's Mam. She's a nurse at the University Hospital in Cork and we all know how well she is known there. So bein' here, well, it's like home to her. She's been nursing for nigh on forty years, I expect. Or close to it."

Sure enough, she was back shortly, a tray of coffee in her hands for everyone, and pastries from the nurses' lounge. "Food to help the wait," she exclaimed when she put the tray down on the small table beside the waiting room chairs.

Worried or not, Sine noted they all tucked into the food as if it would disappear in a moment, which it very nearly did. She suddenly realized she was hungry, despite the food that Henry had bought for her, and grabbed something that resembled a Danish and bit into it.

Eventually, Henry's mam looked up as if noticing Sine for the first time. "Oh, ye're the girl Liam brought to the weddin'. I'm Kathleen, his mam—course, ye likely knew that already."

Sine smiled and shook hands, instantly liking the woman.

41

"I'm Sine," she said, "pleased to meet you."

"It's not goin' to be much longer, I expect. He's been in there for a while now," said Kathleen. Liam's lucky, he is," she said, but gave nothing in the way of explanation for such a contentious remark.

"Lucky?" Henry finally asked. He was frowning at his mother as if she had lost all sense of reality.

"Hm? Oh, sorry, I was thinkin' aloud to myself. But it's true, he's lucky. Lucky he didn't break his neck and lucky, too, that there's a specialist from London here this week teaching a workshop. Another day and he'd be back in London and Liam would have to be taken to Cork. As it is, this fella's an orthopedic surgeon, one of the best, and he's putting Liam's ankle back together. Should hardly be a scar so's not to put off his leading ladies."

Sine giggled at that. "Somehow I don't think a scar would put any woman off," she said, finishing the Danish. "He could probably have scars all over his body and they'd only think he was sexier, more manly."

Kathleen was about to interject when they all saw Niall walk through the door and into the waiting area. The first thing that struck Sine was the visible difference between Liam and his twin. Liam's hair had been cropped short, shaved really, whereas Niall's curls touched the back of his collar, making Sine wish that Liam's did the same. She'd love to run her fingers through those silky locks!

"Ye got the car okay?" asked Henry, and Niall nodded.

"Michael drove us back after we got yer call and we went

straight to the valley to pick it up. It's at your place now."

Henry nodded. "Where's Michael?"

"Right here," came the cultured English voice, and Sine watched as he sidled up to Niall and put his arm casually around Niall's waist.

She wondered at that. How it felt to have someone of the same sex love you that way. But she was too attracted to men, even gay men, if the sight of Michael making her stand up and take notice was any indication, to want to switch.

Looking at Niall made her remember the conversation she and Liam had, just before she left to get help. "Niall, I think we need to sit down and have a chat," she said, wondering if she should wait for Liam to wake up, but time wasn't in their favor.

"What's up?"

She looked uncomfortably around at everyone. "Is there a place we can talk, where we can't be overheard?" she asked.

"If it's about Liam, ye can say whatever it is ye have to say to all of us," Kathleen said, and Sine felt the vibes of a mama bear, loud and clear.

"Oh, no, it isn't that I don't want you to hear, it's just that, well, Liam said this must be kept very quiet, and although I'd rather he be the one to tell you, I don't know if he'll be awake, or awake enough, before it's time for me to leave."

"I'll see what I can do to find someplace," said Kathleen, and marched off, leaving them standing.

"What's it about?" asked Henry.

"I can't tell you right here, but as soon as your mom finds

43

us a room, we can all talk about it. But it really just involves Niall."

"This way," called Kathleen from the corridor. "There's a small boardroom we can use."

The group followed her down the hall and into a room with a round table and some chairs stacked at the side. They each helped themselves to a chair and, closing the door, Sine began to explain. "It's about the film we've been working on." Everyone knew what that meant. It was the latter half of the film, with all the scenes left to do being the ones on the tropical island. "If Liam doesn't do them, he could get sued. The company might not want to wait until his foot is healed before they finish it and that would be way too long, anyway. Could be, what? Six months?"

"Could be, for him to be able to walk properly again," said Kathleen.

"And I doubt they'll agree to scrap the whole thing and start again with a new cast. But there is a solution," she said, her eyes coming to rest on Niall. "You could take his place."

Niall tensed suddenly and gripped Michael's hand. "Not a chance in hell," he said, grim-faced and petulant.

The entire family turned on Niall as if he were a sacrificial lamb. "That's the perfect solution," said Henry, and everyone agreed.

Everyone except Niall.

Michael was quiet, as if he were thinking about it. "She's right, you know. It could work."

"Cop on! Yer all feckin' eejits if ye think I'll do that."

Sine saw the passion with which Niall spoke and wondered why he had never gone into acting himself. His facial expressions carried more weight than Liam's for all that they were twins.

"Why not?" she asked innocently, and felt the family's eyes turn collectively on her. "What?" she said, looking around her as if she'd just become their next meal.

"Sit down, Niall," Kathleen commanded, and Sine was impressed by the power her words had over her children, adult though they were. "There's a problem here and Sine has an idea that may solve it. This is a family matter and we've always solved things as a family. But Sine, ye must know a few things about Niall, first."

At Sine's nod, Kathleen continued. "Right, then. Our Niall's not outgoing. He's the next thing to a hermit, he is, and bein' in public makes him nervous. Now, just imagine him bein' center stage, with a camera on him, pretending to be someone he's not, pretendin' he's not gay. It's like to turn his stomach, it would."

"But I'll be there to help him. I'll think of an excuse to get him some privacy when he needs it," she said.

"And that's not likely to be very much like Liam. He has to be like Liam, has to be Liam, for yer plan to work. The two couldn't be more different if they belonged to different families," Kathleen argued.

Sine nodded in agreement. "I understand that. But with a little help, I'm sure we could pull it off."

"What gives ye the right to ask it of me?" Niall queried,

his mouth a grim line. "Ye're not family. Ye've no interest in this but yer own gain."

"No, that's not true," she answered back. "Liam and I talked this over before I left to get help. It's true it was my idea, but he agreed. He said we should at least try. If you don't do it, we all lose. Especially Liam."

Niall was about to interject when Michael spoke first. "What would he have to do? I mean, is it just a walk in the park? What kind of scenes are you talking about? I know what kinds of films Liam does, and they aren't your '50s style romances with a handshake and a wink. He does full blown nudity, and I'm not certain Niall would like that, much less me. He's my lover after all, no one else's, and I'm not sure I want everyone to see what should be for just the two of us."

"Most of those scenes are done," she answered, and then remembered that there was to be a nude scene by a lagoon. "Except one. But maybe I can convince them to change it," she said quickly before anyone could interrupt.

"Niall," said his mam, "think about it, why don't ye? It's not like ye must make up yer mind right now, like, is it?" she turned questioning eyes to Sine.

"No. Not this instant. But soon. Very soon. Liam and I were going to go back to Galway the day after tomorrow for one more day and then off to the airport for the island shoot."

"So that gives him, what, a day to make up his mind?" asked Michael. He was caressing Niall's hand where it held his in a firm grip.

"About that."

"And what'll I need to do back in Galway?" asked Niall, giving Sine a feeling of hope that not all was lost.

"That one is easy. There's a scene where you're finishing a coffee in a restaurant and then you take Felicia's hand and wink at her, then walk out the door to your motorbike. The last scene is you zooming down the road past the camera."

"Felicia?"

"Felicia McKay. She's the leading actress. I'm the supporting actress. And there's been the odd time," she hesitated, unsure how to phrase things so they'd understand, "well, Felicia's made it known she doesn't do nude scenes. She's got a couple of scars, doesn't like to show them, so she's made it clear, no nudity." She paused to collect her thoughts, and then, "So, when there are specific scenes that don't call for head shots, if it's just body, then I do that. We're built very much the same, so I'm her body double as well as have my own parts."

That seemed to get everyone's attention. It seemed Liam didn't tell them about that.

"You're a body double?" asked Niall. "Is that true?" He was suddenly looking at Sine as if she had two heads.

"Yes, it is. And it's no big deal, trust me."

"So ye've stood naked as God made ye before all kinds of people who work on those films and it doesn't bother ye?" asked Kathleen.

"It's not quite like that, but yes. And Liam has, too."

"That's it, I'm done." Niall began to leave but Michael pulled him back.

"Just wait a moment. We might be able to get this to work in our favor."

Niall looked back at Michael, openmouthed, shaking his head. "No. Ye can't be serious," Niall said.

"Hear me out." Michael then turned to Sine and said, "Do you think you can get me there, too?"

"Huh?"

"If I were to go with Niall, I could help him through this ordeal, because it will be an ordeal for him. But if I were there, it would certainly help. And if you can guarantee us a holiday in paradise afterward, well, we just might consider it."

"Ye're feckin' daft, ye are, if ye think I'll go, even for you."

"But think about it," Michael crooned, taking his lover's chin in his strong, brown hands. "You, me, on a beach under tropical skies. An all-expenses-paid holiday for two. Wouldn't that be worth it?"

"No."

"But it's a holiday we've always dreamed of, and we have time coming to us. We can even do some extra work to finish pushing out the software on time. You know they'd let us. We're the best they've got and they're too worried about losing us to say no. It could be fun."

"Only because ye're not the one in front of the camera, standing around with a bunch of women, pretending ye're so happy ye could cry. They'd be tears of sorrow, and that's the God's truth!"

"It's not that bad, kissing women. Lots of men do it, I've done it. Their lips are quite soft and there's no mustache, at least, not usually," he quipped, and even Sine saw the façade of Niall's resistance begin to crack.

"I tried it when I was a teenager, can't imagine much has changed," he sulked.

"Look," said Michael, standing and pulling Sine close. "I'm touching her and haven't died yet, so watch this." He took her chin in his hand, leaned down and touched his lips to hers, then deepened the kiss.

Sine couldn't help that her hands automatically went around him to slide up his back, her long fingers spearing across his tightly curled hair. And then he stepped back and she felt his energy fade as she opened her eyes. It was just an act, she told herself, and she shook it off to meet Niall's brooding eyes.

But if it was such an act, why did it leave her feeling so empty? Shaking her head and re-composing herself, she said, "And that's it," as if she'd just given a demonstration on how to fold a towel. "Nothing to it. Just smoke and mirrors. You make them believe what they want to believe, and I don't think any one of you in here, except for maybe Michael and me, thought this wasn't the real thing." Her eyes traveled down Michael's frame when everyone else was focussed on Niall. How did Liam phrase it? Chubbed up? It seemed that Michael could swing both ways.

"Here, you give it a go," said Michael, and Niall's eyes widened in surprise.

49

"What, me? Here?"

"Where else? If you can perform in front of your family as an audience, where it's more awkward because they know you so well, then you can do it in front of people you don't know, because they won't know the real you."

Sine jumped in, partly from curiosity and partly because she knew Michael was right. She repeated a phrase to Niall she'd heard Liam say often enough, cupping fingers to palm, saying, "C'mere to me."

Niall cast a glance under furrowed brows to Michael, then stood and walked to where Sine was, slightly set apart from the others. It was as close to an actual rehearsal as she could make it.

"Okay, take a step closer and look into my eyes. Pretend I'm Michael." Niall raised a brow in query and she grimaced. "I know he's taller, just work with me, okay?"

At Niall's tentative grin, she continued, "Think like Liam. Think of how he moves, his confidence, his swagger. Put yourself in his place and let your inhibitions go. I know this is difficult for you but Michael is right. If you can do this here with your family watching, you can do it anywhere and be believable." She put her hand up around Niall's neck and lightly pulled his head down toward her. It was so like the preface to a kiss with Liam that she had trouble keeping the two separate.

Only Niall was so much stiffer, so unwilling to be a part of it.

Finally their lips met. She closed her eyes and forced his

50

lips open, felt him relax a little in her arms and then break off suddenly, just when she thought he'd actually go for a little tongue twisting.

"Enough," said Niall, breathing hard. "It's feckin' awkward with all o' ye's watchin'.'"

Sine put her fingers to her lips. Niall and Liam might be twins but they sure didn't kiss the same. "It'll be okay, though, right?"

Niall didn't answer and there was silence in the room as he went back to sit at the table and Michael put his hands possessively on Niall's shoulders.

"That was convincing," said Kathleen, but Sine couldn't read the expression on her face except to say that, as a mom, she was likely very conflicted in her thoughts.

It was Henry who finally spoke when the silence had gone on too long. "So how are ye goin' to convince the film company to let Michael tag along?" he asked Sine.

"That's the only catch. I'm not sure. We can find grips just about anywhere, same with other crew members."

"Do you need a computer specialist?" asked Michael.

"For what?"

"Well, I'm assuming a lot of the work is digital, and that kind of equipment sometimes needs a lot of help very suddenly, especially if there are deadlines," he answered.

"I don't know," she answered truthfully. "Maybe Liam will, though. We can ask him when he wakes up. But if nothing else, maybe you can be hired as a personal aide, or something like that. We'll think of something," she said.

"Well, then, if you can do that, I think Niall will go, won't you, luv?" He nudged Niall's shoulder and Niall glared back. "But I'll look after him and be the one to say when he's had enough. Sounds like he won't be able to tell anyone so it'll have to be me."

"Sure," answered Sine, "but if he's Liam, he can walk off whenever the mood strikes him. That's what Liam does. If things aren't going well, he literally just says he's had enough, needs a break or whatever, and stalks off. The crew hates it but he gets away with it. So all Niall has to do is be ballsy enough to do it."

"That's arrogance, that is," said Henry. "I'd no idea he was a prima donna."

"Well, he isn't, not quite. But he's well respected enough that when he knows a scene is wrong and people need a break, he'll call it because sometimes the director just wants to push through," she explained.

"Oh, so he's really doing it for others, not himself?" Michael asked.

"Yeah, something like that," she said.

Michael cast a glance at Niall and their eyes locked and held. Sine wished she knew what was going on in their heads but, whatever it was, they weren't sharing. It was as if there was some kind of thought transference going on that no one else was privy to.

At length, Niall said, "I'll only have twenty-four hours to learn to mimic Liam. I could do it when we were kids, because it was so much simpler then. But if Sine will promise to stay close, and if Michael is allowed to come along, then alright. I'll do it." He wasn't enthusiastic and looked more fit to be tied than anything else but he'd agreed, and that was all that mattered as far as Sine was concerned.

The sound in the room began to rise with chatter and congratulations, but Niall stopped them. "At the first sign of trouble, I'll leave. Understood?" This last was aimed at Sine, and she seemed to get where he was coming from but wasn't sure.

"What kind of trouble?" she asked.

"Like if they begin to think I'm not Liam. Or there's complications with an actress, or some such thing. I don't know what I'm up against, but if it goes sideways, I walk."

Sine couldn't get a better deal than that because she knew deep down that no one in a month of Sundays would ever suspect he wasn't Liam. She'd seen how expressive he could be when passion hit. She had only to ignite that passion in him to get him through it, and with Michael there, they couldn't lose. They just had to work on that kiss and get him to relax, like Michael had when he'd been the one to kiss her.

She nodded okay, and watched them file out of the room, back to the waiting room to wait until Liam would wake. As Michael filed out behind Niall, she couldn't help looking at his ass, as fine a piece as she'd ever seen in a pair of jeans, and wonder what that kiss had been about?

Chapter Four

Niall and Michael finally got to their room at a local B&B, glad to be away from everyone else after claiming the need to get some work done so they could leave in another day.

"I'll get the computers," Michael said, tearing his gaze away from Niall's penetrating stare.

"Leave them for now," Niall said, his voice tight with anger.

Michael stood before him, a bronzed god, straight and unafraid.

"That demonstration you and Sine put on. What the fuckin' hell was that all about?"

"Ah, that's what you're angry about. And here I thought it was simply that you had agreed to do something that you so obviously didn't want to do. Do you feel pushed into it?"

"Don't evade my question. Why'd ye do it?"

Michael's own anger rose to the surface at Niall's prodding. "Because you had to be shown. You had to know it's possible to put your own feelings away and just do something you normally wouldn't."

"And ye felt I needed ye to do that for me, did ye? Ye

feckin' neddy." Niall went to the window and jerked the drapes harshly across it, shutting out the night.

"Don't call me a fool and then turn away," Michael said. "I'm no neddy, as you Irish like to put it. I know what you went through, when you tried having girlfriends because that's what everyone else was doing. I remember what you told me, how disgusted you were and how it felt foreign to you."

"And ye don't think I remember that?"

"I'm just pointing out that it's possible for you to go there again."

"Well I did, didn't I? Just to prove to all of ye's so we could get out o' there. But it wasn't that, Michael. It was the kiss ye shared with Sine I'm on about."

"What about it?" He was suddenly looking uneasy. He knew what he'd felt.

"Ye chubbed up when ye kissed. Ye think I wouldn't notice?"

"I was thinking of you."

"Bollocks. Ye were thinkin' of fuckin' her. Or maybe it was the lack ye had the year we began datin' ye were rememberin'?"

Michael had the grace to look ashamed. Michael's girlfriend, the one Niall made Michael give up for a relationship with him; he'd always wondered if Michael loved her more than him.

Michael seemed to know Niall's unasked question. "I didn't love her," he said.

"And do ye fancy yerself in love with Sine, then?"

"Lust, maybe. Not love, there's a difference."

Niall calmed down a little at his lover's words. "Well, that's honest, at least."

"I won't lie to you, Niall. I love you with all my heart and would never lie to you about that. I just can't help a reaction to someone's kiss. She's a fine one, much finer than my old girlfriend. But for you, I'll watch myself, won't let myself get carried away. Because I don't love her. Will never love her. Only you."

"Ye say that now, but we'll be on an island, away from everyone else. Strange things can happen." He stopped for a moment, gathered his wits and tried to control the emotion he was feeling but failed. "God, Michael, when I saw ye all horned up, all I could think on was that I'd only ever seen that reaction with me. And here ye were with someone else, a woman no less, and it all came back how ye made me feel when…"

"I'm sorry. God, luv, I'm sorry." He strode to where Niall was standing and pulled him into his embrace. "I'm so sorry, luv. I never meant to hurt you, and if it makes you feel any better, I felt uncomfortable watching you and Sine together. I wanted to be there, not with her, but with you."

He'd started to rub Niall's arse and it felt good, dreamy. Niall was still feeling upset but Michael seemed to know how to get him out of his funk. His shirt was being pulled from his jeans and he felt Michael's hands, warm, caressing as they stroked his back. His breath was hot on Niall's face as he whispered to him.

"Let's not work right now. We need to do this instead."

Niall was helpless against Michael's touch and even more so when his lover stroked the outside of his jeans where the length of his flute was growing visibly. His breath hitched as those same hands cupped his nads, squeezed, massaged, then popped the clasp and slowly drew the zipper down to release Niall's cock, stiff and eager. Sliding his hands inside, Michael cupped the globes of his arse, pulled him close, and pushed on Niall's jeans until they dropped to the floor, following that article of clothing down until his mouth came into contact with Niall's rigid flesh, and Niall forgot all about being angry.

Michael tasted the pre-cum on the tip of his lover's cock and sighed, part relief, part joy. Niall was so sensitive where love was concerned, and if he was honest, insecure, too. His affair with that girl, or lack, as Niall put it, had nearly torn them apart. They'd been estranged for a time until Michael realized that the girlfriend wasn't filling the gap that only Niall seemed capable of doing. It had taken a long time to woo Niall back.

He pushed the thought of infidelity to the back of his mind. This was the man he loved and no woman could ever take his place. His tongue stroked the side of Niall's cock, and he heard Niall groan, knew he was standing with his eyes closed, relishing the sensations he was creating for him. His lips closed over the silken tip and he took him into his mouth, hugging the shaft, as far as he could.

Niall's hands held Michael's head in place, failing to

get purchase through his short, tightly curled hair. Michael felt those hands do what they normally did when he was getting close. They started rubbing his neck, behind his ears, and then, as they cradled the back of his skull while his own hands kneaded Niall's ass, he heard Niall's throaty grunt, tasted the semen as it began to flow, and sucked until Niall's legs wouldn't support him anymore.

They fell onto the bed and Michael quickly divested himself of his own clothing. While Niall lay languid and boneless from the high of his climax, Michael rolled him over, spread his arse wide, and pressed himself into his lover, eased in the tip, wet with pre-cum, slightly withdrew, and eased in a bit farther. Niall moaned, doing what he could to ease Michael's way by bringing his knees up beneath him. Michael followed the movement, pressed farther inside until he got his rhythm going, felt Niall's body resist the forward push, providing a brace for Michael's thrusts. And thrust he did, riding until he, too, reached his goal. Grasping Niall's hips, he held him close while his climax took him over the edge, his nads shrunk to hard rocks between his legs.

Breathing hard, his ardour spent, he kissed his lover's sweat-soaked back along his spine and up behind his ear. Kissed his shoulders, the back of his neck, tasting the salty sweat that had gathered there. His hands stroked Niall's body, and his cock slid slowly from Niall's arse. It had been so intense he hadn't prepared his lover for his assault and he was worried he'd hurt him. "Are you alright?" he asked, cradling Niall's perfect form against him.

"Mm-hm," came the reply. "Feck, that was good," he exclaimed sleepily.

"Let's just turn out the light and go to sleep. I think we both could use it," said Michael, reaching over to turn the lamp off.

"Right," said Niall, nearly asleep. And then, "Michael?"

"Yeah?"

"I love ye."

"I know. I love you, too."

* * *

Liam lay awake, felt the throbbing of his foot in the cast all the way up his leg, and worried about Niall. Even though Niall had promised he'd do his best to fill in for him, Liam knew the obstacles his brother would face. A nude scene was the least of his worries. All he had to do for that was stand there, get a few shots of his arse, say a few words, and then most of what would follow would be under the covers. It was the under-the-covers part that had Liam concerned.

Niall didn't do relationships well. At least, not with women. He had trouble trusting them, was insecure, and doubted his own ability to cope, not to leave out the fact that he was homosexual. It had driven him underground in his teens, avoiding people and public places as much as he could until coming to terms with his own sexuality. Being a twin hadn't helped because Liam was all over the girls. And the girls? Well, they'd often mistaken Niall instead. He'd thought it funny at the time, but then...

Liam remembered the first time Niall had kissed another

boy. He'd been gobsmacked when Niall told him. But the other lad had come on to him; and to Niall, it had been so easy to allow it to happen.

They'd been fifteen. Liam was out chasing everything in skirts, while his brother was secretly checking out the lads. The day the boy kissed Niall, Liam was reeling from his own experience, his first time with a girl. It had scared him silly but she'd been willing and so they'd waited until her folks left the house, watching from down the road, and knowing her brother was also out, had snuck indoors and quickly done the deed.

It hadn't been a particularly good coupling, when Liam thought back on it. No finesse, no foreplay to speak of, but that was only because they'd been ignorant of all of that. The only thing he really knew how to do was use a rubber. His father had taught him that, whether he'd meant to or not.

Da. What would he make of things now? thought Liam. Niall, finally into a relationship that had him thinking long term. Marriage wasn't an option for him, at least, not in Ireland. But maybe they could do that somewhere else? Hadn't Hank said that it was possible in some jurisdictions in Canada?

He shook his head. Why was he thinking about these things for his brother? It was his brother's business, not his; and yet Liam had always felt protective toward his twin. Niall was tender, his feelings easily hurt. And he didn't understand a lot of the nuances that made up a relationship. He was lucky to have found Michael, who seemed to have a protective streak as well when it came to Niall and seemed to truly care for him. Whatever was between them was solid, wasn't it?

So why was he suddenly concerned that things could go wrong with this setup that Sine proposed?

He tried to rearrange himself in the bed but a bolt of pain shot up his leg and he gritted his teeth against it. He was still gritting his teeth, eyes shut tight against the throbbing, when Sine walked into the room.

"I'll get the nurse," she said, and he opened his eyes to see her walk away before he could react. He had a thing about medication and detested taking anything stronger than an aspirin. But as Sine walked in with the nurse in tow, he knew he'd have to bow down to their wishes. He was beginning to learn that Sine was bossy when it came to some things. The fact that she was still here and not in some pub made him stand up and take notice. Or he would have stood up if he wasn't strung up like a goose.

The nurse followed Sine in, carrying a small paper cup with two pills in it. "These will make you sleepy," she said, handing him the pills, "but they'll at least give you some rest. It's now after eight, so your visitor will have to leave; but I'll give you a few minutes." She seemed a no-nonsense kind of woman, a perpetual frown between her brows.

Liam took the pills, eyeing them skeptically, and then swallowed them down with a mouthful of water. "Ach," he said, "A good porter would help gettin' those down next time."

The nurse turned and left the room.

"Bit of a sourpuss, that one," Sine smirked, one side of her mouth curved into a half smile.

"They work hard," Liam said in the nurse's defense. "Mam says how it's sometimes hard to be friendly when ye've just been puked on and someone can't understand why ye need a moment to clean up."

"Eeew," she giggled. "I guess that's pretty rough for sure. I can't imagine having people throw up on you, or bleed all over you, or stuff like that. Just watching the ambulance guys work on getting your leg out in one piece and all that mess that went with it was bad enough."

"They earn their pay, and that's the truth," said Liam, beginning to feel groggy. "Christ, I don't know what shite they gave me, forgot to ask, but I think I'm goin' to go to sleep soon." He was having trouble keeping his eyes open.

"That's okay. I'll say goodnight now, but as soon as they let me, I'll come back tomorrow."

"Mm-hm," said Liam. She was sounding very far away.

The next thing Liam knew was the rattle of the breakfast cart, delivering the first meal of the day to all the patients on the ward. Mam walked in with his tray, much to the delight of the person whose job it really was.

"How's the leg?" she asked as she plunked his tray down on the trolley and rolled it over to him. "There's some oatmeal here, and toast, coffee, and juice. Ye need to eat it all and keep up yer strength." And then continuing on as she cast an assessing eye over his countenance, said, "I understand they gave ye somethin' to help ye sleep last night. How was it?"

Liam was still trying to get past the first question. The stuff, whatever it was, must have been quite strong because he really just wanted to go back to sleep again. "I don't want to take it again," he managed to get out, "can't keep me feckin' eyes open."

"Hm," answered his mam. "Ye want me to speak to the doctor? I will, if ye say so."

Liam nodded and tried to drift off.

"Liam," she said in a commanding voice that had him lift his heavy lids.

"What?"

"Eat yer breakfast. It'll help wake ye up. Now try not to fall asleep in yer food and I'll see the staff about yer meds. See if there isn't somethin' else they can use that'll be less debilitating."

Liam nodded and watched his mam head out the door, felt his eyes get heavy again.

"Liam!"

His eyes shot open. "Right. Awake. Eat. Got it." He struggled with a spoon of oatmeal and felt like gagging. It needed salt. Dropping the spoon back into the gluey mass, he lay back on the pillow, felt his eyes droop, and gave in to sleep.

* * *

Sine was watching Niall finish his coffee. He was procrastinating, not wanting to get on with what she had termed the "rehearsal." They were at the hotel where she was supposed to have taken a room with Liam but now found herself sleeping alone in the suite upstairs. It was lovely, spacious, and more than fitting for her needs, but the dining room, where they were finishing breakfast along with other hotel clients, was full.

"C'mon," she coaxed. "Niall, people are beginning to stare at you. They think you're Liam, so if you don't want a scene right now, you'll have to hustle."

Niall put the cup down and stared at her. "This is what I'm to do, though, isn't it? Be Liam, be the outgoin' man he is, afraid of nothin'."

"Yes, but…"

"Then if someone asks for me autograph, do I give it? Does Liam? Or how do I handle that? Ye have to tell me 'cause I don't know."

"Right. Okay. Liam signs autographs, usually quite happily," she said in an undertone. "He likes people and encourages interactions with them. So try to be jolly, like no effort is too much to please your audience."

"Feckin' grand," he muttered under his breath. "No matter, I'm done." He stood and pulled his wallet from his pocket to pay for the late breakfast they'd had. He would rather have gone to see Liam, find out a few more things, but he seemed to be Sine's prisoner for the moment.

He paid at the counter and the cashier looked at him and winked. "Loved yer last film," she said.

Niall smiled, winked back, and said, "Ah, thanks, that's grand to hear," and before she could ask for an autograph, he left quickly, Sine following in his wake.

"Why didn't you give her an autograph? You know she wanted one."

"Because I haven't a feckin' clue how he writes his name, for one. I'm sure it isn't like his signature at the bank."

Sine thought a moment. "Hm. We can ask him to show us one."

"Ah, feckit," said Niall.

"What?"

"We're mirror twins, Liam and I. Whatever he is, I'm the opposite. For instance, I'm gay and he's straight. We wear our hair parted on opposite sides…not for looks, but because that's the natural way of it."

"So? We can fix that. It has to be shaved off, anyway."

"That's not all," he continued. "Liam is right-handed. I'm left. I can no more write with my right hand than Liam can with his left. That absolutely cannot be changed."

"Well, that does make things a little tricky. We'll just have to steer you clear of any autograph seekers for now."

"Maybe I can wrap me hand in a bandage, pretend it's hurt?"

Surprising him with a nod, she said, "That might work. Let's think about it."

They arrived back in the room where Michael was closing up the computer. "All done," he said, standing and stretching. "The software's ready to go, I've contacted the team and let them know we're off for a time, couldn't tell them how long because I don't know but said we'd let them know as quickly as we could."

"Grand. One obstacle out of the way."

"Okay," said Sine. "Now your other work. The part where you become Liam."

"Feckit. I was hopin' ye'd have forgotten."

She laughed at that but Niall had been serious. He no more wanted to get on with the rehearsal than he wanted to jump off the Cliffs of Mohr. In fact, he felt he might have a better survival rate if he chose the cliffs.

"Okay, so here's the script. These are the lines you need to learn. Michael," she turned to that man and offered him the script, "it's best if you feed him the lines and I'll help him block out the moves."

They worked for the better part of an hour until Niall felt he had the moves down, at least for the segment they'd been working on. "I need a break," he said, and flopped down on the sofa in the room, then, gazing about him at the room, said, "At least Liam doesn't do things lightly. We can make use of the Jacuzzi later," he winked at Michael, who returned his wink with a grin of his own. Rising, he went to the refrigerator and helped himself to a large bottle of juice, opened it, and proceeded to down the contents.

"Well, at least in that, you and Liam are alike. That's exactly what he would have done," Sine said, watching as he finished it, wiping his mouth with his shirt sleeve, before saying, "Okay. Back to work."

Niall cast her a glance under his brows but then his eyes widened as she began to remove her shirt. "What the feck are ye doin'?"

"Getting ready for the next scene."

She'd said it so matter-of-factly that Niall was stunned.

"C'mon. You, too," she prodded.

"Me too, what?"

"Get undressed."

"Shirt, okay. Jeans, no."

She stopped, her own jeans half off. "Oh, come on, Niall. We're not going to have sex. It just has to look that way."

He couldn't help but stare at her breasts, bared and buxom. She was fully rounded, what anyone with half a brain would call well endowed. And they appeared to be all real. Even he, as a gay man, could appreciate the female form. "Holy shite," he exclaimed as she stood nude before him. "I can see why Liam is attracted to you."

"Why, thank you, Niall." Sine blushed, and Niall glimpsed a softer side of the woman before him. She wasn't a hardened, trained actress all the way through. She had vulnerabilities, he was certain, and it was those softer spots she hid so well that made him like her after all. She was a slave driver when it came to acting, had few inhibitions, but she pushed herself past her comfort zone every time. Could Niall do any less?

"Fine," he heard himself say and then turned to Michael, "If ye don't want to see this, ye can leave. I wouldn't blame ye."

Michael was having none of it. He'd ensconced himself in the arm chair near the window, had leaned back with one foot hooked on top of his other knee. His hands were interlocked behind his head and he was smiling through his words. "Oh no, I think I'd like to stay. Just, when you're finished, we'll kick her out and I'll have a go at you myself. This is too delicious to miss."

Niall felt a reaction in his lower regions to Michael's words. "Ah, feckit," he said, watching his member rise to the occasion. He turned away, embarrassed, and grabbed his t-shirt, holding it around himself, screening his reaction from Sine.

Sine had the grace to share his embarrassment. "I'm sorry," she said. "Usually the guys are too nervous to get a hard-on. There really isn't anything romantic about what we do. It's just acting."

"Yeah, well, try tell that to this 'un," he said, pointing to his body part beneath the t-shirt, rising to the occasion.

"Maybe if I touch it, it'll disappear," said Sine, her bottom lip sucked beneath her upper teeth, an obvious twinkle in her eye.

"I think not," said Niall, and with her threat, noticed that he was beginning to relax. A moment more and the t-shirt came off. He purposely did not look Michael's way. "Right. Let's get at this, then."

They stood facing each other, Michael feeding Niall the lines, of which there were few, and Sine telling him where to put his hands, how to touch, how to move. Comfort in one's own skin was paramount, and his brother was famous. He would have to move into that circle of comfort where he could do no wrong, even with a famous actress in front of him. Would his shyness get in the way? Mam hadn't been joking when she said he was the next thing to a hermit. He shunned publicity, always had. And as Liam became more recognizable, he'd only hid more so that now, only family, their friends, and people that had grown up around them knew that Niall and Liam were twins. To the rest of the world, Niall didn't exist.

He stretched out a shaky finger and touched the tip of Sine's nipple as instructed, watched it rise to a hardened nub and heard her intake of breath. "Like that?" he asked, his voice rough, barely above a whisper.

"Yeah," she nodded, trying to keep her voice steady through the feelings his touch elicited. "Keep going. You're doing it right."

He saw her swallow, then focussed in on the pulse at the base of her throat. He found himself swallowing, too, his throat suddenly dry. He ran a tentative hand down the side of her breast, cupped it, and then put his arm around behind her, pulling her toward him. It was getting easier, he was gaining confidence that he could do this, learning to become his brother, being less afraid of being "out there" because even if he did make a mistake, it would be Liam who would bear the brunt of it. So why not go a little crazy?

He leaned down as instructed and took the nipple into his mouth, then burst out in a fit of laughter and stood up again immediately.

"What?" exclaimed Sine, stepping back, watching Niall try to get his mirth under control.

"Yer nipples are way easier to latch onto than Michael's," he laughed.

A great guffaw came from the other side of the room where Michael was half off the chair in laughter, and Sine joined in. Before long, they were all laughing hysterically, and suddenly Niall didn't care that he was nude. Sine was right. It was just acting. It was going to be fine.

Sine put up her hands in the air. "Okay, I think we have success. Let's finish this up and then I'll leave you guys to it. I want to go see Liam. Just remember that you need to get your hair shaved off before tomorrow."

They blocked out the rest of the moves and this time, Niall found himself moving steadily and easily through it all, never hesitating to touch Sine in intimate places: her breasts, her buttocks, running his hands down her thighs. If he closed his eyes, he could pretend she was Michael, and that helped, too.

She was right. He could do this.

Chapter Five

L iam had been sprung. Mam had convinced the doctor that he could be looked after at home and so here he was, ensconced comfortably on the overstuffed sofa in the front sitting room of Henry's house, flicking through channels on the big screen TV, looking for something, anything to chase the boredom away. His casted leg was propped up before him, two pillows high on a footstool. He still wasn't mobile by any means, and using crutches to get to the bathroom was about as much as he was up for. It would take a few days, he was told, before he could really be up and around.

It would feel like a year.

The knock on the door was unexpected but the person who poked her head in to his invitation of "Come in," was well received.

"I found you," she said. "I called your cell but you didn't answer so I called Henry, and he said you were here. Glad you aren't still at the hospital?"

"Oh, definitely," said Liam in reference to her remark. "What's up? How's the trainin' goin'?"

"Oh, Niall?" At Liam's nod, she said, "Great. I didn't think he'd be able to do it. He was really upset and noncommittal at first but then by this afternoon, he suddenly jumped into it. I think it'll be fine, as long as he doesn't have to write anything in front of anyone."

"What do you mean?"

"He's left-handed."

"Oh, right. Never thought of that."

"It's okay. We'll deal with it if it ever comes up."

"So what did ye do today that changed his mind?"

Sine began to relay the events of the afternoon, and Liam laughed. "Oh feck, I'll just bet he was fit to be tied when he first saw ye undress."

"That wasn't all. Michael was watching and, well, you can guess what happened."

"Chubbed?"

"A bit," she nodded. "But once he relaxed and we got to blocking, he did okay. And then he made a remark about my nipples being easier than Michael's to get into his mouth and we all broke up!"

She had begun to laugh and Liam joined her. "C'mere," he said, patting the edge of the seat on the sofa where he was sitting. He could imagine the sight, her full breasts front and centre and Niall blushing down to his toes. And Michael? Liam had learned of that man's indiscretions, having helped Niall through the rough spots Michael's flirtations with the opposite sex had caused. He felt uncomfortable with Michael being in the same room while that portion of the rehearsing was taking place, able to see Sine as God created her, but Sine seemed fine with it all. In that moment, Liam realized that he didn't know her well enough and decided to immediately remedy the situation.

She sat down beside him and he pulled her to him, fit his hand behind her head and kissed her. Deeply. She responded by opening her mouth to him, welcoming him in and pressing her breasts against his chest.

His tongue found hers and she shuddered in his arms, clinging to him, poised for the next move so that when his fingers strayed to the buttons of her blouse, she placed her hands around his neck, rocking her pelvis forward, spurring him on.

"What are you doing?" she asked, still attached to his mouth, so that her words came out muffled.

"Undressing ye," he grinned, and could feel her grinning, too, even though they were still lip to lip.

"But we're in the front room." She'd barely come up for air.

"No one'll be home for hours yet." He continued to undress her while they kissed, opening her blouse and undoing the front clasp of her bra. "Convenient," he muttered, before breaking off the kiss to take one pink nipple into his mouth and suckling, sending her squirming under his onslaught. "Niall was right. These are easier to find than Michael's."

She threw back her copper tresses and laughed. "How would you know?"

He chuckled his response, then said, "It's easy. He's a man, and unless he's on steroids and looks like a woman, his

73

nipples will be flat and small. Nothin' like these." He then put the other in his mouth, heard her sudden intake of breath, and laughed again. "Help me out, here," he said, struggling to lower the over-sized sweat pants his mam had picked up so he could get them over the cast on his leg.

He lifted his arse and Sine tugged, his manhood standing straight up and ready.

"Shuck yer jeans and hop on," he invited, and he saw the answering gleam in her eyes.

It was awkward, not really comfortable, but Liam managed to slide down enough and Sine managed to spread her legs enough that she impaled herself on him on the limited space of the sofa cushions and began the up and down motions that would give them both release.

"Ye'll have to drive," he said through gritted teeth as he struggled between trying to meet her rhythm and keeping his leg pain-free and still. It wasn't working.

She shifted and he went deeper, a moan of contentment exhaling from her half-opened lips. Straight, white teeth sucked in her bottom lip and Liam could feel her insides clutching his flute.

He pulled her face to his, took her mouth, pressed his lips to her, and mimicked with his tongue what his flute was accomplishing below. She stood on her knees, the motion drawing her up and him nearly out, only to slide slowly back down. He took one peaked nipple of her breast into his mouth, sucked hard, and heard her moan of delight.

Sine repeated the motion; he let her set the pace, knew she

would speed up or slow down, suspend herself where it felt the best because regardless of what she did, he was with her, ready to go at any time. He slipped a lean hand between them, found her sweet spot, and massaged with his thumb, slick with her juices. What he would give to put his mouth there and give her release that way, but she was fully engaged, gripping with her inner muscles, and the result was proving itself.

Her breath came in short bursts, prodded on by his ministrations with his fingers massaging and his mouth on her breast, those full globes of wonder that were all natural. She was wet and slick but tight inside and as the pulsations of her climax registered in his brain, he couldn't halt his own, and regardless of how his leg was feeling, there really was only one brain in action.

He grasped her hips and held her tight to his crotch, felt her spasms subside and clung to her as she leaned against him. "Oh, God, that was good," he whispered in her ear. "Who the hell will do that for me when ye're off with Niall in the tropics?"

They cuddled while they both came down off the high, feeling the room renew itself around them. All time had been suspended; it had been just the two of them.

Eventually, Sine leaned back, still impaled on Liam's flute, pulled her bra closed and began to do up her buttons. "Oh, you'll find someone, I expect."

Liam just laughed. "That'll likely be you more than me. If Niall's to be me, then I must be him; and I don't think I'll fancy a man any time soon."

Sine cocked her head and met his eye. "You know, you two are so similar but so different."

"We are twins," he stressed.

"Yes, but while your physique is similar, and after today, I would know," she laughed, "there are a few subtle differences."

"Such as?"

"Such as this tiny mole on your rib here," she poked at it, a spot no bigger than the head of pin. "It's on Niall's other side, and I noticed he doesn't have the birthmark behind his left ear like you do. Yours isn't very big, but I did notice it the other night. He doesn't have one at all."

"He does, just behind his right ear. Me sister, Ciara, always tells people that's how to tell us apart…the birthmarks. She could just as easily tell people that we part our hair on opposite sides, but she uses that instead."

"Well, from what I can tell, your manly parts are exactly the same."

Liam nearly choked on her words. "Niall really let ye see him naked? I wasn't sure if ye were tellin' it straight or not."

"Uh-huh, and let me touch him, too. Oh, not there," she said when Liam gasped his response, "but his chest, his butt; now that was a nice piece of work, just like yours."

"His arse?"

"Yup."

"What did Michael do?" Liam was in a state of disbelief, his head forward in awe, his stomach muscles taut with holding his torso semi-upright.

She nodded. "He was feeding Niall lines and I was helping him with the blocking. I think that once Niall relaxed and got into it, he was feeling okay about it and then they both just started to enjoy it. I have no doubt, though, that once I left, they went into the bedroom and got it on."

"Like us? Is that why ye came here?" He was part curious, part serious.

"Yes and no," she said, kissing his lips again. "It's just, it's going to be a couple of weeks before I see you again and that's a long time. Especially for you. You might have a new girl by then."

"Ah, me darlin', don't take everythin' ye read in the tabloids to be the gospel."

"But you have a new girl every week. You're always dating someone new."

"Nah, it just looks that way. My publicist likes to show me off as a ladies' man but I'm not really. I'm like other fellas, waitin' to find that one woman I can settle down with." He felt himself slide from her warmth and grabbed some tissues from the pack nearby. "Here."

She took it and they disengaged. He was struggling to haul his baggy sweats up so when she'd got herself tidied up, she leaned over to give him a hand.

"Lift," she commanded, and in the few seconds he could hold it, she'd dragged his clothing back over his arse. He was as tidy as he was going to get.

"Christ, that hurt," he said, shifting his injured leg on the pillows.

"What, the sex or getting you dressed again?"

He laughed in reply. "Sex? Hurt? Not likely, but putting any pressure on that leg just now is not good craic."

"Hm. Well, much as I hate to say it, I have to get going. Niall, Michael, and I are meeting up for dinner. Wish you could come." She was standing, straightening her clothing as she picked up her purse.

"I would, only, ye know Niall and I can't be seen together just now. Maybe after the shoot, but not now."

She nodded in understanding. "I know. Still...." She left the statement unfinished as she finger-combed her silky tresses.

"Call me, every day," he said as she turned to leave. "I mean it. And Sine, c'mere to me."

She stood before him, looking lovely with her long copper hair and ivory skin, the large mounds of her breasts exhibiting perfect cleavage at the top of her blouse. Her flat stomach and rounded hips made her a perfect being in Liam's eyes and he held out his hand for her to grasp. As she did, he pulled her down to his level and pressed his lips to hers.

She answered in turn, tongue to tongue, and Liam could feel himself eager to have her again. Her bag dropped to the floor as her hands clasped the back of his head and then his fingers rubbed the crotch of her pants, felt the tiny bit of moisture that had leaked through, and he moaned. She tucked her hands into his sweats and Liam was glad he'd foregone any underwear. It wasn't practical and would have been too difficult to get over his cast anyway.

They were hard at it, Liam ready to draw her jeans down again when they heard the key in the lock. Sine quickly stood, straightening her clothing while Liam once again struggled to get himself back in his pants. At a failed attempt, he grabbed a cushion and thrust it over his pelvis.

Siobhan stepped inside and closed the door. "Oh, hello, Sine, wasn't expecting to see ye here. Liam, ye must have been glad for some distraction. Would've been boring otherwise." She went to the stairs and with her back retreating up the staircase, her voice could be heard. "I'll take a moment to change and put things away up here so ye's can get yerselves together, like."

Liam and Sine shared an embarrassed look and Liam thought that if anyone could ever turn the color of their hair, it would be Sine right then. Neither could help it. They both burst out laughing.

"Feckit, Siobhan, the mood's gone," he said loudly, knowing his voice would carry up the stairs to where Siobhan had hidden herself away.

"Besides," added Sine, for Liam's ears alone, "once should really be enough. Twice would have been a bonus."

Liam raised a brow and they both burst out in laughter once again.

"Here, let me help you get your pants up so you'll at least look decent, even if you aren't."

"What, me not decent?"

"Never mind, it was a bad pun."

"Ah, don't fash yerself. Come give us a kiss and tell me

ye'll call every day."

"Are you that worried over Niall?"

"Niall? Hell, no. He'll be grand, and Percy Farquharson's the director, a good fella, smart, talented. I just need to know ye're doin' okay. Ye'll be the one keepin' this whole charade together and if it gets blown apart, I need to know because ye'll end up takin' the brunt of it if I'm not there."

"It's only a couple of weeks. A month at most. You'll barely be up and around by then," she protested.

"But if it goes sideways, ye must let me know. I'll get there. If I have to drag this feckin' cast through thirty thousand miles, I'll get there. Ye hear?"

Sine nodded. She looked almost upset, thought Liam, so he pulled her close, kissed her deeply and, forehead to forehead, whispered to her that he wanted her still. "Just because we're to be parted, doesn't mean the party's over."

She grinned and kissed him back, then stood and, once again, straightened her clothing, picked up her handbag from where it had fallen to the floor, and blew him a kiss from the door. "It'll be alright, don't worry." With a wink, she closed the door behind her and left.

Sine walked back to the hotel, glad that it would take her at least twenty minutes. She needed that time to compose herself. Liam had sounded so serious. Was he worried that things could go wrong? She didn't want to be blacklisted from any further work, and that could happen if the bigwigs didn't like what they did, even if it had been in the best interest of the film. It hadn't, not completely, but they didn't need to know that. It was more about protecting Liam from a possible lawsuit.

As she walked, she felt the moisture and tingling in her box, as Liam liked to call it. The Irish had some great sayings and she was building up her own vocabulary, much like memorizing the words to a script. She just couldn't put the letters together to spell something when it came to Gaelic though, as she tried to read the street signs that she passed. Good thing they had English subtitles. Talk about foreign films, she thought, and chuckled to herself.

The moisture between her legs was irritating, despite the memory of what got her that way. It felt like she was walking with wet pants, which she was. Not soaking, just damp. And annoying. A good shower would help once she got back to her room.

She passed the department store on her way back and decided to take a peek inside. It was like any other department store back home, only smaller. But it had some lovely items and she scanned the lingerie with a critical eye. Would Liam like her in something like that, she wondered, taking note of a particularly lacy chemise in a lovely mint green.

Her hand stopped halfway up to the garment and she turned and walked on. Why was she thinking of Liam like that? It wasn't as if he was anybody special to her. She liked him, and she knew he liked her, but she'd been in the business too long to think that a romance that continued through the length of time it took to make a film would necessarily continue. Romances and liaisons happened all the time. Some people flitted from one partner to the next, like promiscuous apes with no mores to fear, and while she wasn't one of those, she had once ended up in a relationship that spanned the life of the film-in-making. That one time turned out to be disastrous for her but she wouldn't compare Liam to the asshole that sent her career in a rapid downhill spiral.

Was Liam really different, though? Did she dare to think that he would be the one man that would make her heart sing for all time? It was too much to hope for as her mind stubbornly recalled that other time.

She'd been working on a film in Manhattan and her role, though not large, had a fair amount of contact with the lead character. She was hoping that it would be the role that would launch her career.

Instead, it had nearly killed it. Jeffrey Harris, the actor, was someone who made her feel weak-kneed when he was near, and seemed to take a shine to her. They'd often talked, she became comfortable in his presence and began to feel closer than just co-workers. He'd was an outrageous flirt with her, eventually taking her to his bed, promising her that she'd be the one in his next film, the leading lady. He'd raved over her hair, her big boobs. She'd thought he was "the one."

And then he dumped her. Before the current piece was even done. She'd gone into his trailer on set, just like she had many times before, and caught him in the act with someone else. He'd simply laughed in her face, said she was crazy to think he'd made any promises to her or offer any help at all. She was a second-rate actress with only nice hair and big boobs to her credit. He'd even said he didn't think she was all that pretty.

It had stung. More than stung. It had cut deeply and to have to go back into work every day until the film was done was like pouring salt in an open wound. When the film didn't bring in the millions it was expected to, Jeffrey had made sure it was Sine who was blamed, even though some reviews had put it down to a poor storyline and Jeffrey's own failure to bring the main character to life.

Then rumors began, rumors of how she'd set him up, worked out a plan to discredit him to his fans. A court case had ensued where three other women came forward, accusing him of fathering their children. It had been messy; her name had been mentioned time and again, and her agent had dropped her like a hot potato. She'd become a liability, and no one, it seemed, wanted anything to do with her.

She'd gone home to Chicago after that, worked a little theatre, and then, at her parents' prompting, decided to look up some family in Ireland to take her mind off things. There were a slew of them, she learned, scattered in three different counties. It was that journey of discovery that had led to bit parts in the filming that was taking place all over the country. The filmmakers either hadn't heard the stories or didn't care, and her varied experience on stage and screen had stood her in good stead. She'd found an agent in Ireland who easily dismissed what they were saying and doing across the pond.

Since then, she'd been careful to never get herself into such a situation again, had avoided relationships almost to the point of being accused of being asexual. No one interested her enough to make her want to take another chance.

Until Liam.

And God help her, she thought she loved him.

Chapter Six

It had been a long plane ride, but after the flight touched down in the Bahamas, they picked up a chartered boat that took them to a small, privately owned island, where the crew settled into grass-roofed bungalows with glass-paned louvered windows that let the cooling breeze from the ocean slip through while still allowing the occupants see out.

The island was small, a speck in the sea compared to the much larger islands where tourists flocked by the thousands. The isle was only three miles long by less than one mile wide, with a small villa at the north end. Along the rocky shore at the southwestern tip, several small huts and bungalows stood sheltered beneath palms, each one concealed from its neighbor by thick jungle growth. On the outside, palm fronds covered high, open-beamed ceilings, giving them an island flare. Each unit was outfitted with a bed and private bathroom but that was where the amenities ended. Meals were taken communally in a large dining hut that also doubled as a bar. Normally rented out to visitors, the film company, in a watertight contract with the island's owners, had scooped up each abode, ensuring the location was secure against unwanted sightseers.

Sine, Niall, and Felicia were lucky enough to have their own huts but Michael, who Sine had been able to get on board as computer-whiz and a helper when needed with the regular crew, would be ensconced in one of the multiple-bed units. That meant that it would be difficult to get him close to Niall but it was the best they could manage without being overt. They were hoping there were some two-bed units but the few existing ones had already been scooped up.

The first day was spent unloading, becoming acquainted with their surroundings, and watching the production crew putting the final touches on the main set, a small lagoon surrounded by palms and punctuated by a waterfall at one end. The production crew, having arrived two days before everyone else, ensured the site was almost ready to go when the actors and Michael arrived.

The lagoon was a site to behold, thought Sine as she took in the stands of palms framing the pond along with several types of flowering plants. Frangipani, hibiscus, and wild unction, some blooms so fragrant they filled the air with their perfume, were on display, covering most of the ground near the water's edge with their beauty. A rocky precipice, crowned with clusters of yellow and red hibiscus at the top and barely twenty feet high, served as the launching point for a small waterfall that fell bubbling and frothy into the pond below. It was a delicious sight, like the stuff of dreams; and with the magic of cinematography, it would look even better, she knew. No doubt the small waterfall would be made to appear two or even three times its actual height.

Away from the jungle and its heavenly pond, the beach started at the rocky southwestern tip, pristine, light beige sand stretching for two miles along the western shore with an expanse of no more than fifty feet between the jungle growth with its variety of palms, Royal Poinciana, and other tropical foliage, and the blue-green color of the Caribbean Sea. Today, the sea was calm under sunny skies and a mild breeze. The smell of the salt water and the sound of the waves rushing the shore filled her with a soul-deep calm that Sine took as a good omen. It would be alright. Niall would make this work and they'd all get to go back home at the end of it with no one being the wiser.

Niall came to stand beside her to stare out at the undulating waves. "Wow," was all he said.

"I know, right?" If she closed her eyes, she could imagine he was Liam, although her body knew differently. They'd managed in Galway quite well, with Niall letting himself go about as loose as he had ever been, according to Michael. The director in Galway had made a few comments; Niall lied, said he was just having an off day, and then tried harder to do as directed. Clearly, it was a struggle for him but they'd managed to finish without raising anyone's suspicions. And tomorrow it would all start again. Niall and Sine were to be in an intimate scene. Luckily, there was no nudity involved, at least for Niall. But it entailed foreplay on his part and she hoped the rehearsal bits they'd done in Killarney would anchor him and make the scene believable, as Liam would do if he were here.

87

"Wicked!" said Michael, coming up beside them, a huge grin plastered across his handsome face. Because he was handsome, thought Sine, and got a familiar twinge that told her there was more to Michael than she'd first thought. "Oh, to have a surf board," he laughed.

"Ye could try body surfin'," said Niall, and both men laughed at that.

"I don't think so, look at those rocks," Michael pointed out.

"Ye don't think a board would get banjaxed on those just the same?"

"Oh, of course it would," agreed Michael, "but it would be a wild ride until it did!"

"Banjaxed?" asked Sine.

"Broken," translated Niall, "into tiny bits."

"Interesting terminology. How did that one come about?"

"What, banjaxed?"

She nodded.

"How the hell should I know? How does any expression come about? It's just Irish," Niall shrugged as if that explained everything, then put his arms around her and Michael and said, "Let's go see if we can round up somethin' to eat. Liam says there's always food on sets, bowls of fruit and the like. I'm starvin'."

They followed the beach a short way until they could see some of the huts through the trees. "The island must be much narrower here," observed Sine.

"There's a map in the dining hut," said Michael. "I

noticed it when I was scouting out the lay of the land earlier. I mean, I had to know where Niall was going to be so I could visit him. So we could, you know…" he said, letting his sentence trail off.

The answer came in the form of laughter. "Yeah, we know," Sine and Niall chimed in together.

Sine didn't miss the caress of Michael's hand as it slid lightly over Niall's butt, nor the look that passed between them. Jealousy rose, a mild feeling but still there, and Sine had to ask herself what she was jealous about? Was it Niall, because he was Liam's twin and would always be close to him, no matter what? Or was it Michael himself, whose black eyes could pierce her to her core, to that place that made her want to jump in bed with him? Maybe it wasn't any of that? Maybe it was just that they had each other, and she was the odd person out, missing Liam?

They sat at a table overlooking the beach, sheltered beneath the shade of a large overhang. Sine pulled out her phone. It was late afternoon and the threesome were enjoying cool drinks at the bar. "I think I'll call your brother, and let him know we're here." She was very careful not to mention his name, still so very aware that it was a dangerous game they were playing.

She waited for what seemed like a long time before looking at her phone. "No signal. I wonder why?"

"Maybe try again later," suggested Michael. "Could just be out for a bit."

"Yeah, but by then it'll be late." She was still looking at

her phone, as if by magic it would work.

"Ireland is a few hours behind us. It'll be fine regardless of the time ye call. Ye know he'll want to hear from ye," offered Niall.

"I guess," she answered, putting her phone down just in time to see Felicia approach.

"Can anyone join in?" she asked, and was met with smiles of invitation.

"What do you think of the place?" asked Sine, by way of conversation. Felicia was not the friendliest of people by nature but her fame had forced her to deal with the flaws in her personality and so instead of the cutting remark of indifference Sine expected to hear, Felicia was chatty, allowed that the island had some great attributes, the best probably being the fact that the bungalows were so well concealed from each other.

"Makes for some great midnight rendezvous," she winked at Niall. Their eyes made contact and she grinned and ordered a drink.

Niall winked back. It was what Liam would do, Sine knew. She only wondered if Niall realized that he'd just given Felicia the go ahead to seek him out later? Well, that would be his problem, and they'd worry about it when the time came. If it came.

In the meantime, there was some work to do, or so Felicia said, and so they headed off to the lagoon where the director wanted to block off his shots for the first scene.

By this time, the properties people had transported

several more plants to the top of the waterfall, filling in gaps, creating a much lusher landscape than the original falls.

The director was calling out orders, checking shots through the squared frame of the thumbs and forefingers of his two hands together.

In an aside to Felicia, Sine said, "That's not Percy Farquharson. Where's Percy?"

"Couldn't make it. Not sure why, but I hear this guy's good. His name's Garry something," replied Felicia, sashaying over to the director, touching his shoulder briefly as she moved past to stand just behind him and off to the side.

The director continued on as if Felicia hadn't even been there. He was in his midforties if Sine didn't miss her guess, wore a ball cap that had seen better days, and with sparse brown hair that stuck out beneath it. His slight paunch was a detraction to an almost handsome face, except that his exceedingly full lips were a big turn-off. She bet they slobbered something fiercely, and realized she was bang on the money when he next spoke.

"It's a slightly smaller area than what I had in mind for this scene," said Garry, wiping his mouth with the back of his hand. "Whoever did the scouting measured this wrong so we'll just work with it. Just means our shots are going to be tight." He squinted his eyes at the scaffold constructed beside the waterfall. "Chuck? You got sight from there?"

The man called Chuck waved his arms. "Be even better once this platform is solid," he said, indicating where reinforcements would be needed on the footings.

"Climb up and see if you can get me one of your famous bird's-eye views. I wanna see right down that actress's top to her big titties."

Everyone standing around, parts of the crew and a few extra cast members, took sidelong glances at Sine, the only actress in that direction, and chuckled. Sine could feel herself blushing and she tried not to let it get to her. So he was a little crass? He wasn't the first director she'd run into like that. Generally speaking, they were a pretty good bunch and by the end of filming, they would all become a tightly knit group, often like a family.

She had no expectations of this group, though. There was something off, and she wasn't sure what it was but despite the loveliness of the island, something just felt wrong. She only hoped it didn't have anything to do with Niall.

Felicia leaned over and said something to Garry, causing Garry to look Sine's way.

"Sine. That's your name?"

He didn't know who she was. Had acted as if she was a nobody off the street, and next to Felicia, maybe she was. Still, his ignorance of her career stung. She'd worked long and hard to get this far, and yet it didn't seem far enough. Maybe that leading lady role would never materialize.

Garry was calling out orders again, "Sine, take your mark here, where this piece of vine ends. Chuck, you got it?" he called out.

The man named Chuck scrambled. The platform wasn't quite ready it seemed and from the way he was moving, he had

92

obvious doubts about its ability to hold a man and a camera steady. He took a lens piece and climbed up the structure, which leaned slightly until he stood on the top, ten feet above the ground. Peering through the small piece, he adjusted and readjusted until he had something he could relate to Garry. "I think it'll work. Let's just get this rig stable before I hoist my equipment up. It's a bit premature to be certain until this thing is solid."

Garry brought his attention back to Sine and Niall. "Okay, let's just do a run-through. We've got a couple of hours before the sun goes down and I'd like to get this one at least rehearsed. The weather has been great but the locals say it's not going to last."

Sine and Niall exchanged a look. Locals? She supposed he was speaking of those from the villa, but there was no time to wonder on that more. Garry was in director-mode and had the crew hopping. Michael had disappeared into the jungle, but could be seen now and then as he did the work he was hired to do.

Soon after, she saw him at the base of the camera scaffolding along with several other crew members, working to steady the structure. Whatever they were doing seemed to have worked because Michael scrambled ably to the top and did several manoeuvers designed to send it toppling to the ground, and when it didn't, everyone cheered. It seemed Michael had suddenly become the hero of the day.

"Right, tomorrow I want every actor in this film to get some sun. Sounds great, right? Don't overdo it. I will have no sympathy for anyone with sunburn. But I don't want a film that shows pasty white characters when they're supposed to have been in the tropics for days." He was eyeing Sine's pale complexion and she grimaced in reply. There had been a lot of outdoor shooting in Ireland, but while their faces had taken on some color from the sun, the rest of their bodies hadn't.

"Sorry. I don't tan; never have, never will. I'll get mildly pink and leave it at that. Okay?"

Garry nodded, then laughed. "Okay by me, spitfire. Just don't burn those boobs." To the rest of the crew, he ordered, "Now let's get this done. I want to see the makeup guy. Where is he? Makeup!"

The makeup man moved his way forward and waited for instructions.

"When we shoot this, I want smudges here, and here," said Garry, indicating areas on Sine's face. "I want her to look like she's been running through the bush and gotten a couple of scrapes, maybe dirt or mud from falling. As for Liam, try darkening him a bit. He's supposed to have been out here for a lot longer."

The fellow nodded and left. Garry looked pleased; things were moving along. "Okay, let's get some blocking done."

They got to work, moving, saying their lines, and by the time the sun was sinking and everyone's stomach was grumbling, they had the basics of the scene down.

Niall hadn't flinched when he had to perform. He was getting used to being Liam, to being as outrageous as his brother could be. His hands hadn't quivered when he caressed

Sine's breast, and when he brought his lips to hers, it was as if Liam was before her, different, yet the same. It brought a sadness to her heart and yet there was an urgency there, too, as if once this sojourn was over, she and Liam could pick up where they left off. That urgency was coupled with a hope she was too worried to explore. Worried that by putting a name to it, it would disappear.

* * *

Hours later, when midnight had long passed, Niall dragged his tired body off to his hut. Too exhausted to even shower, he flopped on the bed in the welcome darkness and cool enclosure of the small space. The night had remained calm and the temperature had stayed steady, cooling only slightly once the sun had sunk below the horizon.

A scratching at the post by his door had him instantly alert, and then Michael's quiet whisper, calling his name.

"Here," he answered, just as quietly. With hardly a breeze, sound carried across the night.

He heard Michael's steps, felt his hand upon his leg as he tried to orient himself to Niall's room.

"I could turn on a light," Niall said, and heard Michael's answering chuckle.

"Oh, wouldn't that just be grand, as you Irishmen would say. We'd have visitors in no time."

"Why? What makes ye say that?" Just then, the sound of laughter carried across the distance from a neighboring hut. "Oh, I get it. There's no filmin' tomorrow so everyone is in party mode?"

"Something like that. I thought we could have our own party here."

"What did ye have in mind?"

Michael grunted but the sound was more humorous than flippant. "Just wait," he said, and Niall felt Michael's hand searching, following the length of his thigh, up his hip to caress his shoulder before cupping his chin and bringing Niall's lips to his.

They kissed; soft, warm. Hungry. A breeze found its way through the opened windows, bringing with it the scent of night flowers and Michael's cologne.

"Mmm, sandalwood," said Niall. "Ye wore it for me?"

Again, a chuckle in the night. "Sure as hell didn't wear for those wankers," he indicated with a nod of his head, barely visible in the moonlight, toward his own hut farther down the path.

"C'mere to me," said Niall, leaning back on his pillow and bringing Michael with him.

Michael followed, and Niall heard him loosening the ties of his cargo shorts and kicking them off before coming to lie on the bed beside him.

Michael's hand stroked Niall's hip. "God, your skin's so warm, and bloody soft."

"Body cream," explained Niall in a throaty whisper, "hopin' ye'd come to me."

"I couldn't wait," and then, "touch me," whispered Michael.

"I want ye. Ye know I do. Just not yet, hm?"

"I don't want to wait. Been waiting all day, just seeing you touching Sine, doing things with her that I wish you were doing with me."

"Tell me," Niall kissed Michael's cheek, worked his way to his mouth, stroked his lips with his tongue until they parted, then pushed his way in, not caring if Michael would tell him anything or not.

Michael pulled back. "I could see from where I was standing. Had a good view. Your hands on her, stroking, much like you're doing to…ah," he breathed.

"There?"

"Yeah." Again, "Aaah. Don't stop."

A muffled sound, a deep breath being exhaled, the word "God," whether in supplication or thanks, it didn't matter.

"Here. In here," Niall said, rolling over and presenting his backside to his lover. He felt Michael's hands on his arse, heard his joyful intake of breath.

"You're lubed already," Michael said, working Niall's arse cheeks like a masseuse, spreading them, readying him.

Then came the feeling Niall had been waiting for all day. For days, if the truth be told. There'd been no chance once they'd left Killarney and now, several days later taken up with preparation and travel, it was their first opportunity and he didn't want to wait any longer.

Michael went slowly, easing himself into Niall, waiting to bury himself to the hilt before taking a moment to cup Niall's nads and stroke his erection.

Niall felt Michael's fingers along the length of his lad,

felt him splay the tip with his finger and spread the pre-cum that had formed there around the head. He sucked in his breath and Michael began moving inside him. Sweat beaded up on his spine; he felt it roll between his shoulder blades and jumped at the searing heat of Michael's tongue as he licked it off the heated skin along his spine.

Pressure built in Niall's groin, but he didn't want it to end yet. "I want to do ye, too."

"In a minute, I'm not done yet."

Those magical hands, thought Niall, as Michael stroked his flute, juggled his nads between his fingers, and tweaked his flat nipples before kneading his pecs. He began to laugh.

"What's so funny?" came the gurgled voice of Michael as he grunted his restraint against an early climax.

"What I said before. You know. About Sine's nipples being a damn sight easier to suckle than yers."

"Maybe I'll have to try one day. Just not right now."

"And never, if I have anything to say about it." It was a point of contention between them. The only point. Michael, Liam knew, could take a woman any time he chose. He had the looks. More than that, Michael wasn't exclusively homosexual. He liked women sometimes, too. And while Niall had been able to swear fealty and everlasting devotion to Michael, he knew Michael would never be able to promise the same thing.

Michael's answer was to squeeze Niall's balls until he cried out.

"It's true, ye feckin' ráicleach."

"Who's calling who a slut, you raaklochk," Michael grunted as he pressed himself harder into Niall's arse.

Niall laughed despite the sensual feelings overtaking him. "Christ, ye'll never learn to pronounce Gaelic, even if ye understand what I call ye... Ah, easy... Oh, that's better...."

"More?"

Niall's answer was to nod.

Pressure built. The sound of the waves on the ocean accompanied the rhythm of Michael's thrusts. The wind blew a cooling reprieve through the room.

"Ah. Ah." The sound of heavy breathing, gasping accompanied by deep, male grunts, and finally, "aah," the long protracted sigh of Michael's release before he laid his body along Niall's back.

Sweat was a glue that held them in place, a lubricant that allowed them to slide effortlessly to a more comfortable position.

Niall felt Michael slip from his arse, took a few moments to regroup, and then...

"My turn."

Chapter Seven

The following morning, as people headed out to the beach after a breakfast fit to satisfy almost any appetite, Niall approached Sine on the path and asked if they could practice the scene scheduled for the next day.

"Remember? It's the one where they're still on the boat, just before it capsizes or whatever," said Niall. "You and I didn't get a chance to go over that before we left and I just heard about it last night. What happened?"

"Oh, that one. Yeah, I remember. They thought they had it but didn't like it or something. Anyway, we have to re-do it. Shouldn't be too hard, just a scene in bed, mostly sleeping," she explained. "Need help with positioning?"

"Yeah, if ye wouldn't mind."

"Not at all." And then, "By the way, I tried calling Liam again last night and nothing. Phones aren't working here. I asked some of the other crew and they said the same thing. That means that if I can't call out, Liam can't call in. Right?"

"True. I thought there was supposed to be mobile service and internet service at the food hut," thought Niall out loud.

"It's all pretty new stuff here, so maybe they just haven't got it hooked up yet. I just wish I could call him or he could call me." She had a strong feeling that she needed to talk to him, to let him know how she felt, but suddenly there was no more time to ruminate on it. They were almost at Niall's hut in time to see Michael on the path ahead.

"Goin' to the beach?" asked Niall, and Michael stopped, spun around, and seeing them, shook his head.

"'Fraid not. We crew people have to work, but I don't have to be anywhere for about half an hour so I stopped in to see what you were doing, only you weren't there."

"Late finishin' breakfast," said Niall, knowing full well that Michael had likely just got out of the shower and was on his way back to his own hut that he shared with three other crew members. They'd been together all night but he wasn't about to let on to anyone, not even Sine.

"You can help us rehearse," Sine invited. Michael returned her grin and the three walked into Niall's hut together.

"Okay, what's this all about then?" Michael asked, removing his sunglasses once inside.

A quick explanation soon had them in position, Niall and Sine in the bed and Michael in the chair opposite, watching and occasionally giggling.

"Spill it. What's so funny?" asked Niall.

Michael couldn't resist telling him. "You look bloody awkward, my dear."

The word "dear" came out "de-ah," which then had Sine giggling. She showed Niall how to re-settle and tried the positioning of his hands on her while snuggling in bed.

Her bikini top was in the way, impeding Niall's ability

to be as comfortable as much as he could be. "It doesn't feel natural," he complained, and from Michael's reactions, it didn't seem to look natural, either.

"Oh, for God's sake, Niall, you look positively awkward. Here, let me show you. Get out of there and watch how a pro does it."

"Just what are ye confessin' to being a pro of?" asked Niall, sliding out from beneath the sheets, straightening his cargo shorts when he stood.

Michael hauled off his t-shirt and shucked his own shorts so he was nude, explaining, "If you get natural, it'll look natural," and then shimmied next to Sine and removed her bikini top, exposing her large breasts above the sheet. "Just watch," he said, a twinkle in his deep brown eyes as he urged her to her side. "I hope you'll excuse me touching you." He kissed her cheek, then pulled her close to spoon around her.

She wasn't immune to the feel of him behind her, only a bikini bottom separating the skin to skin contact that she was suddenly curious about. And then, before she could say what she needed him to do, he'd cupped her bared breasts and showed Niall precisely what he would need to do in order to make the scene appear natural.

"If you put your hand here, on the bottom breast, instead of here," he indicated by moving his hand from the bottom to the one on top, you can still do what Garry wants but you won't be blocking the shot. And then just let this breast rest on your forearm, and you're in business." He lifted his head to look at Sine. "Comfy?" and was rewarded with a grin and a nod.

"How the feck d'ye know that?" asked Niall, rising from the chair to check it out.

"I was watching from over there. Besides, don't you ever watch movies or television? They do it all the time like this," Michael said.

"No. I don't watch much television. Ye know that. At least, not unless it's racing cars or motorbikes or a good football match. Ye know I don't watch the same types of shows as ye do."

"How on earth do you two ever get along?" asked Sine, one long limb above her head on the pillow, seemingly comfortable with Michael's hand on her breast.

"Lots of patience, dear one, lots of patience," said Michael as he kissed her cheek once more, then moved to her mouth and came over her.

"Enough, Michael, I get it."

Michael didn't move.

"Ah, feckit. I'm out of here." He stormed out of the hut, a look of anger and hurt across his features and Sine thought the little display Michael put on was really only for himself alone, and not for Niall at all.

As Niall left, Michael kissed her deeply and slid down her body to take her nipple in his mouth.

Sine gasped and then moaned in pleasure. "Michael, this is not good." He was doing wonderful things to her, things he shouldn't be doing.

"You don't like it?"

"I do. That's the problem. Let's not get carried away. We

both have too much to lose." She was serious. If this was what Niall was angry about, she conceded that he had a right to be.

Michael pushed sheets back and tucked his leg around hers, baring his arse to the breeze. "Then you agree there's an attraction here." It was a statement, something he must have thought he knew for certain.

She looked at him through the cinder colored lashes. "There's a curiosity. That's different."

Michael kissed her again and slid off, for real this time, pulling his shorts on while she sat up and put her bikini top back on. He was watching her, an appreciative smile on his face. "Too bad we can't explore more. I have to get to work, it seems. I think I may be late." And then exclaimed, "Oops," in a flippant manner. Obviously, he really didn't care he was late and the smile he left her with was both cheeky and promising, as was the less than flaccid member he'd quickly covered up by dressing.

After Michael left, Sine stood and picked up her towel where she'd thrown it when they first came in, and took a quick look around to make sure she hadn't left anything else. Then, leaving Niall's hut, she closed the door behind her; and noticing Felicia far ahead along the path toward the beach, walked slowly so as not to catch up. For some reason, she didn't want Felicia to know she'd just come from Niall's hut, even though they had been legitimately rehearsing.

Well, almost legitimately. She felt herself blush at the memory of Michael's body next to hers and was at once angry and at odds with her feelings. Like she'd told him, she was only curious. Shaking off the memory, she tucked her towel beneath her arm and headed for the sand. She wouldn't allow herself much more than a few minutes before covering up beneath the already hot morning sun.

* * *

Liam had waited long enough. Sine had promised to call every day. He'd made her. She'd said she would. And yet two weeks had gone by and she'd yet to call his mobile. He would have known if she had, he'd been bloody well sitting on the feckin' thing all along.

The only thing that kept him calm was the fact that he knew intimately what working on a film was like. Your time wasn't always your own, nor could you account for every second of every day if you had to. Things often moved too swiftly to acknowledge that time had gone by and before you knew it, a week had turned into a month and all promises were off.

But this time, things would be different. He couldn't stand by and let fate determine the outcome. Not now. Although she hadn't called him, there wasn't anything written anywhere that said he couldn't call her.

He dialed the number and waited. Nothing, just a message that said the mobile customer was unavailable. He tried it again, and then just to be sure, a third time. He then tried Niall's phone with the same result.

He finally came to the ultimate conclusion that there was no mobile service where she was, but he knew he could get a message to her via other means. There was email but again, that was assuming there was internet. He knew that lots of faraway places would have internet at one location, the bar or restaurant or something, where people could be in contact with the outside world, but he would need to know her email address for that, and he didn't.

Any other form of contact he could think of would be difficult. He'd have to come up with some ruse, pretend he was Niall and needed to speak to Liam…or something. He couldn't be Liam calling. And he certainly didn't know who the crew members were. In the Caribbean, they'd have a completely different crew with the exception of a few key people, he thought. This was the first time he'd had a chance to go anywhere on a foreign shoot of this kind. He'd made films in France, the Netherlands, and Britain, but this was to have been his first chance at something completely different, and he'd fucked it up good.

He stumbled as he got up from the sofa, grabbed futilely at thin air, and tumbled to the floor, cursing the day he'd suggested climbing that godforsaken hill. He'd done it a million times before so why should this one have been any different?

He waited until the throbbing in his ankle stopped. It was a nasty break, but clean, the only complication being that it had required surgery to insert pins to keep the bone in place. He'd be left with a small scar but it would eventually heal and be as good as new. He just couldn't wait until that happened. His first cast had already been changed to a much lighter one, something they called an air cast. Must be because it was as light as air, he mused, picking himself up off the floor. Light, it may be, but it was still a cast, and still clumsy. He couldn't wait to be free of it altogether.

Henry walked through the front door in time to see Liam dust himself off.

"Tryin' to vault the furniture again, are we?" he quipped, and Liam scowled his reply.

"I'd take it in a millisecond, and well ye know it," he said, not even trying to keep the swaggering tone from his voice.

Henry ignored the comment and asked, "Heard from anyone yet?"

It was as if his big brother could read his mind. "No... nothin'."

"Wearin' on ye, is it?"

Liam nodded.

"So call. What'll it cost ye?"

"It's not money..."

"No, don't be daft, eejit. I'm not sayin' the cost is monetary. It's yer feckin' sanity I'm talkin' of."

Liam looked at his phone. "I tried already. Can't get through." And then, "What time is it there, do ye reckon?"

Henry gazed at the ceiling as if that would supply his answer for him. The thumb and fingers of his hand worked together. "About four hours behind us, I'd say. Not sure, but that's close enough."

"So, it's now six here, so it'll be, what, two in the afternoon?"

Henry winked at his brother and grinned. "Niall would be so proud of ye to have got that one all on yer own."

"Ah, gabh transna ort fhéin," said Liam.

Henry only laughed. "No. I've Siobhan to play with. Who've ye got for yerself? No one. No, mo dheartháir, ye need to learn that one woman can satisfy ye, and tellin' me to go fuck myself won't get ye what ye want. Ye may find ye'll need to go there yerself."

Liam slammed his fist on the back of the sofa, which was entirely counterproductive since the sofa was overstuffed and left no mark, no sound of breaking glass, or anything that would have given him satisfaction. It had even been too soft to hurt himself over. "Ye bollocks, ye know I can't do that! They'll see we're twins. They'll know Niall is not me. Whatever he's got goin' on, I can only trust is still alright."

"Well, ye've got the right of it there. I'd lay bets she's wantin' ye there. Who else to scratch an itch…"

"What are ye sayin'?" said Liam, glaring at Henry.

Henry laughed outright. "Ouch!" he chuckled. "Looks like I've hit a sore spot."

"C'mere to me now," said Liam, bringing his fingers to his palm, as if he was begging Henry closer. And he was. Just close enough that he could lay one on his big brother.

"Don't be an eejit," said Henry, goading Liam. "We both know well that Sine and you've been doin' each other. Siobhan's not blind, ye know, and neither am I. I don't need to walk in on ye, as she did, to know what's goin' on. And anyways, I don't feckin' care. It's yer life, ye're past twenty-one. So if the two of ye's want to get it on, ye have my blessing."

Liam stood up, puffed out his chest, and realized that if he'd had a proper shirt on, he'd have tugged it straight. As it was, it was only a t-shirt and tugging it wouldn't have accomplished anything.

It was a standoff. Contact was eye to eye, and that was how Siobhan saw them when she walked in moments later. "Oh, for God's sake, are ye at it again? Can ye not just talk without havin' a fist fight each time, fer feck's sake?" She went straight into the kitchen, dropped the bags she was carrying on the table, and turned to the two men. "There's more bags in the car. I've been to the grocery store and picked up some food. Seems we've an extra mouth to feed for a time so if ye wouldn't mind, Liam, a donation to the family coffers would not be amiss. And Henry, ye've bigger hands than me. I'd appreciate the help, thank ye very much."

She went back out the door, ostensibly to bring in more bags, leaving Henry and Liam staring at each other, grim-faced.

"Well," said Henry, eyeing Liam's air cast, "I think ye should get some practice on that thing. It's a straight path from the car to the door. Maybe ye should give it a try?"

Liam was left standing in the front room, oversized sweat pants hanging down around his arse and the t-shirt he'd worn for the last few days, stained and smelly on his chest. He was a wreck. A mess. He stank.

But Siobhan's and Henry's words seemed to be the

impetus he needed. Taking a tentative step, he made one step into two, and despite crutches, was soon hauling in his share of groceries from Siobhan's car.

The plastic bag slipped from his hand just as he got it to the table, the contents, a few tin cans and a magazine, spilling across the polished wooden surface. Grabbing a tin in one hand, he managed to stop the magazine from sliding from the table onto the floor without losing his crutches with the other. A photo on the front cover and bold headlines halted his gaze.

Without speaking, he put the runaway tin down and righted the tabloid so he could read it properly. Only then did the expletives start flowing.

"What the hell? Siobhan, what's this?" His look took in his brother's wife, his brother, and Emily, newly arrived.

"Oh, that's my magazine," young Emily said, reaching for it.

"Oh no, ye don't," said Liam, holding it from her and halting her in her tracks with a forbidding look.

"But it's mine," she argued. "Give it to me."

"Not yet," he answered, and knew that regardless of keeping this copy from her, there were thousands more out there, and different ones, too, all with the same sordid stories.

He sat down heavily on one of the chairs at the table, leaned his crutches against the table's edge, and took the offensive magazine in hand. "Liam O'Farrell's Competition," it read, and there emblazoned in a half-page photo were Michael and Sine in bed, clearly together. Michael's arse looked bared to the camera but had been blurred out. Sine was covered, thankfully, her large breasts beneath a single sheet with Michael's hand draped possessively across them. Under the photo's caption was, "more, page 3."

Liam opened the paper and saw a photo of himself and Sine, nude but discreetly positioned so that nothing too embarrassing could be seen. The tousled sheets were strewn haphazardly across the bed; the familiar pattern of the B&B bed covers just visible beneath a beautifully sculpted foot. Her foot. Next to his.

"How the hell…?" said Liam, and never finished his question. He was too angry to say anything while he read the filth that was being reported.

He wanted to rip the sordid thing in his hands to shreds. Instead, he stuffed it into Emily's grasp before gathering his crutches beneath his arms.

"But Uncle Liam," Emily began.

"Not a word," he warned. "Not. One. Word. Ever. Understand?"

The girl nodded, eyes wide. He'd never spoken to her like that before.

Feeling a rage so potent he feared letting it loose, he stumbled out of the house as best he could and down the road as fast as the crutches would allow. He wanted to hit. To run. To do something, anything that would take away the wild energy that had suffused every cell in his body with white hot rage.

No excuse. There could be no excuse for her duplicity. In his fury, her words that morning at the B&B came back full force. "The rumors are true," she'd sighed in his arms, and he, who had loved her from the moment he'd laid eyes on her, had believed it to be akin to somehow lauding him.

He hadn't seen it coming. Hadn't thought that he was just a notch on her list of conquests. He'd been set up. Liam had his own list of conquests but he'd never told anyone about any of them. He was known for that, at least. He didn't believe in kiss and tell. There'd only been snippets here or there of who he was seeing at the time but rarely did any photos accompany the rumors. And when they did, they were stock photos for the most part, publicity pictures taken for whatever production they were promoting, and sometimes resurrected when the tabloids ran out of new dirt to spread around. So he'd never made the front page with overly negative headlines, and had been glad of it. He hadn't realized how glad, until today.

He eventually found himself in front of the old country estate known as the Desmesne, with the gates open and a bit of sun poking through the clouds overhead. Solitude was what he wanted just then and he needed the sculpted paths and walkways of the park-like grounds. He couldn't go running through the underbrush as he so desperately needed to do. Instead, he took the newly laid driveway to the right and followed it along the grand expanse of lawn next to the forested areas. There were gardens with meandering pathways if he wanted to explore them but what he wanted most was the lake.

A half hour later had him at the edge of Lough Leane, where, if he'd had a vehicle and could drive, would have gone to Aghadhoe instead, to view the lake from the site of the old Roman tower, or what was left of it. He'd spent many an hour sitting on the bench on that hillside or roaming the ancient graveyard next to it, under sun or cloud. It never mattered. The view had always cleared his head.

There was no hope for that on this day, though. He'd need to get himself a rental car, an automatic, if he was ever to drive until his foot healed. It wouldn't be weight bearing for at least another month, and even then, driving a manual shift would be next to impossible.

His thoughts returned to Sine. He had never before experienced such devastating heartache from a woman. He'd felt a great loss when his da was killed when his truck rolled over but he and Niall had been boys, only eight. With time, the pain had lessened. Or was it just that he'd become used to the hole that would never be filled when a loved one passed on?

It wasn't the same, though. Thinking of losing Sine was like cutting off his arm. He was floundering, unable to see a way forward, and hindered by the encumbrance of his broken foot, unable to have freedom of movement to do anything about it. He wondered if he'd be able to fly to the Bahamas, find the location set for filming, and see for himself what was happening? He knew, more than most, that what was reported in those rags was often far from the truth.

Yet there had been photos. Pictures of her in bed with Michael. Pictures of himself in bed with her. He knew that photo wasn't a fake. There is only one way they could have

113

been caught together like that and it didn't have anything to do with the production. He didn't believe that one had been photo-shopped, either. If it was, it was a damn good job.

Had someone known it was him and rigged a camera in the room at the B&B while they were out? He'd heard of that before, although not often. Regardless of how many productions were active in Ireland, the actors easily maintained a low profile within the towns and villages they utilized. Most people were happy to leave them be, and smile or nod courteously in greeting. This was the first time Liam had been victimized in such a way. Fame had many costs, he knew, and this was but one.

The evening sky was beginning to darken so he picked up his crutches and cut through the bush on the main path to find the exit gate onto Beech Road. He'd scale the bloody wall if he had to because it was late and he wasn't sure what time the gates would close. He hadn't noticed the posted times when he used the entrance off Muckross Road.

His luck held and he hobbled through the large gate with its wrought iron bars reaching upward between stone pillars, and exited onto the well-traveled road before making his way slowly back to Henry's. "Ah, feckit," he thought, and directed himself off to the nearest pub instead.

Chapter Eight

Niall finally had Michael to himself for an entire night, Michael's earlier indiscretion with Sine forgotten. It hadn't been easy. Truth be told, it had been bloody difficult, but they'd finally managed to make up and find a time to be together. But Michael's talents with a computer were suddenly being put to use. He was often in the production tent, out of sight of everyone, including the crew that had begun to plague his very existence. Inwardly, Niall was glad Michael could escape scrutiny. Michael was a professional, used to dressing in three piece suits and looking like he just walked off the runway of the most prodigious fashion house, a far cry from the jean-clad variety of earthy men who were more often seen in a rough-and-tumble way than the civilized crowd that made up the bulk of both Niall's and Michael's friends. As work on the film progressed, Niall saw less and less of Michael.

He also saw less of Sine. There was something happening there that he didn't understand, but rumors had begun to spread, reasons why she'd relocated to Ireland and jumpstarted her career. Niall really didn't care why she moved; was only glad for her solid presence in the face of the unknown. But with her being shunted elsewhere, for what reason he didn't know, his feeling of security was cracking and he felt the predators honing in on the kill. Only, he didn't know why, or from what direction they might come.

A small smile curved the corner of his mouth as he watched Michael sleeping, the deep breaths almost a snore. Michael had been just as tired as he was and he knew from their lives together that Michael snored only when he was exhausted.

Niall ran the back of his fingers gently across his lover's cheek and chuckled when Michael wrinkled his nose in response; he loved him more than life itself.

Eyes black as night opened, focussed as a smile crossed the strong jaw, dark with a day's growth of beard. Christ, he could be a male model, all sculpted planes and sensual eyes and mouth, thought Niall.

Niall leaned over, took the mouth, soft and pliant beneath his own, and then moved closer, cupping Michael's nads, feeling him chub up in his hand. Michael returned the favor and Niall felt the familiar euphoria streak through him, a sharp jolt of excitement that started at the base of his spine and ran straight to his lower brain.

Michael seemed to have woken in a mood to take charge

116

because he slid down and disappeared beneath the light sheet that covered them. Niall felt his lad engulfed in the hot, moist climate of Michael's mouth. Sensations wrapped his body, the scent of the cool morning air before the heat of the day took over, bearing with it the smell of moisture from the rain that had pelted down during the night. Birds had begun to chirp and call through the jungle outside as the sky took on a lighter hue.

His mind had stopped working as Michael worked his magic. Pressure built, his nads tightened as every fibre of his being tensed beneath the onslaught of Michael's mouth.

Michael's tongue played him like a musical instrument and Niall was no more able to stem the flow than he would have been able to stop the sunrise. Both were inevitable, and both grand. The first rays of daylight pierced the open window as Niall quietly vocalized his release in heartfelt sighs and sounds of completion, then lay back on the bed, sweating and breathing hard.

Michael poked his head up from his place near Niall's groin. "Good morning, luv," he whispered, a gleeful grin spread across his handsome features.

Niall held out his arms, and Michael gladly crawled the short space into them. After the turmoil of the last few days, it felt good to be in Niall's arms again. He longed for them, hated leaving the one he loved to the mercies of the unruly crew. Individually, they were manageable, a few of them quite friendly. But Michael was no stranger to bullies, having grown up unashamed of his homosexual leanings, and could pick a troublemaker out of a crowd a mile away. And this crowd was full of them.

He turned and rolled beneath Niall, caressed him as he urged him to go back to sleep. Witness to the fatigue that was beginning to plague him, Michael knew no other way to help ease the burden that Niall carried. They'd been working for ages on this arse-hole of an island, an island that had them all enthralled at first. But as time wore on and technical troubles began to surface, the short space of time allotted to do the work was soon used up and the production began to run on the contingency fund.

It was no one's fault. The equipment had been housed in a tent that looked sheltered enough to withstand the heavy wind and rain that had come, but sadly, was not. A portion had worked loose and within a short space of time; with the wind picking up speed and people running for cover, no one had thought to check it out. An entire canvass panel was torn off and two cameras and some audio equipment had to be flown in to replace those that had been damaged by the torrential downpour. They'd had two such storms since beginning their work, and if they'd had a chance to finish in the allotted time, all would be well, they could go home. But now they were behind and other storms were building. If they didn't wrap up soon, the production could be in jeopardy.

Michael kept it to himself. No need to tell Niall and have him concerned he was putting Liam's livelihood at risk, even though it wasn't his fault. But Niall would think it was. And Liam wouldn't know anything until it was all over.

Briefly, Michael wondered how Liam was doing, if his foot was any better? Henry had described in great detail the moment they extracted Liam's foot from between the rocks. It had made Michael's skin crawl and he couldn't help the sensation that sent a shiver up his spine.

"Mmm?" asked Niall, snuggling closer into Michael's arms, a questioning look in his sleep-filled eyes.

"Nothing. Go back to sleep. It's too early to get up yet." He snuggled down with him, knowing he needed to be up and out of there before they were discovered. But morning was just breaking and the few housekeeping staff wouldn't be around for at least an hour yet. He felt his eyes becoming drowsy again and kicked the covers off his over-heated body. He loved cuddling Niall, but it was already warm out and Niall had a heat that was all his own.

Minutes later, Michael's eyes closed tightly in sleep.

* * *

The pub was getting full. It was half six, he soon realized, and the taproom was lively with customers. A one-man band was entertaining at the front, so Liam made his way through the crowd to an empty seat at the bar and ordered up a pint. The bartender poured the stout three quarters full, then left it to rest until the black solidified beneath the layer of head before drawing the rest. Setting the pint glass down, he filled an order of whiskey for one and a shandy for another. Then coming back to the stout, which had now turned to its customary black finish, placed it on the counter in front of Liam.

Liam nodded and paid for his drink, then took a deep draught, nearly spilling it when he felt a hard slap across his back. "Well if it isn't Niall, and all alone tonight. Where's yer man?" asked a familiar voice. "And what's with the hair? I almost took ye for Liam just now, though he's away, I take it."

Liam swatted the man's hands off his newly grown hair, where thick fingers were tugging at the emerging strands. He sighed in dismay as he recognized an old mate of his brother's, Connor Grady. "Ah, Connor, nice to see ye. Michael's away just now," he said, knowing it was true. He really wished Connor would go away, too.

"I see. So, me and the fellas was wonderin'...ye know, what's in them tabloid papers? It must be true, if ye're here and Michael isn't. I mean, did ye see?"

Liam was about to say he had when Connor bellowed to his mate at a nearby table. "Johnny, let's see yer woman's newspaper." The man named Johnny handed it over to Connor, who made a big fuss about turning it to the correct page. "Here, right here. See?"

It was a different paper than what Liam had seen before. This one's headlines read, "Another Side to Liam O'Farrell," above a photo with himself and Michael in bed.

No, not himself, he corrected. Niall. The other two photos he saw in Emily's paper were present here, too, along with a story about too many choices for Ireland's famous son. Liam choked on his stout. "Jaysus feckin' Christ," he swore. "Has he no shame?"

"So, it's true then," said Connor, and before Liam could add anything, said, "It's sorry I am to hear that, me lad. I'd hoped it was a mistake."

Liam pushed the paper away. "I don't know. It might be," he mumbled under his breath, then downed the entire glass of stout with one breath, banged the glass on the counter, and wiped his mouth with his sleeve. Quickly gathering his crutches, he began to hobble out the door.

"Where ye goin'? Ye just got here. Hey, what did ye do to yer foot? Thought I heard something about one o' ye's breakin' yer foot but thought it was Liam. Guess it can't be if you're here, eh, Niall?"

Liam only nodded, teeth gritted. Whatever calm had come over him from working out his anger before was nothing to what he was feeling now. "Feckin' Michael, feckin' Sine. Feckin' all o' them, the lousy, feckin' lot o' them," he muttered under his breath as he step-thumped his way back to Henry's. Behind him, he was sure he heard the familiar laughter that accompanied jokes about arse bandits. It galled him to his toes that for tonight, the jokes were about him. How in feckin' hell did Niall and Michael stand it?

There were two reasons he didn't go back to challenge them and make them take back their words, he grudgingly acknowledged. One was because there was no sense in it; he was at a distinct disadvantage with his foot in a cast and he didn't need a fist fight to add to his woes.

The second reason was even simpler. Whatever jokes they might tell of homosexuals, Liam knew that if you wanted someone to stand by you, as crass and relentless with their teasing as those fellas were, they were the ones who would be there to defend you. It was the only thought that kept him sane on the road back to Henry's.

Chapter Nine

It was the end of another hard day at the office, thought Sine, wiping the sweat from her brow where the copper strands had plastered themselves against her skin as if liquid glue had been applied. She lifted the damp hair from her shoulders, exposing the back of her neck to the heated air. Nightfall had come and it was cooling off but hadn't yet spelled complete relief from the torturous sun.

A shower would feel good, or a dip in the ocean even better, although it was now dark and swimming in black water was never something she was keen to do. Picking up her flip-flops, she thought she'd be fine wading in the surf. It reminded her of the surf she'd seen when she was a kid and they'd gone to Maine for a holiday. The beach there was a smooth stretch of sand where the shore rose up to grassy filled banks, similar to some of the beaches she'd seen in Ireland. There was something about an Atlantic coastline that didn't seem to vary much regardless of what side of the ocean you were on.

There was no grass here, though, just endless beach until the jungle encroached on one side, the ocean on the other. The length was such that a sunbather at one end would be hard pressed to see someone at the other.

She knew if she turned around she could head straight to the dining hut, but she wasn't ready for supper yet and didn't much care if there was anything left by the time she got there. While the production crew in Ireland had been a dream to work with, this crew seemed bent on the destruction of certain people's careers, hers and Liam's in particular.

Unfortunately, Niall was taking the brunt of it and there didn't seem to be anything she could do to deflect it. Her own situation wasn't good and it was taking all she had to stay above it. Even the director was beginning to look sideways at her, as if she was suddenly not the one he wanted in that role anymore.

Well, too bad, she thought, wading in to watch the water lap at her toes with one wave and wet her legs half way up her calves with the next. The director didn't have any say. At least, this one didn't. They wouldn't redo the entire film because this guy didn't like her. Again, that feeling that something was off was centered around him. He didn't seem to be up to the standards that he should be for a film of this magnitude. He was playing favorites and it seemed a little late in the game to be trying that. Besides, she had a sneaky hunch that he and Felicia were getting it on, and wondered if that was behind Garry's direction choices.

Well, more power to Felicia, she thought, trying hard not to care, but the fact was, she did care. It cut deeply. Not that she wanted to be the one in the director's bed. No, never that. She just wanted to be the lead in a film, to be special enough to warrant the attention a lead actor got. Feeling replaceable or facing the possibility of being cut from a project was not comforting to someone whose persona was completely opposite of what she portrayed every day. Always being out of her comfort zone was wearing at times but she had to do it, had to be the extrovert that was not her personality at all.

Niall knew how she felt and had tried to shore up her diminishing reserves more than once. He was in the same position. She saw him struggle with it every day, and as if her thoughts of him had called him to her, she heard his voice over the shushing of waves at the shore.

"Sine."

She heard and, turning, saw him striding toward her. "Were you looking for me?" she asked, thinking at the same time how she wished he were Liam; wished that she could just put her arms around him and give in to her desires.

"Yeah, sort of," he said, rubbing his shaved head and scratching at a fresh mosquito bite. "Feckin' blood-suckers," he ground out. "If I still had my hair…Christ, it itches."

"I have some stuff in my hut if you'd like to use it."

Rubbing his hand over the offending spot, he said, "Alright. Anything to take the itch away, even for a bit."

They walked the shoreline toward the area where the huts were discreetly disguised within the jungle, but none of them too far from the shore. The surf was always audible, no matter where they were.

"So, why did you come looking for me?" she asked, and he answered her with a shrug.

"Michael's been shanghaied again. Told me earlier that the whole digital unit is banjaxed. They need another but haven't any choice about it right now. He'd taken it apart, thinks he's fixed it and now trying to put it back together, hoping it'll work."

"And you don't want to help?"

"I'm Liam, remember? I don't know anything about computers except how to use a feckin' phone. And even then, some of it's above me," he laughed.

Sine laughed along because she knew it was true. It still didn't make sense that Niall could work his way around a computer like he was a part of it and Liam could barely use his phone. In that, they were truly opposites. As a change of subject, she said, "Well, if it's company you're after, I'm afraid I'm not much."

"He was pretty brutal with ye today. I thought ye grand, but that's just my own opinion," he said, grinning at her. His teeth showed more than the rest of him, except maybe his eyes, she thought. It was dark enough, and like Liam, Niall had been blessed with extremely white teeth. Couple that fact with the tan he'd taken on over the last few weeks and the only way he could effectively hide in the dark would be to shut his eyes and keep his mouth closed.

It was her turn to shrug. "He's the director. His seems to be the only opinion that counts, not like back in Ireland."

"No. I'm not keen on this fella, don't really know why he was chosen, and it doesn't matter. He's here, we're nearly done, and soon we can go home." They had arrived at the gap in the trees that led to the huts, the lights outside each unit turning on automatically at nightfall.

She led the way through the short, serpentine path that curved around large palms and branched off a few feet before the entrance to her hut, so much like all the others. A small, covered porch led to a doorway that when left open, allowed breezes to flow through the hut, cooling it against the heat of the day. Although rustic in appearance, it had amenities that put it far above a camping scenario. The bathroom was basic, outfitted as it was with a shower, sink, and toilet. Niall's room, Michael had told her, had the benefit of a bathtub as well, but who would want to use it when the ocean was so close by? But Niall had intimated the other day that he was happy to have a tub. He'd had a very devil-may-care look in his eye just then that told Sine he hadn't been alone in it.

Opening the door wide, she flicked on a light against the darkness that surrounded them. Immediately dozens of insects began to invade the space and both she and Liam raced around, closing shutters and doors, making sure that no gaps existed where bugs could enter, then did what they could to eradicate the interlopers. That done, Sine went into the bathroom where she kept everything from hair brushes to medicines and pulled out the package that had her anti-itch cream in it. She came back out with the tube of cream in her hand just as the lights went out.

"Oh, great. Now what?" she said to no one in particular. She didn't expect an answer.

Niall looked around. The only sound was the rising wind,

and within minutes, they both knew a squall was about to hit. "I wonder if it'll be very bad?" said Niall, having taken the tube from Sine's hands and smearing a small dab of cream on the bite. His bristly pate would feel strange beneath his touch, Sine knew, because she noticed it every time she touched him there when working. But in order for him to be Liam, it had to be shaved.

Sine peeked through a crack in the shutters and quickly drew back in again. Like most storms here, once they began, you were effectively held hostage where you were for many an hour.

"Look at it this way," smirked Sine, "you could be stuck with the director in his hut, or up at the dining hut still having to be Liam, instead of with me."

Niall laughed outright. "Oh, that's rich, that is. You're no more entertainment for me than…"

"Than what?" she queried when he hesitated, her mouth shaped in a tight moue that was discernible in her light-hearted voice.

"Ah, feckit. Nothin'. It's just, well, if ye miss Liam half as much as I miss Michael—and he's here beside me most of the time, mind—well, then I feel for ye. That's all."

"Well, thank you, Niall. I'm very happy to hear that at least one person understands how I feel."

"Do ye love him?" They were standing on opposite sides of the room, she just from the bathroom with the anti-itch cream not yet put away; he, with his torso bared to the waist, a bronzed god with flashing blue eyes just visible in the faint glow from the emergency light in the wall socket.

Do ye love him? The words echoed through her brain and touched her heart. Sine couldn't deny what she felt any more than she could deny Niall the truth. Tears started in her eyes, and for once, she was powerless to stop them. She was beginning to notice that where Liam was concerned, all bets were off.

"C'mere to me," he said gently, holding out his arms, and Sine, confused and miserable, slipped into his embrace and buried her face in his chest. She smelled the masculinity of Niall's skin, felt the moist warmth of his sweat on her cheek, and choked back a rather audible sob.

"It's not fair," she sniffed, "I love him so much and he doesn't even know it. I don't think he would care, even if he knew."

"Ah, that's not true, and well ye know it. Liam's not like that at all."

"I'll bet he's got a few women on the go; I'm sure I'm not the only one."

"Ah well, that may have been true before, but not now."

"What do you mean by, 'not now'?" Did he know something she didn't?

"It's nothin' I can say for sure, just from what I noticed when I saw the two of ye together back home."

"And?" He was holding her close and rubbing her back, much as if she were a small child. Even if Liam had been doing the same thing, she could have told the difference. There was tenderness, but no sexual meaning in the action from Niall.

129

He looked at her upturned face and smiled, his expression limned in the yellow glow of the light protruding from the wall socket, and tucking a strand of copper behind her ear, smoothed the sweat-moistened tresses softly with his fingers. "Well, I think I know my brother better than anyone, and though he hasn't said a word, which I wouldn't expect him to, I can tell you're special to him. I'm almost never wrong when it comes to Liam."

She sighed and hoped it was true.

A knock on the door startled her and she jumped in Niall's arms. He turned and opened the door a crack, noticed it was Michael and let him in, a howl of wind virtually throwing him into the room.

"Quick, close the door before we all get blown into the bathroom," he said, struggling to get the door closed against the strength of the gale that had begun to blow with vigor.

"I hadn't noticed it was so bad out there," said Sine, sheltered as she'd been with Niall's body. She'd felt safe within his arms and almost rued Michael's interruption.

"Got anything to drink?" asked Michael. "I would have stopped at the dining hut but everything is battened down."

"You know, I think I have a six-pack of something I bought on our way to the island. I don't think it's what you're used to but it's better than nothing. Besides, it's been here for, what…three weeks? It needs to get drunk."

She went to the small fridge and opened it up, and sure enough, there were six bottles of locally brewed beer that promised to be one of the best, according to the label. Pulling it out, she glanced at the carton as she set it on the small table beside the fridge. "It's a 'Black Beer'd Stout'," she quoted. "Thought it looked interesting. Help yourself. Two each. Get ready to party." It was all said tongue in cheek although she would have loved to have really let loose with some good Irish brew.

The men each picked one up, squinted through the dark at the bottles, and then popped the caps, each taking a long, first swig. It was warm in the room and the stout was cold.

Niall was the first to swallow and speak. "Hmmf. Not bad," he exclaimed.

Michael was taking his time. "Not bad," he agreed. "It's definitely different than ours but I like it."

Sine took a sip of hers and had to agree. Then, since there was only one chair and a bed in her small room, she took the chair and let the guys have the bed. It was like being a voyeur on an intimate scene, although neither one was doing anything untoward.

The darkness continued but the battery in the emergency light was still working, still a dull glow in the blackness around them. Each of them had drunk their two bottles and now sat sleepy-eyed and slightly hungry. But as no one could leave the shelter of the hut for fear of being washed away by wind, rain, and tide from the thick of the storm passing through, they agreed to hunker down where they were at least safe.

The storm raged on and Sine tried to curl up in the wicker arm chair, eventually settling for arranging a pillow against her back and flopping her legs over the padded arm. It wasn't overly comfortable but it was better than the floor.

"It's your bed, you know," said Michael, standing and stretching. "I don't mind taking the chair. You and Niall can have the bed."

"I don't think so," she replied. "As valiant a suggestion as that might be, I think you'll soon find your long legs too much for this chair. I'm a lot shorter than you, so I think this is best."

"Michael's right, though," said Niall, almost a disembodied voice in the dark room. "This is your room and here we are kicking you out of yer own bed."

Sine laughed. "There is no way either of you are going to fit in this chair. You're too tall. So forget it. I'll sleep here, you guys keep the bed."

"The bed is big enough for three," suggested Michael. "I'll go in the middle, you both can have the outside. It isn't like we're going to be nude," a hesitation, and then a hopeful sound to his voice accompanied by a teasing chuckle, "are we?"

"Yeah. Right. I think I'll just stay here," she said, stifling a yawn with the back of her hand.

"Alright. If that's what you wish, but just remember that it's your room and if you get tired of the chair, there'll be a spot on the bed for you."

"Mm-hm," she said, and tried hard to let sleep overtake her.

* * *

Michael lay on the bed beside Niall, wanting to bring him close, feel his warmth despite the heat inside the room. The outside temperature had dropped with the incoming storm and was approaching a tolerable level but true comfort inside had yet to be achieved. He soon heard Niall's deep breathing and knew he was asleep, so he tried to relax himself as much as he could without waking him, and closed his eyes, hoping for sleep to claim him.

An hour later he heard Sine whisper, "Michael, are you still awake?"

"I am." A slight shifting on the bed, the rippling sound of the sheets pierced the dark, the wind and rain an ongoing racket outside.

"Does the offer still hold? My back is killing me."

He chuckled, knowing she wouldn't be comfortable in that chair for long. It was time he manned up, so invited her once again. "Come over here. I'll take the chair."

"No, don't. You won't sleep, either. I'll just use a small corner." She made her way through the dark with the wind still howling outside.

The sound of rain lashing at the windows and against the door was somehow comforting to him, like rain on a tent when camping, but the weather didn't seem to be letting up at all and he briefly wondered how well the electronics were holding up. All he knew was that he'd been able to get things working again but for how long, he didn't know.

He moved over so Sine could get on the bed and heard Niall sniff and mumble in his sleep. Turning to face Sine, he

133

spooned himself into Niall, Niall's front to his back, felt his lover's arms pull him into a hug, and would have been happy to fall asleep that way.

Still, sleep eluded him.

Beside him, Sine had finally dozed off on her back, her soft snores a counterpoint to the storm outside. He watched her breasts rise and fall in the glow of the emergency light, just enough to see by.

He'd seen those breasts bared before and knew she was well endowed. Not only that, but there was no artifice at all, every bit of breast was hers, and he felt himself grow hard with the memory of her naked body, standing before Niall, training him for the mission of impersonating his brother.

The training had worked. When it finally came to doing that scene, Niall had pulled it off. She'd done a good job, getting him over his fear of being naked in front of people, of being intimate with a woman. Briefly, he wondered what it would be like to sleep with her; wondered if she'd be interested.

He quickly dashed that thought. It would hurt Niall and destroy the love they shared and nothing was worth that. But still, the thought lingered and he placed his arm across her midriff, his thumb reaching up to lay against her plump breast.

Sine moved in sleep, slid closer, and as he was spooned into Niall, she turned and spooned into him.

His body responded, chubbed up, as Niall would say, but luckily, Sine didn't wake. He felt his erection there between them, rigid against the softness of her arse. If he shifted, he could slip between her legs; but to do that, he'd have to undress, and so would she. As much as he told himself he wanted it, he knew it wouldn't happen.

Hours later, they woke to a grey dawn, noticing that the lights had come on while they were sleeping. They must have been tired enough to sleep through the change, especially with two beers on an empty stomach to help out.

"Didn't we close all the shutters?" asked Michael, noticing one was pushed wide open, the window beyond it letting in a cool, refreshing breeze. "You didn't open it, did you?"

Sine blinked the sleep from her eyes. "No. They were all shut tight so the bugs wouldn't come in."

"Well, this one is open. I wonder how that happened?"

"Maybe someone was lookin' to see if we were all here and alright?" suggested Niall.

"Maybe," allowed Michael, but he wasn't so sure. Going to the door, he opened it and poked his head outside. No one was about and the beach was strewn with debris from the storm. The wind was still up but had lessened greatly. Clearly, the storm had passed.

"I need to change," said Sine, going to the bureau in the room where she'd unpacked all her belongings. It seemed an invitation to the guys to leave, so they did, promising to meet her at the dining hut when she was ready. It was breakfast time and they were all hungry, especially having missed dinner the night before.

Sine closed the door behind them and went back to the opened window. It had been closed. She knew it had been closed, so why were the louvered panes now open, and why were the shutters, so securely in place the night before, pushed apart?

She quickly changed into something more relaxing, a light, summer dress that hung loosely and made her feel pretty. Its leafy design in green, gold, and white complemented her coloring, and the straps, which separated her breasts and supported them, let the rest of the dress hang loose, allowing air to circulate beneath. It was one of her favorites, something to boost her flagging confidence.

Donning the dress, she left the hut for some breakfast, but not before walking around to the side where the window had been opened. She checked the ground, looking for some signs of intrusion, but there was nothing out of place that she could see. Even the ledge looked fine, although she noticed that the window could be pushed open from the outside just as easily as from the inside. She hadn't locked it, had seen no need.

With that bit of information, she turned her back on the hut and went in search of food. Her stomach was making particularly loud noises.

Chapter Ten

Niall was just finishing his coffee along with Sine and Michael when one of the grips, a man named Bruce that Sine seemed to take a particular dislike to, swaggered in. He glanced at the threesome, cupped his nads in a rude fashion, and grinned lasciviously. It made Niall's skin crawl.

"Morning, folks, sleep well?" he asked of the threesome.

Without directly answering, Niall nodded, as did the other two. None of them liked Bruce. Even many of the crew appeared to dislike him, or at least, avoid his company when they could. Still, there were a few that could be described as his cronies, who seemed to be just as crude as Bruce himself and didn't mind keeping company with him.

Niall didn't care for that bunch, and was pleased that when it came to nude scenes, the set was usually closed off to most except the essential people. Bruce was never included in that group, and for that, Niall was grateful. Still, he wondered what had been said amongst the crew when off on their own time. Did they talk about what they'd seen? Compare his body to others or discuss him in a lewd fashion? He didn't know, and furthermore, was happy not to know. How his brother took it all, he'd wondered more than once.

Felicia walked in just then and glanced at the three before helping herself to coffee and a pastry. She strode purposely toward their table, sitting down next to Sine, who was on the opposite side of the table from Niall and Michael.

"You three sleep okay?" she asked, and at their nods, said, "I did, too. It's always good to be with someone when there's a storm up, especially here. It was pretty wild."

Niall felt the bait, wanted to ignore it but couldn't. "Ah, but I'm sure ye had a good night with his nibs, eh?"

There was silence for the space of a heartbeat and then Felicia burst out laughing. "Liam, you are too funny! How did you know?"

Niall just shrugged. Liam wouldn't give a fig who was sleeping with whom, so for once, he'd be cavalier about it. "Doesn't everybody?"

"I guess no more than everyone knows that you three sleep together."

All three heads came up at once and a chorus of, "What?" filled the air. Others seemed to have heard the exchange and were suddenly quiet.

Niall jumped into the fray, skipping ahead to throw cold water on anyone's ideas that a threesome was going on. "Ah, ye must be talkin' of last night?"

It was Felicia's turn to shrug.

"Well, we were all just caught in a storm and not willin' to risk our necks tryin' to get back to our own huts. This place was shut up tight so couldn't go here, and I just happened to be at Sine's getting somethin' for a terrible bite, see?" He offered his head for Felicia to look at, which she did.

"Well, I can see you've got a good bite there. You should put some more stuff on It. Looks like it could get infected."

"She's right, you know," said Sine, sipping the last of her coffee. "It does look pretty bad. Makeup is going to have quite a time disguising that piece of your head," she laughed.

Niall felt her words, as if they were trying to ease the situation. So how better to ease something than to meet it head on? "So, as I was sayin', we all three met there, Michael comin' lookin' for a place of refuge since this was all shut down. We eventually just fell asleep, waitin' out the storm," he said.

"And you're sure that's all that happened," grinned Felicia.

No one was surprised at her comment and they all agreed in shrugs and mumbles that yes, that's all there was to it.

"If ye're lookin' for sensationalism, Fee, ye'll not find it here," said Niall. "If ye'll remember, since it was likely you who opened the window to look, we were all clothed."

Felicia was taken aback, "What, me? I didn't see you guys, I was just repeating what I'd heard."

"Nothing like the rumor mill to keep things interesting," mumbled Sine as she took another sip of coffee.

That seemed to be the end of that particular conversation, Niall was pleased to note, and chalked another one up to his expertise at jumping into Liam's personality. It had been extremely difficult at first but as time went on, it was easier to

S. M. Cross

pretend to be something he wasn't. He only hoped it wouldn't backfire.

"Michael."

They all turned to see the director walking toward them. Michael looked at the three others, quirked an eyebrow, and said, "Time to go. Guess my fix didn't stay fixed." He downed the last of his coffee and followed the director out.

While Niall and Sine concentrated on their the last of breakfast, Felicia's eyes followed Michael out. One corner of her bottom lip met her tongue between her lips and she furrowed her carefully sculpted brows in thought. "So, how did you guys meet Michael, anyway? I know he came on board in Ireland, but I thought he was just going to be another part of the crew that flew here, not some computer whiz kid."

Sine shot Niall a look that said she'd handle it. "Michael is a close friend of one of Liam's brothers. You know, there's a lot of boys in that family," she laughed in an effort to keep the conversation light and happy to be able to tell Felicia something that woman didn't already know.

"No, I didn't know. How many?"

"Three others," said Sine, not mentioning that Liam and Niall were twins. "Anyway, Michael happened to be available, you know, kind of in between jobs, and said how he'd love to be able to work on a film set. We, that is, Liam here, introduced him to the director, and when the producers found out that Michael knew a lot about computers, well, that clinched it. He was only too happy to have him along for this segment."

"Hm," said Felicia, and Niall wondered about her sudden friendliness. "I guess we can be grateful for his help. Garry said the unit was broken, didn't know if it could be fixed; but Michael seems to have got it working, at least for now."

Niall nodded his agreement. "He told me it was banjaxed."

"Banjaxed. That means 'broken' in Irish, doesn't it?"

Niall laughed, "Yeah, sort of. It's not Irish as in Gaelic, but it is a truly Irish expression. I think hangin' around with me brothers has taught Michael a few expressions he wouldn't normally use."

"So you've known him a long time, then?"

"Yeah," said Niall, and left it at that.

"I wonder if we're going to work today?" said Sine, hoping she could effectively change the subject of Michael's relation to Niall. Too much information in the leading star's hands would not be a good thing.

"Don't know, the weather's still iffy," said Felicia, and Niall shrugged and stood to go.

"I'm off for a shower. Sine, can I borrow some more of that cream from ye?"

"Sure. I'll get it for you. Come on."

They left together, feeling everyone's eyes follow them out the door. Waiting until they were a good distance away, Niall said, "What do ye make of that?"

"Not sure," said Sine, "but I checked the window because I know we shut it tight last night. It can be opened fairly easily from either inside or out. And I didn't lock it. Just closed it and the shutters. Someone obviously opened it while we were sleeping."

141

"Obviously. But what I want to know is, why?"

Sine shrugged and they continued on their way. The storm, having blown through, was beginning to give way to sunshine. It was going to be another day in paradise, after all.

* * *

Liam was struggling to maintain his cool. Being Niall wasn't at all fun. He couldn't ogle the women the same way he normally would, at least, not outwardly. Niall wasn't like that. Niall would look at women, enjoy their beauty, and then ogle the men with them. That's what Niall would do. Furthermore, other gay men in town who knew Niall would often come on to Liam, thinking him Niall, stroking his arm in a familiar fashion or easing him down into a chair at the pub as if he was some sort of cripple who needed help. The crutches were a bother, he thought, and made things difficult at times, but he was not so bad off that others needed to pull chairs out or be so solicitous of his comfort.

And yet, that's what was happening. Everywhere he went, people would hover over him. As Liam, he was used to the deference paid to a well-known actor, but as Niall, computer geek and introvert, he was not. It got under his skin, irritated him so that instead of the congenial outlook usually expressed in his features, people more often saw a scowl.

"Yer face is goin' to freeze that way," said Siobhan one morning, almost a month later.

"I don't feckin' care," snarled Liam over his breakfast.

"Have a care who ye're talkin' to," came Henry's retort.

Liam apologized and settled into himself.

"It's hard, I know," said Siobhan, trying to soothe things over like she always did. Never one to mince words, she called a spade a spade but when tact was needed, came through with that as well.

"No, ye don't really know, although I appreciate the effort," said Liam, dripping frustration. "I think I'll head back home. I can't be around here anymore as Niall. It's drivin' me over the edge."

"And how are ye goin' to manage? Ye can't drive, ye can't but manage one bag at a time for groceries, and ye're really no bother here. Stay at least until ye've got rid of those crutches and can have a proper walkin' cast," she suggested.

"I can drive," he insisted, "I just need to rent an automatic."

"It's no never mind to me what ye do," said Henry, "but ye still can't be yerself. Ye've got to be Niall at least until he shows up back here."

"Feckit, Henry, I'll go ape-shit waitin' that long. They're overdue now and I've no idea what's goin' on. None," he finished.

"Do ye know where they are?" asked Siobhan.

Liam nodded. "Yeah, on a privately owned island somewhere in the Bahamas. Somewhere. That's the catch, I don't really know where. I just know it's privately owned. I'm certain I could locate it if I flew into Nassau. Someone would know something," he said.

"Charters would maybe be a place to start. What about gettin' in touch with the fellas from the crew here? The company would certainly know," offered Henry.

"That they would. But I'm Niall. And what would Niall be needin' to know for?"

Henry shrugged. "I'm sure ye can think of somethin'."

Siobhan got an idea. "What if ye pretended to be yerself, just this once, callin' from that island and sayin' ye needed to have somethin' sent to ye, but needed to know how to tell them where ye were. Would that work?"

Now it was Liam's turn to shrug. "Don't know. Could give it a try, I guess." He pushed his chair away from the table and rose, gathering his crutches under his arms. "I'm goin' for a walk. Maybe it'll help me think," he said, hobbling toward the door.

No answer came from behind him. He hadn't expected any. Henry and Siobhan had gladly taken him in while he recovered enough to be on his own. The crutches were definitely awkward but he continued on, more convinced than ever that if he acquired a rental car, it would make him more independent, and then maybe, just maybe, he wouldn't be such a grouch.

He could go now, he thought, and then realized that he had his own ID in his pocket, not Niall's. He could no more rent a car than he could fly to the moon. The only thing he and Niall had exchanged were passports. They each kept all their other ID, not thinking there was any need to switch that much of it.

The other option, he knew, was to get either Henry or Siobhan to rent a car for him. That would be easy enough.

His thoughts had kept hidden from his conscious mind exactly where his footsteps were taking him and before he knew it, he was on Main Street where throngs of visitors were taking in stores full of Irish souvenirs and trademark goods. There were decent restaurants, too, Liam knew, but he wasn't hungry and he certainly didn't want to be mistaken for himself. No one but close friends and family knew that he had a twin, let alone a mirror twin. He'd managed to keep that much out of his limelight profile.

About to redirect his steps, he caught the headlines in yet another tabloid rag. The photo on the front caught his eye: the three, Niall, Sine, and Michael, all snuggled up in bed together, Michael's hand cupping Sine's breast.

Anger rose up so deep inside that had he no awareness of where he was; would have thrown a crutch through a window if he hadn't cared about causing a scene and wouldn't need the feckin' thing to walk away with. Turning abruptly, he nearly knocked a woman down and he apologized profusely, felt his face flushed in anger and embarrassment, and thumped his way rapidly down the street, hoping no one would stop him for anything. Behind him, he could hear the muttered words, "looks just like him" and knew he'd have to beat it off somewhere fast.

Just then, one of Niall's friends drove by and recognizing him. Liam waved him down. "Connor," he called and then whistled loudly so that the car stopped. Liam hobbled over and pleaded, "Can ye help me out?" He didn't particularly like Connor but knew he could rely on him to help out in a pinch. And if this wasn't a pinch, he didn't know what was.

Connor seemed to take in the gathering crowd and grinned. "Ah, they'll be onto ye like shite to a blanket, thinking ye're Liam. Best get in," he offered.

Liam wasted no time, and balancing on one foot, opened the rear door, stuffed his crutches in first, and slid in beside the other person next to him. "Sorry, didn't know ye had company," said Liam as he closed the door solidly behind himself.

"It's no bother," said Connor. "Just Johnny. Ye recall Johnny from the other night at the pub?"

"I do," he said, nodding to Johnny and acknowledging Connor's current girlfriend in the front seat.

"So, where ye off ta?" Connor asked.

"Nowhere special," said Liam. "Just away from here." He indicated the masses swarming the streets and slowing traffic to its usual crawl.

"Oh, if ye've time then, how 'bout stopping by my place? We were just headin' there. I've a computer I'd like ye to look at. It's been acting up and I don't know what's the problem."

Liam froze. He hoped his expression of shock didn't give anything away but he quickly covered it up with an excuse. "If ye don't mind, I can't do it today. I'm just not feelin' myself," he said. It was true. He was not only not feeling himself, he was certainly not feeling like Niall. Niall, who could fix anything related to and including computers. Liam was daft when it came to electronics. He could paint, draw, play any number of musical instruments, and perform in

146

front of live audiences with a gleeful thrill. But he couldn't fix a computer. He could use them, write on them, even look at pictures on them and surf the net. But what he couldn't do was anything that involved fixing them. He could barely change his password without Niall's help.

"Ah, that's too bad then. I'd ask yer beau, Michael, but he's on that island with yer brother."

"Yeah," said Liam. What else could he say?

"Shall I drop ye off at Henry's or would ye like to visit for a bit with us? We may take in the pub later."

Liam wasn't even tempted to stay with them. "I wouldn't mind if ye just took me back to Henry's. I'd appreciate it, really."

A few minutes later he was deposited at Henry's door and met Emily coming down the walk.

"Hi, Uncle Liam," she called, and Liam flushed in frustration.

The man named Connor poked his head out the window. "Ye'd think she'd know by now how to tell her uncles apart," he said, and Liam, just wanting to get out of what could turn into a sticky situation, didn't respond to him other than to thank him for the ride.

"Hi, Em," he said, watching the car drive away. "Maybe ye could remember I'm supposed to be Niall when we're outside?"

Emily blushed and apologized. "Oh, I'm so sorry, I clean forgot. I hope I didn't get ye into trouble?" she asked.

"Nah, I don't think so. He just thought ye couldn't tell

Niall and me apart is all. Just remember for next time though, eh?" Noticing another magazine in her hand, he said, "So what've ye got there, now?"

"Ye don't want to know," she said, moving ahead of him to go into the house.

"Maybe I do," he said, following her.

"No, it'll just make ye angry again."

"I promise I won't. I saw another in town just now. It fair set the crowds on me, thinkin' that I was Liam. Which I am, but they can't know that. Furthermore, they can't know I've a twin. How the hell I managed to keep it all a secret until now, I don't know. But I feel like it's all fallin' down around me ears and there'll be reporters at the door any day now."

"There might be," she said, opening the door and holding it for Liam to hobble through.

"What?" He stopped just inside and then side-stepped so she could shut the door. "What makes ye say that?"

Emily shook her head. "Just some things I've heard. People asking questions and the like."

"What people? Where?"

"In town. I was in one of the hotel restaurants, just curious like, to see what their menu was, and I overheard some fella askin' questions about ye. Ye know, like had anyone seen ye around?"

"They were reporters?"

She nodded. "I think so. One had a camera at a table and he was doin' somethin' with it, and the other was writing on a tablet. He had a small wand that looked like a mini recorder and he and the other fella were chattin' about ye. When the waitress went over to them they asked if she knew about ye and seen ye around."

"Me as Niall, or me as Liam?"

"You. Liam."

"Ah, feckit. Bloody predators, they are." It was worse than Liam had thought. Having lived relatively quietly until now, he could feel his fame closing in on him and he longed for his home by the sea, off by itself on a strip of land bordered by high cliffs to the front and a thick forest to the rear. Few knew there was a cottage there, let alone an estate owned by one of Ireland's famous sons.

But he couldn't go back. Not yet. He was too dependent on others with his foot still unable to bear weight without the use of crutches, and a big, hulking cast, light as it was, on his foot. Another two weeks. He had to hide for another two weeks.

And he still hadn't heard from Sine.

Chapter Eleven

He was able to take almost anything, Niall thought, except the attentions of a famous personage such as Felicia McKay. She'd been at him all day, her intentions perfectly clear. Up until now, she'd been content to be in bed with the director. Literally. But they must have had a rift because, despite the scorching temperatures of a Caribbean summer registering the outside temperature a sweltering hundred degrees he was sure, he would swear on a stack of bibles you could freeze water within an inch of coming into contact when those two were together.

And it seemed he was her next target.

She was standing beside him, rubbing his arms after yet another torrid scene on set. They'd both been almost nude but he had no worry of his body's reaction to her nearness. Regardless of her beauty, he was no more turned on by her than he would be to a feisty mare. Both might be beautiful, and he did love horses, but neither attracted him in that way.

That, he reflected, was likely what made working with her tolerable. She was a looker. A fine woman, because to call her a lady would be a lie. She was the kind of woman you'd admire in a painting or perhaps a statue. A marble statue. She was about as warm as that. He didn't doubt she'd be all over him in bed if he was interested. But he wasn't. She had her own game plan, one he was not privy to. Perhaps Liam would have known, but he himself sure as hell didn't. The last thing he wanted was complications arising from his actions that would affect others, his brother in particular. He was certain, would lay bets on it, that Liam loved Sine. Yet Liam's past with Felicia was no secret. Just how involved Liam had been with the actress was anyone's guess but if he had to guess now…well, he felt like a fly about to be caught in the spider's web.

It was late, and she was following him to his hut. Now what was he to do? They stopped at his door and he turned to look at her. "I need to sleep. It's been a long day, and I'm tired. Especially after not getting much sleep last night." It was the wrong thing to say. He knew it as soon as the words were out of his mouth.

"Oh, I was under the impression you had a good sleep last night, cuddled as you were, all three in the same bed."

As agreeable as he normally would be, Niall couldn't let her gain the upper hand. "We asked ye before, how ye would be knowin' that?"

Her response was to shrug. "Oh, like I said, just what I've heard," she said in a nonchalant way.

"Well, ye know what I think of rumors, eh? I don't hold much store in them at all."

"Are you saying they aren't true?"

"I'm sayin' it's my own business, and no one else's."

Her hand moved to stroke his torso, something she did during their scene together. Only, in their scene, her hand had followed the hard planes of his stomach down to cup his manhood. At least, that's how the story went. He wasn't too keen on anyone other than Michael touching him there and made at least the first part of that thought very clear when they were blocking the scenes. "Ye can make it look that way," he'd said to her, quietly, just for her ears alone, "I'm just not keen on bein' touched there, hm?"

She'd obeyed. Partially. The director had other ideas, wanting the tell-all shot. So he'd endured her hand being on him while the camera came close. He wanted to boot the cameraman out of the way but he was essentially a good guy, intent on his craft and not one to gossip about what he'd seen. As a talented cinematographer, the fella was just fine in Niall's books.

Felicia, though, was different. She had that look in her eye now, the look of a predator. The same one she'd worn on set.

"Sorry to disappoint ye, Fee, but I'm just not interested tonight."

She stood back, glaring at him. "Not just tonight. Every night. You haven't looked at me the way you used to since we came to this island. Even before. You said you'd take me with you to your brother's wedding but you took Sine instead. How do you think that made me feel?"

How could he explain his brother's feelings for Sine? Would Liam go to bed with Fee if he was in love with Sine?

He wanted to think not, wanted to stake his own reputation, and therefore, his brother's, that Liam would evade Fee's clutches just as he was trying to do. But his hesitation must have given her the footing she needed because Felicia shot back with more venom.

"So, that little would-be starlet has you by the balls, has she? How's she in bed? I'd wager you've been there several times with her already."

"Actually," said Niall, quite truthfully, "I haven't taken her to bed at all. So don't pretend to know me. And don't bother to think ye've any claim to me, either. I'm not interested."

Her hip came into contact with his, her hand cupped his arse and squeezed. "You seemed pretty interested the last time. We had a good romp in the hay, or don't you remember?"

Last time? She must be referring to time spent with Liam. There were obviously things he didn't know about his brother after all and the depths of Liam's interest in Felicia was just one. To cover up his ignorance, he feigned courage, determined to evade her grasp. "I remember just fine. Like I said, I'm not in the mood is all."

It was obvious from her next move that she wasn't finished with him yet. "Let me in, just for one drink, and I promise I'll go away." Her breasts rubbed up against his chest and she stepped into him, pushing him toward the opened door of his hut.

Niall felt her warmth and for one moment was tempted, if not for anything more than he was lonely for Michael.

Michael had been taken away early that morning to work on the computers and hadn't been seen since, yet Niall had heard his voice of frustration when he walked by the production tents. No one could swear like Michael when electronics got the better of him.

"Fine. I've a couple of beers in the fridge, ye can have one of those." He backed through the doorway and she followed him in. While he headed straight to the bathroom to empty his bladder that had been full an hour ago, she went directly to the fridge and pulled out the beer.

He came out to see her outstretched hand and gladly took the frosty can. Touching the tip of the can to hers, he toasted out of habit more than to be polite, "Sláinte," and took a healthy swig. In fact, downed half the beer in one go.

Felicia was impressed. "Wow, you were thirsty," she remarked with a glint in her eye. "Are you trying to get drunk on me?"

"Drunk? On one can of beer? Not likely. It'd take a dozen of these for me to feel them. Don't ye know there's no one can drink like an Irishman?"

She giggled uncharacteristically. "I was kind of hoping you would. Maybe then you'd see what you have, right here, right now."

Suddenly feeling very mellow, and very sorry for being rude in wanting her to go away, he apologized. "Isn't like me to be rude, I'm usually very accommodating. It's just, well, I guess I've had enough of this film and just want it to be done."

"It is dragging on, but we should be finished soon, don't you think? I mean, Michael is working on the computer and Garry is thrilled that he's here. Wants to hire him full time, I hear."

"Yeah, well, you'd know," he said, and then felt ashamed of himself all over again. What was happening to him? He took another healthy draught and another quarter of the can was gone. His eyes began to bother him, he couldn't focus quite right and he seemed to have no will of his own where his body was concerned.

It suddenly dawned on him that she must have spiked his drink while he was in the bathroom because he'd never had this kind of reaction to anything before. He tried to ask the question but his tongue was too thick to work.

"Hey, how ya feelin', hon?"

There wasn't a worried tone to her voice, it was more… he couldn't think straight. In some part of his mind, he knew her angle, knew what she had planned. But he couldn't voice it, had no control over what was happening. So when she walked over to him, pushed him back on the bed and began to undress him, his hands, instead of pushing her off, pulled her to him and began to undress her, too.

"Oh, honey, yeah, come on, that's right," she soothed as he lifted her shirt off and bared her breasts. She stood and pushed her shorts down and kicked them off, leaving her naked to his gaze.

Niall's vision completely blurred. In his mind, he saw Michael, was wondering why Michael's voice was different but had no notion why. "C'mere to me," he said, naked and ready for his lover.

Felicia took the two steps to him and pushed him farther up on the bed. He was ready for her, or for Michael, said his brain. Only he couldn't understand why Michael was facing him instead of away. He needed him so much, couldn't contain the erection he had much longer without going off. Everything was incredibly intense.

He felt his body engulfed in the moist depths of a canal and couldn't help himself. His muscles had a will of their own and he began to pump with his hips, while the figure in his vision seemed to ride him hard, breasts bouncing as the rhythm increased.

Breasts?

Niall's hands reached up and touched the nipples. They, at least, were real, and he folded himself upward to take them in, heard the gasp of surprise from the vision and then felt his mouth being captured, tongues swirling and darting. An immense euphoria overtook him and he felt his body let go, rigid, unable to stem the cry that echoed throughout the small room.

The figure on top of him collapsed, his flute buried deep within. Michael, oh Michael, he thought, we've never had it so good.

He hadn't realized he'd spoken the words out loud, hadn't known that he didn't have Michael in his arms.

He fell asleep or passed out, only to wake in the morning staring into Felicia's big golden eyes. "Good morning, Big

Boy," she crooned, a smile crossing her features from ear to ear.

Niall sat up suddenly, his head swimming in pain. "What the feck? What are ye doin' here?" He put his head back on the pillow, willing the drums in his head to quiet.

"Not expecting me? Maybe expecting Michael instead?" she asked, seemingly very sure of herself.

"I've no idea what ye're on about," he said, "but I think ye better leave."

"Leave? But it's just getting interesting. How about you tell me all about you and Michael?"

"How about ye just leave?" He didn't care about polite anymore. His head was hurting like all the bean sidhes that ever lived had been let loose inside his skull, screaming their warnings, only they were too late.

"I'm just getting started. You know, the Liam I knew would have jumped at the chance to take me to bed, but you didn't. You've changed, Liam, and I don't know why. Or maybe I do. Maybe you've decided you're gay? Is that it?"

Christ, she was onto him! Or not him as Niall, but him as Liam. What impact would that have on Liam, to be thought gay instead of the man that all Ireland, and the world, thought him to be? Liam would kill him for destroying his reputation!

"Look," he said, "I don't know what you're on about or what it was you put in my beer, but if you don't get out of this bed and out of this hut, I will personally throw you out and your clothing after you. I don't give a fuck if ye're naked or not. Let the world see ye as ye are."

There was a soft rap on his door. "Niall?" came the hoarse, deep whisper from the other side, "Are you in there?"

"Niall?" asked Felicia intently, still not having moved from the bed. "So maybe you aren't Liam after all. What kind of game are you playing?"

"It's no game and Niall happens to be my middle name. Now leave off." To the door he said, "I've company just now. Give me a moment."

Minutes later, Felicia walked out the door and down the path toward her own hut. Niall stood in the doorway, wanting to hit something. He didn't know if his cover had been blown. Didn't know what had happened last night. All he knew was that he was in shite deep enough to bury him. And Liam.

Michael eased around the corner once Felicia was gone. "Did she stay the night?" he asked, and a look of wounded emotions crossed his face so rapidly, Niall wasn't sure he'd really seen it.

"Don't fash yerself over it," he said. "There was nothin' in it."

Michael pushed his way into the room. "Nothing in it? What? Are you saying you slept with her?"

"Keep yer voice down. My head's about as big as a beach ball."

Michael, he could tell, was furious. "You slept with that bitch," he accused, "and now she's going to tell all, just because I fucked up and called you Niall. If I'd known, had any inkling that you were with her, I would never have blown your cover, and well you know it. So don't come on all innocent with me. I know what she's like. I've been listening to Garry sing her praises in bed the whole time I've been working on that fucking motherboard. We need to be done and away from here, sooner than later. And if it doesn't happen, I will leave here, with or without you. Because I've had it."

He was about to step away when Niall grabbed at the collar of his t-shirt and hauled him into his hut, closing the door solidly behind him. Spinning Michael about, he pulled him into his embrace and plastered his lips to Michael's, working at him until Michael opened his mouth to let him in.

What followed was a session of lovemaking for desperate times. Niall needed Michael badly, needed to banish the memories of the night before.

Michael needed the reassurance Niall's lovemaking provided, because where Niall was concerned, he felt very insecure. In Michael's eyes, Niall could get any guy he wanted. Part of it was Liam's fame but he knew there was more to it than that. As introverted as Niall was, there was a sweetness about him that radiated beyond the furrowed brows of secrecy. He had a magnetism that invited people in, even though his outward expression might say otherwise.

But not so Michael. Michael's heritage set him apart and put some guys on edge. They didn't like his swarthy looks or they feared his Middle Eastern roots. And yet Niall hadn't cared. Niall had seen past all that and loved Michael for who he was. Only, Michael had always thought that it was just a matter of time before Niall showed him the door. So

159

Michael had cultivated other relationships, tried to have one in the wings to hop to should Niall ever leave him, but they were always women because for Michael, no man could ever replace Niall.

Niall had grabbed Michael's nads, immediately drawing his thoughts away from his insecurities, and rolled them around in his hand, sending amazing sensations zinging through his body. He moaned his pleasure, felt Niall slide down his body to take his cock into his mouth.

It didn't take long. No sooner had he come than he was turning around for Niall, allowing him entry into that part of him reserved for Niall alone. Niall was rough, there was pain, but Michael didn't care. Soon, there was only pleasure and he felt Niall reach his climax, held firm while the convulsions wracked his lover's body, then allowed him to relax against him.

Their breathing slowed, and Michael turned in Niall's arms. "Let's get a shower," he said, and Michael nodded.

"My head is killing me," remarked Niall entering the bathroom with Michael right behind. He went to his kit on the shelf by the mirror and pulled out a bottle of pills. "Christ, I hope these work. Whatever that bitch gave me last night did a number on my head."

Michael stopped before climbing into the shower. "Niall, did ye make love with her?" It was a straight forward question and yet Niall hesitated. "Niall? I asked…"

"I know what ye asked. And I can't quite tell ye. I think I did, but the whole time, I thought it was you. Only, I couldn't figure out why ye were facing me, and yet I was inside ye. It was all very strange."

Michael turned back to the shower, trying to hide the emotion playing across his features. It cut him to the core to think that Niall had slept with someone else, and a woman, no less.

"Michael." Niall put his hand on Michael's shoulder and turned him around, saw the tears and was instantly contrite. "Feckit, Michael. I had no desire to sleep with her. I'd let her badger me into inviting her in for a beer. She must have doped the beer when I was in the loo. I never would have taken drugs, have never taken drugs. Not for any reason and ye know that. Tell me ye believe me?"

Michael nodded and blinked away the tears before they could fall. He let Niall hug him and then they entered the shower and washed themselves clean. For Michael, it was like washing away the pain of knowing Niall had been with a woman. But it didn't take away the worry of what might follow.

Chapter Twelve

Y ou don't have to say a thing," said Sine when she saw Niall approach her at the breakfast table. She was half finished, tired of waiting until he showed up for her to begin.

"Eh?" he asked.

"Fee's already told everyone who'll listen about how she spent the night with you and how you called out for Michael right when you climaxed. She certainly isn't shy about spilling details."

Niall's face paled and Sine felt sorry for him.

"This is all my fault," she continued. "I should never have suggested it. They might have gone for you taking your brother's place if they knew he'd broken his foot," she said quietly, careful to not mention names.

Niall pushed his plate away and concentrated on his coffee. "I guess we'll just have to wait and see what happens," he said. They both picked at their food and before long, left their plates almost untouched to meet on set as scheduled. It was to be another day of work, hoping the computerized unit would last, worried the electronics would give out again.

At midday, they all broke for lunch and Sine went down

to the beach. Dark clouds were gathering off the horizon and she wondered if they would pass the island by or hit it like they had before. If the storm came toward them, she had no doubt it would land sometime during the night, if not sooner. She'd done a lot of sky watching since arriving nearly a month ago, and was getting pretty good at reading the signs.

Michael squatted next to her on the sand. She hadn't heard him approach and started when he spoke.

"Care to share your thoughts?" he asked.

Sine glanced at him and for the millionth time wondered how it was he could be so desirable to women and yet not want anything to do with them. Like Niall, he was clearly gay to those who paid attention. She sighed, and said, "It's all over, isn't it? The rumors, I mean."

Michael nodded. "Yeah. They aren't nice, but I don't know there's anything we can do about them."

Sine had been thinking long and hard of a way to crush the rumors, to make people believe that they weren't true at all. So far, she'd come up empty. But somehow, Michael sitting down beside her gave her an idea. "People are saying Niall's got a thing for you, is that right?" She looked at him through the curtain of her long, straight locks.

"Not quite. Just that he's hiding the fact he's gay, even though he's got this persona of a real lady's man. Remember, they're comparing him to the Liam they knew last year, and for some, the Liam of just a month ago. That Liam wouldn't have turned down an opportunity to bed Fee." He stopped abruptly, as if just realizing what he'd said in front of Sine.

163

"Never mind," she said, waving off his indiscretion like she would an errant fly.

"Sorry. Really, I mean." At her reaction, he took a deep breath and continued. "Anyway, if he wasn't in the mood, he would have done something to appease her. As it was, she had to trick him into going to bed with her, finally resorting to drugs to do it for her because otherwise, he wouldn't have. And furthermore, he didn't care. That's the part they're talking about. The fact that Liam suddenly doesn't care about women."

"Yes, but he called out for you while he was drugged. That says something, don't you think? And it must have made an impact on Fee because she's absolutely spiteful now."

"True. She seems convinced he and I are lovers and that we're hiding it."

"What if we deflected their talk; did something to make them disbelieve what she's saying?"

"Like…?"

"I don't know…like maybe a rumor that you and I are tight?"

"Could work, I suppose," said Michael, mulling it over. "I promise I'll think about it but whatever we do, we'll need to have Niall in the loop. And that's the other thing," he cautioned, and at Sine's raised brow, said, "we must be very careful what we call him. Fee heard me call him Niall this morning. She's thinking something's up. We can only thank God that this island is as remote as it is."

"No news from home?" She was hopeful, but not

expecting a miracle. Michael had access to the internet, and therefore mail.

Michael shook his head. "'Fraid not, love. He might have emailed Niall but I usually have someone looking over my shoulder at what I'm doing so I can't take time to get into any email string. But take heart, I'm sure it's just that Liam is waiting for your return."

"I don't get it. He said he'd call, every day. And without cell service, I get that. But he hasn't even left a message by some other means."

"I'm sure there's a reason, and I'll check when I get an opportunity," he promised, rising. "I have to get back to that motherfucking motherboard," he quipped, and Sine couldn't help but smile. If Michael's smirk was anything to go by, it was turning out to be the most challenging project of his entire computer career.

* * *

Michael was up to his eyebrows, ready to pull his curly, black hair out by the roots. The motherboard was being particularly difficult. Short of building a whole new one, he was coming up blank in solutions.

"Can I help?"

Michael looked up to notice one of the grips standing over his shoulder. "Unless you're a computer genius, I don't think there's much you can do."

"I worked a little on my own computer at home. I'm good at soldering. Sometimes it takes two hands or another pair of eyeballs."

"Well, eyeballs I'd be grateful for. This thing is going to make me go blind before much longer."

"Well, I'm Japanese-American. It's said we have eyes that detect more color than others, so, maybe I can detect a problem with the connections where you can't."

"You're Japanese? I thought you looked a little Asian, but certainly not the typical Japanese look." The fellow, named Sam, really didn't look Japanese. His eyes seemed to lack the epicanthic folds that characterized Asian people and his nose had a bridge higher than expected of that race.

"Yeah, I know. My mom's not full Japanese. I take after her dad, who was white and as English as could be. By your accent, I take it you're English as well."

Michael laughed. "Yeah, born but not quite bred. My grandparents on one side came from Saudi Arabia. My dad's full English, a Londoner to the core. I grew up in Kew Garden."

"Your grandparents are Arabs?"

The raised brows and Sam's light brown eyes gave Michael pause to think. His background had never been a problem before but in this day and age…

"So, you ever get accused of being a terrorist or anything? You know, found yourself on some no-fly list?"

Michael laughed but a prickle of nerves twitched in his gut. "No. Never. Not even a hint. But then, I live in Ireland now, and there's very few places a terrorist would want to hit. So, no. I'm not a terrorist. Wouldn't ever want to go that route. I mean, look at it this way…do you ever stop to think that maybe some Americans still hate you for the Second World War?"

Sam shrugged off the comment. "Yeah, I see what you mean. Sorry, I didn't mean anything by it."

"No bother. Forget it. Let's just get on with this."

An hour later, they'd made some progress and Sam left to go back to his own job, leaving Michael to the rest. Michael had a funny feeling about Sam, that as friendly as he'd seemed, and he had helped, there were storm clouds ahead on the not-so-peaceful island.

* * *

"Every feckin' day, Henry, I said to her, 'Call me, every day,' and she said she would. What does that say about her and me? About us?"

Liam's had at least one whiskey too many, thought Henry as he listened his brother rail at the world.

"There's likely a good reason, Liam. Ye can't expect miracles where there are none."

"And what's that supposed to mean?"

"No bother. Forget it. Ye'er too in yer cups to listen." He was thankful both Siobhan and Emily were out. There was some sort of festival on in Tralee and he thought it grand they would go together. Just like a mother and daughter should, although Siobhan was just at an age where she could have a child still if she wanted to. But having adopted Emily as a ten-year-old seemed to be enough for them. Maybe Siobhan couldn't conceive, he didn't know, but there'd never been any talk, of either wanting or hoping for a child. And so here they

167

were, with a teenager on their hands and Siobhan feeling her way, much like Henry, through the years of parenting a teen.

Liam was acting like a teenager. He was good practise. After all, Henry had helped Mam raise the lot of them, him being the eldest when Da was killed.

"Look," Henry said, tired of hearing the same story for the millionth time, "just find out where they are and go. It's no never mind to me if ye stay here or go there, but ye can't sit and do nothin' anymore. Ye'll drive us all crazy if ye do."

"How?" asked Liam, his voice risen in exasperation. "Tell me how I'm to find them if I'm Niall and not me?"

"Christ, ye're thick as a brick, Liam." Henry took a swig of his cola and shook his head. He wasn't the first one to question why one of the twins could be so adept at electronics and media options and the other so inept. But it all came down to the mirror twin thing. Some mirror twins had even been born with their organs on opposite sides.

Luckily, that hadn't been the case with his brothers, but in all other aspects, they were true mirror twins...the birthmarks, the parting of their hair, writing with opposite hands, just to name a few. The list could be extensive if he really thought about it. "So there's no mobile service?"

"No. At least, I don't know."

"Would GPS tracking work?"

Liam shrugged.

Henry chastised himself over that one. Why was he asking such stupid questions? Niall would know, not Liam.

"Do ye think, if we searched for Niall's phone, that we

could pick up where they are? I know ye have yer phones interlocked that way."

Liam just shrugged and Henry knew his brother was about to take a much needed nap.

"Look, I'll just go to the phone store and talk to Kevin. He's the best and he knows ye both. So have a nap, be sober when Siobhan and Emily get home, and maybe I'll have some good news for ye."

Liam was out like a light before Henry left the house, draped across the sofa, his injured foot propped up on the arm at the end with extra cushions beneath.

Walking down to the phone store was easy for Henry. Unlike Liam, he didn't have a broken foot, nor did he have to worry about people recognizing him for his famous brother. There were similarities, of course, but no one, ever, would mistake Henry, a good ten years older, for either Liam or Niall.

He was just about to enter the phone store when someone passed by with the latest tabloid in hand, and blazoned on the front page was yet another photo of his brother in a compromising position. Henry didn't care about that; he was more concerned with how those photos were making it out if there was no internet. He was really no better than Liam when it came to things like that but he did credit himself with a few more marbles than his actor brother.

Kevin, the very man he needed to see, was just finishing up with a customer. On seeing Henry, the portly twenty-something fellow waved him over. "What can I do for ye today?" he asked, brown eyes smiling behind a pair of black-rimmed glasses. A geek he might be, but no one could deny that Kevin knew his stuff.

Henry got Kevin into a corner where they were less likely to be overheard, and explained what was happening. The second best thing about Kevin was that you could tell him anything and know it would go no further.

"Bring me his phone," he said once Henry had explained, "and I'll see what I can find out."

Most of what Kevin had told him meant nothing to Henry but when he heard the words, 'bring me his phone,' he decided he didn't need to know more anyway. Kevin was his hero. Kevin would fix it and do what Niall or Michael would do, if they were here.

Later that night, after seeing everyone else off to bed, Henry sat up watching late night television. Not much was on…just that crazy show where the discs slipped off to the next level and determined how many points would be won. He'd just switched the channel over to it and had already forgotten its title.

A sound on the stairs made him turn his head and he saw Siobhan in the shadows. She was wearing her dressing gown, the light-weight one she liked to use for summer, and characteristically, probably nothing underneath. She, like Henry, always slept in the nude.

He patted the seat beside him and she came to stand before him.

"Are ye comin' to bed soon?"

170

"Not really tired yet," he said, and felt guilty that he might be keeping her awake. "Are ye missin' me, then?"

"Mmm," she answered, a smile curving her full lips, bringing out the dimples on her cheeks.

He parted the robe and placed his hands on her broad hips and wondered again if she'd regretted that they'd never had a child. "C'mere to me. I'll make ye feel good."

She stepped closer as he placed a kiss on her navel and then parted her legs to feel her warmth with his tongue. Her sigh was all the permission he required and he indicated the sofa beside him. She lay down, legs up in the air, and Henry feasted on everything she had. Neither heard the small creak of the stair, nor saw the head peek around the corner, eyes wide with interest.

Fifteen-year-old Emily was getting the education she'd been curious about of late. One or two of her friends had confessed to having gone for a ride and although she knew the basics of sex, the particulars were sorely lacking.

She kept quiet and watched, slightly out of sight behind a large potted plant at the base of the stairs, just in line with the sight of Siobhan and Henry having at each other but effectively screened from their view. Long tapered fingers spread the leaves just enough to view the goings on.

Henry's mouth was between Siobhan's legs and he was doing something that had her adopted mam gasping and bucking beneath him. The next thing Emily saw was Henry standing and quickly undoing his jeans, then pushing them down to fling them off his feet, his drawers quickly following.

171

She'd never seen Henry's arse before, and was more than curious when he bent over, the tip of his flute just visible, his nads hanging loose between his legs. His flute was ramrod straight and Emily's eyes widened even more. She would have gasped if she'd not been desperately trying to stay hidden, so she covered her mouth with her hands instead so no sound could be heard over the volume on the television.

The angle changed and, for a moment, Emily saw Henry, full front, and felt a tingling sensation between her legs. She loved Henry like a father. He was someone she could trust and she'd never been in a position before to think about him sexually. It had never crossed her mind. And while seeing him naked and ready for sex didn't elicit longings for Henry in her bed, it certainly awakened her to the possibilities of some of the fellas she'd seen at school and around town.

He'd turned again, was doing something with his hand to Siobhan's privates. And then he was sliding into her and they were both panting and grunting. Suddenly Henry's arse tightened, dimples showing in his taut cheeks, and his nads disappeared between his legs somehow. Siobhan was gasping again, and Henry was grunting.

And then sounds of, "Aaah," and "Feckit, Henry," were heard as he relaxed on top of her, Siobhan's legs giving up their grip around his waist to lie languid along his sides.

"Jaysus, Siobhan, that was deadly craic!" exclaimed Henry as he began to withdraw from her body.

Emily knew it was time to go. She didn't want to be discovered and she wanted to remember, to go over everything she'd seen, like a video playing over and over again. Turning, she tiptoed back up the stairs but couldn't help the one creak that always seemed to be there.

"Did ye hear that?" asked Siobhan, cleaning herself up and straightening her robe.

Henry cocked his ear but the house was silent around them. "No, nothin'. Just yer imagination, I expect."

"No, I'm sure I heard it," she insisted.

"Well, everyone's asleep, just you and me awake, so my guess is, it's ghosts."

"Ah, ye're as daft as they come, Henry O'Farrell, but I love ye anyway."

They embraced, and Henry pulled her closer. "Let's go upstairs and do this all over again. I don't think I've had me fill of ye yet," he grinned. "By the way, why did ye come down? Just horned up?"

A blush met his gaze, a barely concealed smile that widened to a gaze, and Henry picked up his clothing from the floor.

"Are ye not goin' to put somethin' on, then?" she grinned.

Looking at the rumpled heap of clothing in his hands and back at Siobhan, he said, "If the two upstairs really need an education, then here it is. Otherwise, I believe I'm quite safe in me own house."

Siobhan stifled a giggle and led the way up the narrow staircase and into the room they shared to start all over again.

Chapter Thirteen

Michael was miserable. He understood Niall's explanation of what had happened but every time he thought about it, it cut a little deeper. Felicia was running around saying contradictory things. One minute she'd praise Liam's, or rather, Niall's, sexual prowess, the next she would call him a girlie-boy, accusing him of being Michael's lover. Which he was. Only no one was supposed to know. Niall was supposed to be Liam and so all day, in order to debunk the rumors that were spreading, Niall had buddied up with Felicia, all but proclaiming her to be off limits to even Garry.

Garry, it seemed, didn't really care. It looked like he had his eye on Sine, and that didn't bode well. What was it that turned a bunch of film production people on a deserted island into sex-crazed idiots?

And then there were the new rumors, something about Sine and whatever happened in Boston. Or maybe it was New York? Michael didn't know, and didn't really care, but it was causing difficulty with the filming. More than once he'd seen her face, drawn, looking frustrated. Or maybe it was pain, as if she was trying hard not to cry. Whatever it was, her scenes were not going well and he'd heard Garry in the production tent, reviewing them and making bold comments on how he could find a better actress in Amsterdam's Red Light District.

So here he was. He'd finally got that motherfucking motherboard repaired, at least for now, and just when Garry was ready to get going again, other things began happening. People were looking sideways at each other, mumbling and grumbling without saying much but clearly looking miserable. Michael didn't know what was going on but thought it had more to do with some storm that was brewing here on the island amongst the inhabitants and nothing to do with the storm that was brewing off shore. He shifted his weight on his feet, then realized he'd kicked a cable as he made to move out of camera range.

Bending down to realign the cable, a voice behind him, clearly not meant for his ears, was saying something about Sine. He was crouched down next to the large electronics cases when he heard them mention "Manhattan," and then Sine's name mentioned followed up with "fucking Jeffrey Harris." At least, that's what he thought they'd said. It was difficult to listen to a conversation behind you as well as concentrate on what was going on in front of you, because for some reason, Garry had just told Sine to take five, and she stomped off the set looking like she'd just lost her best friend.

Weirder yet, it seemed that Felicia was being pulled in to do the scene instead. Yes, they looked alike in many ways, although Michael had intimate knowledge of Sine's breasts and therefore knew that hers at least were real. He wouldn't swear that to be true of Felicia's. But why would Garry make a switch? There was suddenly a lot of chatter between the script writer, the continuity person, and a dozen other people.

It was a crazy business, this filmmaking industry, and Michael was sure that once it was all over, neither he nor Niall would want anything to do with it ever again.

A loud bang was heard, and everyone either jumped or ducked instinctively. It was as if the largest light bulb ever invented had just exploded, leaving a portion of the set in the dark.

Garry swore and people scrambled. It was the third time one of the large lights had gone. Michael only hoped they had enough replacements for it because power fluctuations on the island, especially surges, seemed to be the norm. As they waited for the light to be changed, it was clear Garry was in a mood as he joined the conversation going on behind Michael.

"Are you shittin' me?" he scoffed, and then Michael heard what sounded like the clipboard Garry had been holding had just been thrown to the ground. "God dammit, I thought she was familiar, just couldn't place her, you know? Shit, now every fucking thing I've ever worked for is down the fucking toilet because some little whore can't keep her legs together."

"They had her blackballed, state-side," said one voice that Michael recognized. He was sure it was the grip that had made gross comments and leered at them the other morning at breakfast. The guy named Bruce. "No one wanted to touch her after that little episode. It was pretty messy, and I should know. I was there."

Bruce was there? When Sine was blackballed?

"If that's the case, I want that little bitch off my set tonight. I'm not sacrificing my career for the sake of this shit-hole."

Michael didn't wait to hear if he was referring to Sine, their location, or the movie, but quickly made his way to Niall's hut, where he hoped to find him alone.

Luck was with him. Niall was just out of the shower, having finished his work for the day but the grin that had begun to form on seeing Michael soon disappeared.

"He wants her off the set?" Niall asked, his brows knit in a mixture of confusion and anger when Michael told him what he'd overheard.

"I've no doubt it's what he means to do," said Michael, "and I also think that were Liam here, he wouldn't let Garry get away with it."

Niall finished drying himself off and flung the towel on a rack, not bothering to see if it landed there or not. "Are ye sayin' it's my fault things are goin' this way?" he asked, and Michael blushed because he knew that's exactly how it sounded.

"No, I'm not saying it's your fault. But perhaps you could step in for her, you know, challenge the changes. Garry's running the show, and…"

"That's right," Niall retorted, "Garry's runnin' the show. Period."

Michael, not one to stand down from anything, took a step closer to Niall and glared up at him. Michael, though tall, was a good inch shorter than his lover. "I think you, as Liam, could influence Garry. You could show him the error of his ways. If he has his way with this, it'll change the entire script into something the original writer didn't want. It won't be a story about a triangle anymore. It'll just be you and her, and I know you don't like 'her.' So you need to do something."

Niall stepped away, clearly angry. "Michael, I love ye, God knows, but right now, I need ye to leave. I have to think on this."

"Grow some bollocks, man, you need to act now!"

"Leave! Get out," shouted Niall, pointing to the open door. "I said I need to think on it."

Michael turned to go, hesitating just long enough to say, "Just don't wait too long or it could be too late." He strode out of Niall's hut, saw Felicia walking toward it, and turned to go in the other direction. He didn't care to talk to her; right now he didn't care what she wanted with Niall. He had an opened bottle of whiskey in his hut that he'd brought from home and if it took all night, he was going to find the bottom of it.

Niall felt horrible. He'd just sent the only person he truly loved out of his hut, and the way it was all heading, maybe out of his life. This was not like him. He didn't do things like this. He and Michael had never argued like this before. Had pretending to be his brother brought about changes to his own personality?

Maybe he'd better go after Michael and apologize? He hated to see him hurt and he knew he'd hurt him badly. Michael was the outgoing one, the one who made the decisions and was somehow always right. This time, though, it had been himself dictating what course they would take and Michael had just given him a clear warning that should he hesitate, it could all go very badly.

A fleeting thought passed through his brain that perhaps Michael knew something he didn't and was quite correct when imploring Niall to act now. Ah, feckit, he thought, and quickly donned shorts and a t-shirt to go after Michael.

He wasn't three steps out of his door when he ran into Felicia, her arms outstretched in greeting. It was unavoidable. She, was unavoidable.

"Hi, handsome," she cooed, "going somewhere?"

Niall hesitated. What would Liam do? No, scratch that. He knew exactly what Liam would do and so he put aside his initial impetus to smooth things over with Michael, and pretended to be Liam. "Ah, nothin' that can't wait a bit. What's up?"

"Isn't it obvious? I thought we could get together, like before."

"Ye mean like before, when ye doped my beer." He was done playing nice after kowtowing to her all day, hoping to dispel the rumors she was spreading. Instead of pleasing her it seemed to do the opposite.

"Oh, don't be angry with me," she pouted. "It was just a little pill, no harm done." She made to put her hands on his waist but he held her off.

"I don't like any pills, little or not. I detest takin' medicine of any kind. Even aspirin, which I had to do this mornin' to get rid of the headache your little pill left me with. No harm

179

done, my arse," he exclaimed, and turned to leave her there. At least he knew that about Liam. When it came to taking medicine, no matter what the reason, both twins were in agreement.

"But, I didn't mean any harm. You just needed to get into the mood, and you did." She had him in her arms then, back against the wall of his hut before he knew how he got there.

If it was possible to have cold sweat on a hot day, then Niall had it. He felt it trickle down his spine and resisted the shiver that threatened to follow. "Look, I can't just now, I, ahem, I've no condoms," he lied in a conspiratorial whisper. He kept pre-lubricated ones because sometimes it was just better that way. For Michael. But she didn't need to know that.

"Hm, there was a whole bunch in there the other night, I swear I saw a new pack." She was rubbing his abdomen, tucking her long fingers inside the waistband of his shorts.

"Oh, right. I forgot, I guess." This wasn't going as he'd hoped and with Michael off in a snit and Sine nowhere to be seen, he feared he was alone in this. At least it answered a question he'd had about last night but just to be sure, he asked anyway. "About last night…"

"Hhmmm?" She was busy, seeking lower inside his shorts.

"Feckit, Fee, not in broad daylight." His protests met with deaf ears.

"Then inside. Come on," she urged.

Niall had to stall, her hands on his flute notwithstanding.

"Did you put a condom on me? I don't remember. I mean, it's not like I was myself, eh?" It really was getting difficult to think straight with what she was doing.

"Of course. I'm not stupid. Think I want a kid any time soon or catch whatever might be going around? So, come on," she cooed, having slid her hand fully inside his shorts. "There's technical trouble on the set and we're putting off shooting until tomorrow. We have time before dinner for some fun."

He wanted to take her to task insinuating that he could be carrying some STD but his mind was too busy working out defensive moves than to worry about defensive talk. And admitting he knew she'd drugged him had no effect on her whatsoever. She hadn't even batted an eye.

Felicia moved her body in front of him and was pushing him back toward the open door. Niall knew when he was trapped. His inability to think fast in social situations meant that he wasn't quite up to talking his way out of things like Liam could, and so he backed up, gave in, and only hoped that when it came time to do the deed, he was really up to it.

Fee wasted no time in divesting Niall of his clothing, and soon he was before her in all his glory. That was nothing new. He'd been on set with her like that, but this was a completely new scenario. He wouldn't be drinking his way out of this one.

Stepping toward her, he felt his hands shaking. He hadn't made love to a woman for a long time, not since he was a gangly youth, trying to fit into a straight lifestyle. He'd always wondered why it hadn't meant anything to him, had felt no connection, no joy in the act other than sexual relief. If he'd had a blow-up doll, the feeling would have been the same.

So here he was, about to replay the scenarios of his misguided youth and he was as nervous as all hell. His fingers, feeling more like ten thumbs than anything resembling fingers, drew the zipper slowly down the back of her dress. He looked into her eyes and could read her mind. She wanted this, wanted him to be the lover that she remembered. But that lover had been Liam, and as well as Niall knew his brother, what Liam did or didn't do during sex was a mystery to him.

Maybe he could please her with a "slam-bam, thank ye, ma'am," but he didn't think so. She seemed to be the type that wanted it drawn out and fulfilling on several levels.

He began with her nipples, figured that was pretty standard, rubbing the pads of his thumbs lightly over the peaks, bringing them to hard little nubs. Even Michael liked that and apparently, so did Fee. She moaned her pleasure and leaned against him, taking his lad into her hands. Despite his nervousness, he felt himself chub up. At least something was working, he thought.

She grabbed his nads, rolled them in her fingers, and Niall felt himself move toward her. And then her hand moved up, grabbed hold of his lad and tucked it between her legs. The heat and moisture he felt there spurred him on. But in his mind, it wasn't Felicia he saw in front of him, it was Michael. As long as he could maintain that image, he might get through this after all.

He left her breasts and ran his hands down her back to cup her arse. It was full and round, soft beneath his touch, muscular, but in a different way than Michael's. His lover's arse was all hard planes when in the throes of sex, but soft when he wasn't pumping with his hips…Niall felt his body mimic his thoughts, felt his hips move as if powerless to stop.

"Onto the bed. Let's get on the bed."

Felicia's urging penetrated Niall's brain and he picked her up before throwing her bodily onto the surface to watch her bounce once before lying sprawled before him, legs open in invitation.

"Michael, ah, Michael," he thought, and used the silent plea to keep himself stiff as he grabbed the condom from the drawer and rolled it on.

And then he was inside her, moving, feeling nothing but the rush of pleasure, because that's all there was. Felicia was moving beneath him and he barely heard her begging, "My nipples, oh Liam, you know how I like you to take my nipples."

His brain wasn't functioning other than to keep his lower half moving, but he recognized the urging in her words. A small voice inside his head cautioned him against seeking his own completion before she had hers, so he slowed down his own movements, ignored the tightening of his nads, the frisson at the base of his spine that signalled his readiness, and concentrated on her needs instead of his own.

Minutes later, he heard her breath hitch, felt her insides tighten around him, and shortly thereafter felt her legs encase him in a grip that demanded he stay inside her.

Feckit! Feeling himself suddenly dwindle, he knew he was going to have to fake it. The excitement that had him ready, that of being in a warm, moist canal, was suddenly gone with her climax. And so he kissed her, kissed her like he would have kissed Michael, let himself slip from her body and pretended all was well.

"You didn't come," she said afterward.

Niall had nothing to say.

"You always come. Are you okay?"

He had to give it to her, she appeared to be seriously concerned.

"Oh, it's nothin', was just distracted at the last minute. The past few days the pressure's been on and it's just gotten to me, I expect."

"Oh, well, here, honey, let me do you. It isn't fair that I came and you didn't."

"Nah, don't fash yerself. It's alright, really."

"No, I mean it," and before he knew it, she'd pushed him back down on the bed and went to town on his lad.

Despite his misgivings, despite the fact that she wasn't Michael, he couldn't deny the pleasure she gave him with her mouth. In as little time as it took to throw back a splash of whiskey, she had him chubbed up and ready to toss his load.

Then, suddenly, it was over, he'd climaxed as she sucked him dry, and the sweat that had built between his shoulder blades was drying on his skin.

He'd need another shower.

Breathing hard, he opened sex-softened eyes to see the woman before him, her deep golden eyes so close to the same color as Sine's but so far from Michael's nearly black orbs.

He felt sick. Whatever they'd done was done. He needed her gone, needed to figure out where to go from here. And he sure as hell wasn't ready for her next words.

"Why don't I move my things in here for the next few days? We've only got a couple of things left to do and it would be so nice to spend whatever time we have left here together."

Niall stood there, openmouthed, willing for words to come. Any words. On a long, drawn-out exhalation, he finally said, "Ah, no. As lovely as that sounds, I need my space. This hasn't been the easiest job I've ever done so, I thank ye for yer kindness, for wantin' to be with me, but I really need to have some time alone."

She seemed to consider it, to accept it, and Niall thought that was a little unlike her. He fully expected an argument of biblical proportions.

"Alright, then," she said, as if they'd just talked about the weather, "if that's the way you want it. I'll just go see what Garry's got going on. Maybe he won't be too busy for me."

With that, she threw her dress back on, and only then did it dawn on Niall that she had come to him commando, a fact that had failed to register on his brain when he first pulled her dress from her.

As he watched her march out his door, he wondered what else would come about because of his actions. The interlude hadn't gone badly, at least, not as badly as he thought it could have, but it clearly hadn't gone the way she'd wanted it to.

No matter, it was suppertime and he was hungry. It seemed at least that part of his anatomy was working and after taking the time to shower and change, he made his way straight to the dining hut where he noted Sine off to the side, her face a study in unhappiness. She looked like she was barely holding it together and she suddenly stood, red-faced and upset, stalking out of the dining hut, leaving her dinner and whatever was upsetting her behind.

And then he heard the rumors, the rumbling and laughter amongst the crew, not even caring that the subject of their banter had been seated just feet away. Niall felt an anger so raw and intense, saw exactly what Michael had been on about, and knew he had to act. He may not have the outgoing personality of his brother but he was a protector at heart, had a nurturing, caring personality, and if someone was threatened, as was clearly the case here, he had to step in.

Standing amongst the throng of diners, he banged his fist on the table and even Garry took notice, Garry who would blithely ignore anything that didn't have to do directly with the film.

Niall looked about, felt his face flush red beneath the tan, and waited for the throng to stop their chattering before he spoke. "I have had enough of the rumors and intrigue that have plagued this set from the moment we set foot on this godforsaken island. What should have been an easy two-week stint has turned into a month of vicious lies, and I'm sick of it. Sick of almost everyone here. Ye're bollocks, the lot of ye, if ye think this is okay what ye're doin'. It's not, and ye're all acting like school kids. So just stop. Have a care for someone else's feelin's. We're here to do a job, not see how many scars we can inflict on someone. We've a film to finish up, and believe me, when it's done, I hope to hell I never see any of ye's again!"

He turned to where Garry was sitting, a smug smile across his ruddy cheeks, chuckling as he chewed, openmouthed. In his late forties, Garry's thinning hair was perpetually covered by the worn baseball cap and this time was no different. He took the cap off now and flipped it backward, whipping his sweaty forehead with the back of his hand. "It's just a little sex, Liam. God knows you're not immune from that from what I've heard."

"What I do or don't do is my affair and no one else's, and I certainly don't manipulate people over it. I've never spread rumors, and never will. And you, as the de facto ruler on this set, ought to know better than to let things get out of hand. There's a beautiful woman out there ye've allowed to be destroyed right under yer nose. Ye've condoned it."

"She did that herself. No one forced her to play the whore, it was all her."

"Ye don't know that. And I'm willin' to bet if ye were to take a careful look into it ye'd see it was all that gligeen that did it, the one with the three illegitimate kids from women who are now suing him for child support. Doesn't sound like much of a stalwart citizen to me. Sounds more like a loser. A lot like you."

187

Garry stood suddenly, knocking the table in front him over and froze, hands clenched to fists at his side. "Who are you calling a loser?"

"If the shoe fits, as me mam would say…" and he raised his fists to match Garry's. A fist fight was something Niall could relate to. How many times had he had to fight his way out of a situation? Growing up gay wasn't exactly the easiest route in life. "Go ahead," said Niall, licking his thumbs before wrapping them round his own fists, held up and in front, the way Henry had taught him.

"Now hold on just a minute," said Garry, uncurling his fingers and backing away once he noticed Niall's, the way they were expertly held up. "We don't need to have no more trouble. Let's just all cool down and talk this over."

"Time for talkin' is done. We have a couple more scenes to do on this feckin' film and then it's over. I for one will be glad to see the back o' ye. All o' ye's."

He stood tall and strode over to the sideboard and grabbed a sandwich from the cooler. He didn't have the stomach to stay and eat with the rest. Even Michael, it seemed, had shunned the company at dinner, and though Niall craved his presence, knew Michael had gone to lick his own wounds, much like Sine.

Seeking solace as his only company, Niall left the hut and the silence behind him.

Chapter Fourteen

The night was silent, the heat cloying. With barely a breeze through the palms to cool the sweat that had beaded upon Sine's fevered skin, she sat on the edge of her bed in the dark, fanning herself with the script. The script she was tempted to shred to pieces. But more than the discomfort of a hot night, she missed Liam with a passion she hadn't thought was possible.

She'd seen Niall every day on the set, and rather than be a source of comfort, his presence was a reminder of all that she missed. It wasn't possible to miss someone that much if you didn't love them, was it?

Was it pangs of wanting, leaving her feeling hollow and uncertain, only because it had been a trying day? People were on edge. A big storm was expected, but more than the weather, someone had asked her about her last film. While she'd played it down and said very little, she was certain she'd been identified as the woman who'd given the film and Jeffrey Harris a bad name, even though the bastard deserved it. She'd been blackballed for it back home. What were the chances of her being ostracized for it here? And yet it seemed that way. She felt like she was being shunned.

Then she and Garry had a disagreement over that stupid scene in the lagoon, just before the big spot went out. Everyone had witnessed their argument, heard Garry order her to take five to think about it, meaning "get the hell off the set," and then promptly replaced her with Felicia. The fact that Felicia and Garry were in bed together, both literally and figuratively, was well known. But there was something else going on. The more she thought about it, the more it only made sense that someone here had known about her past and was talking.

It could have been one of the grips. There was that one guy who looked kind of familiar, had eyed her up and down, and though seemingly friendly, was the kind of friendly you didn't want. Like someone looking you over as if you were a prime steak and they were just looking for a place to have a barbeque.

That evening, Felicia had sought her out, had confronted her and accused her of being the reason the film had not brought in the big dough. Sine remained silent and hadn't flinched. No, not then. It wasn't until Felicia told her that she was aware Sine had played hooker for the star of that film that a crack began to form in her façade. Felicia produced a few more tales and before Sine knew it, the whole sordid mess was being retold throughout the cast and crew, of her and Jeffrey in bed together, fabricated tales intertwining with fact until it was all a mess. A big. Fucking. Mess. And everyone heard about it at dinner.

She hadn't tried to fight back. There was no use. It was

their word against hers, and because the actor was such a big draw at the box office and she a virtual nobody, there was no way she could be in the right as far as they were concerned. She'd left the dining hut then, her dinner barely touched, but she didn't care. She had no appetite for their lies and little enough for the food that suddenly seemed tasteless.

She stalked back to her hut, showered, and crawled into bed. The one good thing about the tropics, she thought, was that nightfall was early and sudden. The sun hit the ocean and boom, that was it. Complete darkness.

But she couldn't sleep. Her thoughts kept her up all night until she'd finally begun to cry because she wouldn't cry in front of them; she'd grown thicker skin than that and wouldn't give them the satisfaction. But here in her bungalow, she was alone. Just her and the night.

God, she missed Liam!

Her mind wasn't done with her yet, though, because there was Michael. He'd stayed pretty much in the background, doing what he was told to without complaint. But something had changed this afternoon. There was a tenseness in his manner when he approached his co-workers and she hadn't seen him since she left the set and no one had seen him after that. What was that all about? Sine hadn't heard about any reason why, no rumbling amongst the crew, which was usually the first sign of trouble. You'd hear things, sometimes just a word or someone grumbling. But this time, no one said anything, as if they had nothing to say about Michael.

So where was he?

As if her thoughts had made him appear, she heard his voice calling in a husky whisper through the bamboo screens and open windows of her bungalow. "Sine? Are you awake?"

"Michael?" She wiped her tears and sat up, throwing her robe on over her nakedness, and dabbed at the trickle of sweat that rolled between her breasts.

"May I come in?"

"Yeah, sure. I'm too hot to sleep anyway." It was a lame excuse but she didn't care and met him at the door, not bothering to turn on any light. The moon was up and full but seen only now and then with the clouds scudding rapidly across the sky. Without any other light, he wouldn't know that she'd been crying, she thought.

"Have you been crying?"

So much for the cover of darkness, she mused to herself, and sniffed again. "Yeah. How'd you guess?"

"Could've been the way you sound, like you've a terrible cold or something. Are you okay?"

At any other time, his cultured British accent would have her reliving every word, but this time it had no effect on her. She heaved a great sigh and sat on the end of her bed. "I will be, I guess. I just don't know anymore." She couldn't help it; the tears began in earnest, flowing freely down her cheeks.

Instantly, Michael was beside her, a box of tissues from her bedside in his hand as he enfolded her in his arms and held her close. "Here, take one," he said, and waiting until she blew her nose, began to coax the story out of her.

"They all thought it was my fault," she said, crying and

192

blowing and sniffing all at the same time. "But it wasn't me. I wasn't the one who leaked it out that he had all those broken hearts behind him and more than one woman who'd accused him of fathering her child. They just assumed it was me because there was no one else to blame. I still don't know who ratted him out."

"Well, that likely isn't going to matter now anyway," he observed, still holding her close, rubbing her arm lightly with his hand.

He smelled of sweat, of the scent of something exotic like sandalwood, and she remembered Niall saying that he loved Michael's cologne. If that was it, then so did she. Her thoughts brought her round to the fact that Michael was sitting on her bed when he should really be with Niall. "Why are you here?" she asked suddenly, lifting her chin from where it had been tight to her chest.

"Oh, nothing, really."

"Come on, you made me tell. Now it's your turn."

The silence was broken only by a quick gust of hot wind that lifted the bamboo curtain and let it drop to clack loudly against the wall like a primitive instrument in a jungle band. Michael finally spoke. "Wait a moment." He left her side, went to the opened doorway, and leaned down to pick something up.

"What are you doing?"

"I thought I'd bring this along. I was kind of looking for a sympathetic ear, and in case I didn't find one, was going to polish off the rest of this by myself." He held up what was left of a bottle of Irish Whiskey that Sine knew, from being around Liam, was very good.

"Where did you get that?" she gasped in surprise.

"Brought it with me. Sure can't buy anything like it in this godforsaken place," he said, eyeing the thatched-roof canopy above them. "Got any glasses?"

Sine shook her head. "If you want a drink, I'm afraid you'll just have to swig it from the bottle."

"Alright. I'll go first, and then you."

She laughed through her sniffles. "Oh no. I'm not touching that stuff."

"It's good. It'll take your mind off things."

"I don't think I'd like it."

"You haven't tried it. Here," he passed the bottle to her and watched as she took a sip, and then, "Well?"

She leaned her ear to her shoulder as she thought. "It's not bad. There's a nice glow that kind of warms you from within. Yeah, maybe it's not so bad after all, kind of like the stuff I had in Cahersiveen with Liam," she allowed, and then took another sip. "So, what's the deal with you?" She handed him back the bottle and waited for his answer.

"It's the fact that I'm an Arab."

"You're English. Only half-Arab, not even. And as far as I know, you were born in England."

He nodded. "As were my parents and grandparents on one side. My grandparents on the other side were Saudi. But that was a long time ago."

"So what brought this up?" She took the bottle from his

proffered hand and downed a healthy mouthful.

"Some of the crew have it in their heads that I'm related to terrorists and am therefore, likely, a terrorist myself. They were threatening to turn me in if I didn't leave."

"But you have an English last name."

"I know, but that doesn't make a difference with some of those guys."

"So that's it? They won't include you because you're part Arab?" She really didn't see the problem, and taking the bottle back, had another sip.

"No. That's not it, not really. It's part of the deal, but not the whole thing. You see, they don't want me in their bunkhouse because they found out I'm gay, and I sure as hell can't go to Niall right now." He took the bottle from her and downed his own mouthful, and then just for good measure, took another one.

Understanding dawned. Sine knew how some of the guys felt about gays. They were a macho bunch, the kind that would do almost anything to appear more masculine than the rest, screw anything with two legs and a skirt. Mostly, they just liked to beat the shit out of each other for fun, just like naughty school boys. "They're afraid you'll come on to them," she guessed, and he nodded.

"Something like that."

"Ridiculous."

"Tell that to them."

"Why don't you stay here? I'm not afraid you'll come on to me. You're gay. You're Niall's lover. It'll be alright."

"With one bed?" he asked, eyeing the queen-sized bed they were seated on.

"We'll just keep to our own sides. It's the best I can do because we aren't trying the chair thing again and I wouldn't suggest the floor. Have you seen the size of the bugs they have here?" She shuddered at the thought.

"Mmm, well, if you think it's alright."

"It'll be fine. Oh, wait a sec."

"What?"

"I have to find my pj's. I took them off. They're over here somewhere," she giggled.

"You don't have to dress on my account. I don't have any pj's."

"You have gonch."

"Gonch?"

"Underwear. You have underwear. It's kind of almost okay, like a swimsuit," she giggled again.

"If I'd thought of it, I would have brought one. But I really didn't think of it."

"We're in the tropics. How could you not?"

Michael's response was to shrug.

"Okay. Fine. You keep your gonch on and I'll find my pj's."

Out of the darkness came, "Or we could dispense with both."

Her head shot up. "Huh?"

"Well, we know there isn't anything between us. It would simply be a way to solve two problems."

"And what two problems would that be?"

"The first, and I'll admit it's a very selfish problem, is that it would show those idiots that I'm not gay; that they're completely wrong."

"But you are gay. They aren't wrong," she yawned. Why was she feeling so drowsy all of a sudden?

"Yes, but if they thought I had slept with you, they'd begin to wonder, don't you think?"

"No. I don't. And it would only compound my own problem."

"What, the one where you went to bed with the lead actor?"

"Yeah. That one."

"I'm not the lead actor. Couldn't we just pretend we had a thing going? It would certainly take the heat off of Niall."

That made her stop in her pj search. "What's up with Niall? I mean, I know we talked about a decoy plan to get the heat off him, but I thought he'd had it figured out with Fee." Niall was her project, her promise to Liam, and she didn't want to let him down. But as far as she knew, Niall had things figured out for himself.

"The crew keep looking at us; at him and me. I think they're trying to put two and two together and I think Niall is having difficulty keeping up the pretense of being Liam."

She sat down heavily on the bed. "Good Lord. Now what do we do?" Her head was feeling fuzzy. "Hand me the bottle. I think the numbness is wearing off." She took another healthy swig and handed the bottle back, watching as Michael upended it, finishing off the stuff.

Then Michael stood over her, his nearly six-foot frame silhouetted briefly in the flash of moonlight streaming in the open window. His sculpted muscles were limned in gold, his eyes blacker than the night around them. Her heart began to beat a tattoo in her chest.

She swallowed, felt the lump in her throat. More than anything she wanted Liam, and he wasn't here. But Michael was. And everything was all her fault. Now she really would be responsible for ruining a film and likely an actor's career as well. Not only that, two other people would fall prey to the ugliness that were tabloid magazines. But it could all be proven to be unfounded if Michael shared her bed. And it had to be convincing. All it would take was for the maid who came to straighten the bungalows every day to find them together. They all knew the maids were the largest source of gossip on the island. It seemed easy enough. And Michael was safe. Wasn't he? She looked around for an excuse, any excuse to send Michael away, but her emotions kicked in and she started to cry again. She missed Liam terribly. A big lump of self-pity stuck in her throat and she coughed it out, like a big sob.

Michael held out his hand and Sine took it, felt the warmth of his fingers as he entwined them with hers and pulled her up to meet him. His fingers tilted her chin up, and then his lips came down over hers. She responded. It was so wonderful, he was so warm, so gentle. The kiss was so nice, except there was no chamber maid there to witness it. Just the clouds above.

He didn't stop with a kiss. He pushed her robe from her shoulders, exposing her ample breasts, then took one of the curvy globes in his hand, balanced it as if weighing it, then smiled a toothy smile, a predator in the darkness.

Sine sucked in her breath but didn't move. His mouth bent down, took the ruched nipple between his teeth and teased it, then rolled it around his tongue until she gasped for its release. She could feel his cock, engorged and straining against his pants, and Sine now knew that what she'd seen in the hotel room was for real. Michael swung both ways and tonight, it seemed, she was his next conquest.

"Michael," she gasped between pleasing sensations that were rocketing through her body, "I don't think this is a good idea."

"Too late," came his reply, and then, before she could say more, he'd laid her bare before him and had worked free of his shorts, those items that looked like they could be a pair of short pants or a swimsuit. Swimsuit indeed! He was naked beneath them.

"No. Maybe we shouldn't," she began, but Michael was very persuasive, and she was very drunk.

"I'll be gentle," he said. "It'll help with your missing Liam."

"No, it won't. I'll just feel guilty."

"About what?" His lips were doing wonderful things to her nipples. "You don't think Liam is celibate, do you?" he said between nibbles. "And honestly, not according to Niall, he isn't. And if he told you otherwise, well, maybe you shouldn't be so naïve."

Did Michael always talk like that, like he was slurring his words? He was becoming difficult to understand. "Huh?"

"Exactly. Now shush."

"Shush?" He was kissing her, and oh, she knew it was wrong, knew she'd regret it in the morning or maybe sooner, but for now, she wanted it. She'd make amends later. Besides, he was right, she thought. Michael was right. Liam had said not to listen to the tabloids, but weren't those stories always based in truth, at least somewhere? She and Liam had never said they'd be faithful to each other; he'd never asked her for that promise. He could have, but didn't. And she'd said that she fully expected he would have some other woman by the time she got back and he never refuted that. Or did he?

She was feeling confused. Maybe it was the whiskey? She missed Liam. But maybe she was just horny, and Michael was here, and shit! It was so complicated.

And then he was stroking her down there, spreading her with his fingers, readying her, priming her. A moment's hesitation while he laid her on the bed, plumping her pillow, making her comfortable. He came over her, kissed her, had her completely under his spell. The room rocked dizzyingly for a moment, then righted itself again.

Then a gap of time, a few seconds, and she heard the rip of cellophane and knew he'd put on a condom.

"Here we go, luv," he whispered, pressing into her slowly, stretching her with his size.

She wanted to tell him to stop but it felt so good, the

pressure, his cock sliding into her, her body welcoming him.

And then it was too late. He was inside, pumping, and Sine, without any effort on her part it seemed, was going to climax. A part of her didn't want to. She wanted to remain pure for Liam. But Liam wouldn't be celibate, wouldn't stay true to her. Everyone said so. She was nothing. A nobody. And only a gay man wanted her.

She climaxed, and announced it with a primordial scream into the night. Then it was over and Michael was breathing hard on top of her. How had it happened? She didn't know. She only knew she felt horrible, and any tears she'd cried before were nothing to what she felt like letting loose now.

The wind was whipping up the palm trees that surrounded the bungalow and sending the bamboo shutters to clacking against the wall in a furious fashion. Anything that wasn't tacked down was being blown around both inside and out of the little hut. Fat drops of rain began falling, going from a lone drop to a deluge within seconds. The storm was upon them, in more ways than one.

Michael held the woman in his arms as she cried herself to sleep. He felt like the world's biggest wanker, and perhaps he was. He'd betrayed the man he loved with the woman his lover's brother wanted. He had no doubt that Liam wanted Sine but he did doubt that man's ability to love only one woman. Liam hadn't done it yet in all the years Niall and he had been together. So why would this little nobody be treated any differently?

He hadn't thought about making love to Sine when he'd

wound his way through the bush to her bungalow. He'd really only been looking for a place to crash and a sympathetic ear. But then she'd been crying already and had admitted to wearing nothing under that skimpy little robe. That, coupled with the now empty bottle of whiskey, had blurred the lines of reason. It had all been too much for him and the solution to both their problems seemed to be so easy: just make everyone believe that they were lovers. It would stop all the rumors.

Except for one. He couldn't help but agree with Sine when she said it would only deepen the case against her. Now they'd know she had loose morals. They already knew she'd slept with that actor just for the publicity she'd get. Only it wasn't true. She wasn't loose, she'd thought she was in love with that fucking arsehole.

She would definitely be on the losing end of this one.

And then there was that other little thing that nagged at him. She loved Liam. As if he'd called her name just then, Sine sniffed.

"Sine?" he asked quietly. No answer came back except her deep, even breathing and the sound of the storm outside.

He could still salvage her pride. He could skulk back to his bed and his roommates could go fuck themselves.

"Bunch of fucking wankers," he mumbled to himself, and decided it wasn't worth getting swept out to sea from the storm just to try to get back to his hut. With the clouds covering the moon and the fury of the wind and rain, he'd never make it back in one piece. But what was he going to do about Sine? Did everything she sacrificed just now add up to victory for Niall? Possibly, but was it worth it? He doubted it.

He felt lower than the lowliest snake in the grass, and no matter what he might try, he could never make it up to her. He couldn't undo what he'd done. Not that he'd wanted to. He loved Niall fiercely and wouldn't trade him or what they had together for anything, yet he'd enjoyed discovering Sine's passion. Liam was a lucky sod, but it was going to take everything he had to fix the mess they'd...no, he corrected himself, only he had created this mess. Sine was innocent, and somehow, he'd have to make the world see that she'd been the victim all along, and staying the night with her, to be found by the maid in the morning, was the only way to do it. Otherwise, this whole interlude would be for naught, and Michael had to make their sacrifice worth something.

The rain had brought with it cool winds and a dampness from the splatter through the openings in the bamboo screens. The room was protected from outdoor moisture but the floor near the door would be wet in spots, he knew.

He took a moment to stand at the open door and take a leak. No one would notice a bit of piss in the face of all this rain. He didn't even bother to shake it off. Wet was wet.

He made his way back to the bed, dried his legs and feet off on his shorts as best he could and crawled in beside her. Sine stirred but didn't waken, so he curled himself around her in a protective manner, winding his legs between hers and cupping her breast with his hand. Pulling her close against him, he drew the light sheet over them, gave himself up to sleep, and dreamed he was Judas Iscariot.

Chapter Fifteen

A squeal and rapid apology from the maid woke both Sine and Michael with a gasp. Michael reacted first, covering Sine with the sheet, briefly noticing the imprint his fingers had left against her breast. He must have been holding on to her all night.

"I come later," said the maid, a tiny lady with Asian features, looking embarrassed and scurrying away as fast as she could go.

Bright sunshine poured in through the open windows, which was odd. First, because it had been storming like the world was coming to an end and now there was sunshine. And second, because Michael knew there had been shutters there last night. He sat up and looked around as if willing them to appear out of nowhere.

"What are you doing?" asked the sleepy voice at his side.

"Looking for the shutters that were on that window," he replied, making an effort to see without moving too much. He had a helluva headache.

"Oh, there," pointed Sine. The blinds had slid beneath the small bureau on the wall near the bathroom, and just the corner of the shutter was visible against the similar-colored wood of the floor. "I guess the wind must have torn it off. It blew pretty hard."

"I wouldn't know. I don't think I moved since passing out beside you."

Sine sat up beside Michael, careful to keep the sheet over her breasts. "I woke up at some point. There must have been lightning because I remember a flash. No thunder, though, unless I slept through it."

"We were pretty wrecked."

"Yeah. I think I know what the inside of a toilet tastes like. Yech!"

"Well, maybe we should go get breakfast. I'm starving."

Sine was silent beside him. And then, "You go ahead. I'll wait until everyone else has eaten and then I'll grab something."

"But the maid was here, she'll have started spreading rumors about what she saw. You know how fast these things work."

"Yeah, I know. I just don't feel like being ridiculed right now. It takes a lot to make me want to hide, but it takes a long time to recover, too. You know?"

"For me, personally, I don't give a fuck. How about I get you something to eat and bring it here?"

"Okay, if you feel like it."

Michael got up and dressed, feeling her eyes on him. He turned and was rewarded with her winning smile. "You know," he began, "if I were straight, I'd keep you for myself."

"Yeah, I could probably go for you, too. But I realized something last night."

When Michael didn't answer but lifted a brow in question, she finished by saying, "I love Liam."

He smiled, a soft expression. "I know." And then he was gone out her door, and she was left holding the sheet above her breasts and feeling like crying again because for once, for just this once in her life, someone knew who she really was and had been kind.

* * *

"Where were you last night?"

Michael put his tray opposite Niall's on the table and sat down facing him. "Taking refuge from the storm," he answered, careful to keep his voice down so as not to be overheard.

Niall, staying just as quiet, said, "Hm. Seems the maids are talkin' about findin' you and Sine together. At least, that's who I think they meant when they mentioned the girl with hair the color of a copper penny and described you as something out of "Lawrence of Arabia."

Michael laughed outright; couldn't help it. "I've been called lots of things in my time but Lawrence of Arabia isn't one of them."

"It's true, then?"

Michael's laughter died down as soon as he looked into Niall's deep blue eyes. Oh God, he thought. Niall had the loveliest eyes, and now, with anger so heightened he could hardly keep it in, they'd gone the color of a haunted sky, and Michael knew he was in trouble.

"Well, um, we just thought it would be a way to deflect

certain rumors from you. We meant to tell you, to bring you into the loop."

"So ye went to bed with my brother's woman, and ye thought I'd agree to it?"

"Well, not exactly. I mean, we didn't…"

"Don't feckin' lie to me, Michael," Niall stressed, trying to keep his voice down. "This is me ye're talkin' to, not some plonker out there who can't see beyond this table."

"We did it for you," he hissed.

"Bollocks! Ye did it for yerself. Ye've hurt her even worse than before. Now she's got another stash of rumors followin' her around, and just when I thought I had everyone in hand last night."

That brought Michael up short. "What do you mean?"

Gritting his perfectly white teeth, Niall leaned closer to Michael. "Do ye not see how perfectly subdued everyone is this morning?"

For the first time, Michael noticed the atmosphere. It was subdued. It was quiet, normal. Just people having breakfast, no jocularity over someone else's misfortunes as had gone on for the past month.

"Holy fuck," he said. "What did you say?"

"I merely turned into a parent, told them to stop acting like school kids and grow a brain. Told Garry off, too. If there was such a thing, I'd have his licence, I would. No one should have to put up with that bullshit crap. He thought it was all 'just sex,' as he put it. But he refused to see what was happening beyond his own langer. The feckin' eejit's so full of his own shite he can't tell when he's down a quart."

"I'm gobsmacked. I don't know what to say."

Niall threw his napkin down. "No? How about 'goodbye'?" He left the room and Michael, who was suddenly so shocked that he couldn't move, remained frozen with the sugar container in hand, ready to pour into the spoon.

Eventually, his mind began working again and he put the container down without knowing if he had put sugar into his coffee or not. A quick sip told him no, but he suddenly didn't care. Going over to the sideboard, he loaded a tray with two coffee cups and a carafe of fresh brew, some Danish pastries, and a dish of fruit and headed back to Sine's hut. How the hell could everything go so bloody, fucking wrong?

She was dressed by the time Michael got there and though he was enduring his own hurt from Niall's tongue lashing, he knew Sine needed his support. She had no one else.

He put the tray on top of the bureau and handed her a cup of coffee. In his jumble of nerves and the scrambled condition of his mind, not to mention the remnants of a massive hangover, he'd forgotten any cream or sugar.

"It's okay, I learned to take it black long ago. For some reason, location filming often results in the coffee being there but the cream and/or sugar missing. So I gave up. Besides, I kind of like the almost bitter taste, especially when you lace it with Irish whiskey." She managed a brave smile, and Michael had no doubt she was wishing there was something left in the bottle to demonstrate her words with.

"I thought you hadn't ever had it before?" he asked,

208

taking a bit of a flaky pastry, trying vainly to catch the crumbs that fell to the floor. He remembered what she'd said about bugs and cast a worried eye out for fast moving critters.

"Just once. But I used to enjoy Irish coffee before I realized it kept me up half the night."

Chuckling, Michael asked, "And how long did it take you to realize that?"

Now it was Sine's turn to giggle, "About two years."

They ate in silence and Sine asked, "Did you mean what you said? I mean, about, if you were straight?" She didn't want to elaborate. Couldn't.

Michael watched her for a moment and dropped his eyes to finish his pastry. "Yes." He was tempted. God, he was tempted. But he loved Niall so damn much it hurt, and he could never keep up a dual relationship with them both. Everyone would be hurt. Much more hurt than they were right now.

"Are you alright?" he asked her, watching as her eyes seemed to turn glassy with unshed tears.

"Yeah," she said, taking a swipe at them, catching any moisture before it could turn into something more than just a bit of water in her eyes. "I just don't know where to go from here. I mean, I left the States because of all that shit, and now it's started here. I thought I'd be safe. Thought that whatever was happening over there would stay there. I guess what they say is really true. You can't run from your past forever. I just wish it would die," she finished quietly, and Michael knew she was talking of the rumors and stories of that other time.

209

"Hold your head high...how does that song go...'don't cry out loud'?"

"Funny, I always loved that song. I just never thought it would ever apply to me."

He put his cup on the bureau and walked over to her, put his arms around her, and held her close. "You are a very special woman, Sine," he said, rubbing her back and kissing the top of her coppery head. "Don't let a bunch of fucking fools make mincemeat out of you, just because they're jealous of the talent you possess. Do you know," he said, setting her apart a little way but keeping her in his arms, "Niall went to bat for you last night."

That surprised her. "He did?"

"Yeah. Told them all off. Garry, too. Guess Garry didn't know the effect all this shit was having on the principal actors."

"Yeah, well, Garry wouldn't noticed a bomb going off unless it blew Fee out of his arms."

"That's my girl," grinned Michael, sensing the Sine he knew, the stalwart woman with more courage in her little finger than all of the crew put together, begin to return.

"Guess it's time to see if I get to be in the final scene or not. If yesterday was anything to go by, I might as well leave right now. I'm all packed, anyway."

For the first time, Michael saw her bags stacked beside the bed. "You aren't going to stay around for the next day or two and just relax in the sun? It's all been arranged, you know."

"I don't care. I couldn't relax here any more than I could

210

go back to Manhattan and go through all that shit again. No. I'm going to leave, either before that scene is shot if I'm not in it, or after. I just want out of here."

Well, I don't blame you." Taking her by the hand, he said, "Come on, I'll walk you to the set. I have to make sure that motherfucking motherboard is still working, anyway."

* * *

Liam hobbled onto the dock with a little help from Tristan and waved goodbye to their chartered sea plane. Money could buy a lot of things, after all, and between him and Tristan, they could afford almost anything they wanted.

Before Liam had made the trek to Galway to visit with Tristan James, the film's producer, and confessed all that had gone on, he'd taken Henry's advice and gone to see Kevin at the phone store. Kevin hadn't been able to find Niall's phone because, as he told Liam, it wasn't turned on. But in the end, it hadn't mattered. Tristan knew the exact location.

The scene in Tristan's office that day played over again in his mind.

"It's not somethin' I'd ever have done if I didn't feel like my back was up against a wall," Liam had told him.

Tristan hadn't been happy. "I could sue your arse and have your union card for this but I'm too thankful you're here to worry about it. That being said, I don't know what the union will say about your brother."

"The union will have no cause to complain. Sine was able to get him a card before they left. It took some scramblin', but she managed."

"That makes it easier, but still doesn't address what's going on over there. Have you heard anything?"

Liam sighed and gripped the handles on his crutches in his fists. "Not a thing. I made Sine promise me to call me every day but there's been nothin'."

Tristan shook his head, his shoulder length, blond hair tied back in a low ponytail and coming loose. He looked, much as he always did, like he had just run in from somewhere and was on the verge of running out to somewhere else. He was a man of limitless energy who thought that sitting at a desk for more than five minutes was torture.

"Doesn't surprise me. There's no mobile service there but there is internet, or should be. It's a new company on that island. They're just getting a hotel business going where people can rent bungalows along the beach. All meals are taken in a central bungalow or hut or something and there was to be internet and mobile service there but they weren't able to get it up and running. Some kind of delay, don't know what it was but obviously, with the filming going on and their agreement to stay away during production, they haven't made any progress."

"Someone has internet. They've been sendin' things out to the tabloids."

"You've seen them, then?" Tristan's blond eyebrows shot up.

"I have, and it makes me want to kill someone." Liam felt his anger rise, knew his face was flushed. His cheeks felt hot and he was filled with a restless energy. If he was able, he would have taken himself off to the nearest gym and made good use of their punching bag. But he was here, in Tristan's office, watching as that man juggled papers on his desk, obviously looking for something.

Finally, Tristan held up a piece of paper in triumph. "Aha! Here it is, my travel itinerary."

"You goin' somewhere?" asked Liam, suddenly curious because he was going to need Tristan's help to get to the island.

"I was getting ready to head to the Bahamas myself to take a peek at what's happening there. Care to join me?"

Liam had nodded. "I would."

"Good, because I believe there's more to the story than just suddenly having to replace Percy."

That had surprised Liam. He hadn't known Percy, their on-location director, had been replaced.

At Liam's raised brows, Tristan said, "For some reason he's been put on a no-fly list. He didn't find that out until he got to the airport, so it must have happened after we had all the tickets arranged. Then, get this." He hesitated to put his thoughts into words, stressing them with a raised hand, "Felicia said she knew of a director that fit the bill, and against all warnings, I okayed it because we needed someone. I couldn't risk not doing those sequences that were so vital to the story. The only reason I didn't go personally was because my wife took sick and has been hospitalized for the last few weeks."

Hearing of his wife's illness, Liam was suddenly

concerned. They were friends, had been for a long time. "I'm sorry to hear. Is she goin' to be alright?"

"Yeah, she is now, thanks for asking, but it was touch and go there for a while. I didn't dare go anywhere, just in case." His eyes met Liam's and a complete understanding of the seriousness that had kept Tristan in Ireland was conveyed. "But now, she's back home and her sister has come to stay with her until I get back. I've got to go and get to the bottom of all this shite the tabloids are pouring out. I want publicity for the film but this isn't the kind I want." He indicated the small stack of magazines on his office desk, and Liam had understood.

That was two days ago, and here they finally were. Liam looked around but it was Tristan that pointed the way.

"Through there," he indicated with an outstretched arm, a finger pointing toward the gap in the trees where the path was easily discernable. "I'll be along shortly."

Following Tristan's directions, he step-thumped up the path that led to the walkways, and found the private huts that lined the beach, discreetly hidden behind dense foliage.

The first thing he noticed, when finding his way along the huts, was that they all seemed deserted. Maybe he was late and they'd left already, but no, Tristan had said they were still filming, and weren't expected to leave for another couple of days. There was a mail packet boat due in after six, he'd said, that serviced the villa at the other end of the island, and Liam could catch that one back if he wanted to leave. Tristan, it seemed, was going to stay until everything was cleared up and packed up.

214

So Liam continued on until he heard voices, and then followed the sounds to the lagoon where the familiar sights of a movie set lined the otherwise pristine pool. Staying hidden in the dense foliage, he made his way cautiously to a viewing point taking careful note of camera angles so as to avoid being in a shot.

Sine was standing, facing Niall. Niall was bare chested and dressed in ragged bottoms, befitting the stranded traveler he was portraying. Sine was garbed in a tattered dress, barely covering her ample breasts, as she was also a stranded traveler and needed to be as bedraggled as her counterpart. Of Felicia, there was no sign.

"Playback," called Garry, and music poured through the giant speakers. "And…action!"

Sine's hand caressed Niall's face as he tilted his head down to kiss her. The music swelled, the kiss deepened and his hands skillfully pushed the tattered fabric from her shoulders.

Liam was impressed. His brother had fit in and done as good a job as he himself would have, thought Liam, relaxing on his crutches.

At the end of the take, Felicia sidled up beside Garry and whispered something in his ear. Garry's head shook an emphatic "no," a movement that Liam could see even from across the pool where he remained hidden. What was she up to? He didn't know, but he knew she could be calculating and manipulative and was beginning to get the feeling that all was not well.

Two grips stood head to head while Garry was obviously going over something with the script writer and continuity people. From his spot behind the lush greenery, he was in a good position to overhear their conversation, although he hadn't understood who they were talking about until Sine's name was mentioned. Worse, they were snickering about her, and one said, "Yeah, found with that Arab fellow, buck naked in each other's arms."

"I wondered about him for a while…thought maybe he was limp-wristed but if he's with her then…"

His voice trailed off and Liam cursed the breeze that ruffled the plants and created susurrations loud enough to hide their words.

The wind died, and apparently, as Garry was still occupied, the two had kept up their conversation and were now focussed on Niall, whom they thought to be Liam.

"Wonder what Liam thinks of them, being found together like that?"

The other shrugged. "Why should he care? He's doing Felicia."

"Isn't she doing Garry?" came the other's question.

"Damned if I know. I think they're all doing each other," to which both men laughed.

Liam was gobsmacked. He wanted to go over to the two, ask them to clarify what they were saying, had a million other questions to ask, but mostly, just wanted to plant his fists in the middle of their faces.

A movement across the way captured his attention, and

Liam watched as Sine was handed a robe for her shoulders. He saw her pull it over herself, push her arms through the three-quarter length sleeves, then belt it securely at her waist, and was thankful that at least someone was on the ball where she was concerned.

The robe shimmied over Sine's sun-drenched skin, and though a light silky material, it was too hot for the weather but hid her breasts from everyone else's view. She'd never had a problem with nudity before, of feeling self-conscious in front of others. But now, being the center of attention and the object of so much salacious talk, she'd grown wary of any attention, overt or otherwise.

Standing off in the shadow of a light reflector, she sipped a cold drink when Michael came up beside her and put his arm around her. The movement was more than friendly, and seemed to declare her off-limits to anyone else. She didn't move away, didn't do anything to dislodge his nearness. Leaning into his strength, he pulled her closer and put his head to hers. Anyone who saw them would think them a couple in love.

Garry called for her. They were ready to do it again, trying the scene from a different angle.

Michael caught her chin with his fingers, brought his lips to hers and kissed her, a chaste kiss but lovingly given, then met her eyes, winking before he released her. She hadn't quite given up; was holding on just long enough to finish, and hoped to hell it would be over after this last take.

Niall's countenance had turned red with anger but Sine

was beyond caring what Niall thought anymore.

"What was all that about?" asked Niall in an aside while they faced each other and wardrobe tucked Sine's dress back into place.

"Nothing. Just…nothing." She smiled wanly at the wardrobe girl and waited until she'd finished fussing.

"If we're ready, people," said Garry loudly in a bored voice. "We're losing daylight."

People chuckled. They wouldn't lose daylight for at least another four hours.

The action began again, and so engrossed was Liam in watching his brother do something so out of character for him that he hadn't noticed people gravitating toward himself and whispering amongst themselves. Like Niall's original look, Liam's hair had grown but not to the length that could disguise him completely. As people jostled their spots in the circumference of the pool, careful to stay out of camera shot, Liam hadn't noticed them moving closer; he was now exposed to their stares.

Chapter Sixteen

The shot was done and Garry confirmed it. "That's a keeper," he called, then, under his breath, muttered, "thank Christ," as people began to disperse.

Sine took the robe from the wardrobe woman, thanked her, and left, presumably to go to her hut and change. Liam's eyes followed her as she traced a path through the bush, unknowingly heading straight for him. Her glance quickly took in the crutches, and then Liam himself, and gasping her surprise, she was at first joyous. Liam was here! But as she took in his expression, recalling Michael's closeness scant minutes before, she was soon filled with obvious confusion. He didn't look at all happy to see her.

It didn't take her long to put two and two together, thought Liam. She knew he'd seen Michael beside her, kissing her, looking after her like they were a couple. "It's true then," he said, and she knew what he meant.

Her mouth opened, then closed, and, as words seemed to have failed her, she turned to run headlong down the path as if she couldn't wait to get away from him.

The crowd that had started to form around him while he was watching the filming now followed him toward his brother. He didn't care.

Michael, who had stopped to look at the computer once again to make sure all was well, was about to leave when Niall stopped him in his tracks.

"Wait," Niall called, and Michael halted, turning to face him.

"I don't think we've anything more to say to each other, Niall," said Michael, not caring now who heard him. He was through playing games.

Niall hesitated. "I just want to know what that was all about; you, with Sine a few minutes ago. It's not like this is new behaviour for ye, Michael. Ye've done this to me before and I thought we were past it. Guess not, eh?"

What could he do, thought Michael, that would make it alright again? "I'm doing the best I can, luv. I'm trying to protect her, protect you. And somehow, I've ended up hurting everyone. I just wanted her to know there was someone in her corner."

"There is someone in her corner."

Both turned at the voice they knew so well. "Liam! When did you get here?"

By now, the crowd of onlookers included almost everyone on the set and all were gawking at him and Niall. Even Garry had stopped what he was doing to join the group.

Liam, Niall, and Michael looked about them, at the group that had formed, at Garry who was looking nonplussed.

The twins did what they had always done: stood fast against the odds.

And Michael joined them, for once not having to stand on his own.

"What in hell is going on? And if he's Liam, who the hell are you?" asked Garry, pointing at Liam.

"I'm Liam O'Farrell, and if ye are who I think ye are, ye have a lot to answer for. As for this guy," he gestured with his head toward Niall, "this is my brother, Niall, my twin. A mirror twin."

"What the hell is a mirror twin?" asked someone in the crowd.

"I'll explain it to you very quickly," Liam addressed the anonymous speaker. "We're mirror images of each other, including sexuality. So, if you've noticed anythin' amiss, it's because he's gay, tryin' to play a straight role, and doin' a damn fine job of it." He was staring straight at his brother, wanting him to know how proud he was of him, although Niall was looking anything but proud and had turned his head as if his worst secret was out. He was feeling like he was that fifteen-year-old once again, thought Liam, and newly aware of who he really was.

The mumbling through the crew continued but Liam ignored them. His focus was on his brother.

"So Niall, what's amiss?" he asked, and Niall only shook his head.

"Everything," said Michael, answering for him. "It's completely fucked up. All of it."

Liam sighed and gritted his teeth in frustration. "I've heard a few things, standin' over there, watchin' the filmin'.

221

I think we have a lot to talk about. Garry," Garry looked up, his face a mixture of the unknown. It was hard to tell what he was thinking. "I'd like ye in on this, if ye wouldn't mind."

A streak of red hair retreating down the path caught his eye and he called out, "Felicia!"

She turned at his voice, looked at him as if scrutinizing him and immediately her demeanor changed. "Why Liam, it's really you! I knew all along something wasn't right." As if she had just noticed the crutches, she exclaimed, "Oh, baby, what happened?"

"Long story for another time. I want ye to come with us," then added, "please."

"Sure, hon, whatever you say,", she sidled up to Liam to take his arm but he shook her off.

"I can't hold ye and maneuver these feckin' crutches, so ye'll just have to walk on yer own, like." He was really minding his manners because in about five minutes he was going to get to the bottom of the rumors and it wouldn't be pretty.

They walked into the dining hut, and even though dinner was about to be served, kicked everyone out and locked the door. Faces peered in the windows but Liam didn't care. He needed to know what was up before any more time passed.

"Who'd like to start?" he asked, but didn't hear the contrite voices he was expecting.

"What the fuck are you up to, you slimy sonofabitch?" exclaimed Garry. "You trying to pull one over on me? Is this some kind of joke?"

A banging was heard on the door and a loud voice called out, "Liam, open the door, it's Tristan."

At Liam's nod, Niall unlocked the door and let Tristan in, then locked it behind him once again.

"I think I've seen enough," said Tristan, his voice a quietly lethal tone, "to barring a whole bunch of people from ever working in this industry again. But as I have witnessed the professionalism of Liam's interactions with people in the past, I'm going to let him handle this one for now. Liam," he indicated with a nod of his head, "the floor is yours."

Thanking Tristan, Liam shook his head at Garry, who had taken on a nervous twitch, biting at his fingernails while he waited. Garry, a man who could attract women when he wanted them, looked anything but a man any female would like to be seen with. He was suddenly flushed with worry, and for a reason.

"No, Garry, this is no joke," Liam informed him, picking up where the conversation had been left. "The simple fact is that I broke my foot right after my brother's weddin' and we sent my twin brother, Niall here, to fill in for me. And from what I witnessed out there, he's done a fine job."

"He's been a pain in the ass," said Garry, a petulant look crossing his tired features.

Niall took exception to being called out. "I have not. I'll have ye know it's yon crew and her that's been the pain in the arse." He pointed out Felicia, which surprised no one, not even Fee herself.

"Sure, blame me. But it was that little whore that started

everything. She was pulling the same tricks here as she did on her last film, which, if you'll all remember, made that film flop at the box office and got the lead actor some very negative publicity. Why, it almost ruined his career." She was doing her best to look the injured party, pouty lip and all.

"Bollocks," shouted Liam and Niall together. Liam shot a glance at his twin. Never, in all their lives, had Niall been so vociferous, so Liam gave him the nod, and Niall continued on.

"That young lady has more talent in the freckles on her nose than you'll ever have in yer whole body over a lifetime. She's a decent, caring young woman who just happened to fall for the biggest arsehole on the planet. All she ever did was try to stick up for herself and her biggest mistake was thinking that maybe, just maybe, he was the only arsehole out there. Turns out there are a few more, some right here in this room."

"You filthy girlie-boy," she spat, and in one swift move and despite his crutches, Liam had her by the straps that held up her skimpy top.

"I have never, ever hit a woman, but by God, ye bring me so close that if I wasn't the man I am, I'd level ye now. Never…I repeat, never, refer to my brother like that again."

Michael, who had been quiet up to now, stepped beside Niall and slipped his hand in his, twining their fingers together. Niall shook off Michael's hand and stepped away. It seemed that all was not quite forgiven.

Liam dropped Felicia like a hot coal and turned to Garry.

"And what's this I hear ye're doin' both Fee and Sine? Is yer own wife not good enough for ye?" He really didn't believe Sine would allow the man to touch her but the rumors…

"I never touched that little whore, and my wife is none of your business." Garry's face was turning red and Liam knew it wasn't just from the heat.

"It's my business when ye use people. Especially the people I love."

"Oh, hon, thank you, I…"

"I didn't mean you," said Liam to Felicia. "I meant Sine and Niall, and even Michael here. But you, Felicia, have been as much a party to the shite that's gone on here as Garry."

Garry sighed in resignation. "Well, Liam, you're right there. I haven't been the man I should be. But this fucking job has doubled in time; doubled, no, make that tripled in budget; and all because we've had more than our share of technical troubles. And being stuck on this shit-hole of an island hasn't made things easier. But I'll tell you true, if it wasn't for Michael here, this whole project would be down the tubes. He kept us up and running these last couple of weeks."

Liam looked at Michael and the corner of Liam's lips turned up somewhere between and smirk and a grin. "The last I heard, you were just a crew member, stagin' or somethin'. That's a bit of a promotion," to which Michael shrugged and nodded.

To Garry, Liam said, "Ye'll want to make certain his paycheck reflects that, hm?" He glanced over at Tristan while he spoke and saw the producer shrug and nod, an indication

225

that while he would think about it, he knew Liam was right. Michael deserved to be paid more than just a stagehand's wages. A technical expert came at a much higher price, and if it wasn't for Michael, the entire film might be a write-off.

Garry began to mutter something about the budget but Tristan's broad Oxford accent halted him. "Don't think I haven't got the power to veto whatever you might come up with. You weren't supposed to be the director on this phase. I don't know what happened to put Percy Farquharson on a no-fly list, but I'm going to find out because I'm very curious how a two-bit director of B-list films gets to work on something this big."

Again, Garry made to interject but the looks he was getting from Liam, Niall, and Michael made him shut his mouth, much like a codfish that had given up its last breath.

Liam had been looking around, curious that Sine wasn't in attendance. "Where's Sine? She should be here to help clear things up." With everything that had gone on, Liam himself wasn't sure how he felt about Sine at the moment but he knew she hadn't been guilty of anything to do with jeopardizing the film.

"I'll go get her," said Niall.

"No, don't bother," said Michael, "she's gone."

"Gone? Gone where?" asked Liam and Niall at once.

"Left the island. The mail packet left at six and she meant to be on it. It's now nearly seven."

Niall turned on him, "Ye bollocks, ye. Ye knew all along she was goin' to leave and ye never said naught. Ye've left

226

her thinkin' she's ruined."

"I've told her I'll protect her, and I will," said Michael, defending his silence where Sine's leaving was concerned. "She told me earlier that she meant to leave as soon as filming was done, that she didn't want to stick around here one minute longer than necessary; and I couldn't see any reason why on earth she shouldn't do just that. We had no notion you were coming, Liam. None. Maybe if we'd known…" but he didn't finish, and Liam felt the frustration rise.

"Whatever has been goin' on here has hit the tabloids in a very big way out there," he pointed out. "The rags are full of photos from this island. What I want to know is how they were taken and how those feckin' things got off the island?"

"Photos?" asked Niall. "Ye mean in those feckin' magazines Em likes to buy?"

"The very same," said Liam, his eyebrows furrowing deeply as he remembered every new rag that went on the stands and what it did to him inside.

All eyes turned to Felicia and Garry, standing side by side and looking guilty as hell.

Michael sighed. "I think that's our answer," he said. "Garry's really the only one with internet here."

"You could have sent anything you wanted, Michael," accused Felicia. "You worked on it day and night."

"I did. And as a professional, I know better than to snoop into people's private emails and the like, so I never even tried. Had I any inkling that something of the sort was happening, of course I would have looked. I would have stopped it."

Liam had been thinking about the photos in the tabloids, the type of photos, all intimate, as if staged. But they couldn't have been staged, so then…what?

"Who took them?"

No one said anything but Felicia was wearing a "go ahead and try me" look.

Liam did just that. "Felicia, I asked a question. And if ye don't think I can't blackball ye the way ye did Sine, think again."

"I didn't take them," she said, and while Liam believed her, he knew she was hiding something. "But ye know who did. Furthermore, I think ye were workin' in tandem, sabotagin' this film, discreditin' other actors, me included, and makin' yerself come up all roses. I wondered why it was always Niall or Sine, and even some with Michael in those photos, but never you. I'll bet ye won't want to tell me that, would ye?"

The people outside started banging on the doors, wanting to get in. Liam was aware Felicia hadn't answered his questions but with dinner held up, he knew he'd have a worse problem on his hands if he didn't unlock the doors.

A glance at Tristan and Liam knew he was thinking the same thing. "Tristan? You have anything you'd like to say?"

"Not at the moment. But I can tell you that there will be an investigation into the matters here so no one will be going anywhere for a couple of days. We've at least that much time before the charter arrives to take everyone back to Nassau and I intend to get to the bottom of this before then." His gaze fell directly on Felicia and Garry, and though Garry lowered his eyes, scuffing his sandaled feet across the floor, moving invisible specks of dirt, and looking shamefaced, Felicia's gaze was haughty, as if her fame could protect her from her own destructive actions.

Liam gave Niall the okay to open the doors, and the crowd outside made their way in, taking sideways glances at everyone already in the room while making their way to the counter to get their food. Liam went to a table and having sent a silent plea to Niall, waited at the table while Niall brought two plates full.

Tristan had left the dining hut, to do what, Liam didn't know but he had faith in Tristan's abilities to take care of everything from here on in.

Michael threw some food on a plate and made to leave the dining hut but Liam caught him before he could escape. "Michael," he called, and Michael stopped, changed direction to meet Liam at his table.

"Sit with us. Tell me what's going on," Liam invited.

"No." Michael cast a wayward glance at Niall as he was in the business of filling two plates with food. "There's nothing for me to say now that would change anything."

Liam understood. "No, I don't want to get between what you and my brother have goin'. I want to know about you and Sine. What's goin' on there?"

A long sigh escaped Michael's lips. "I've ruined everything. Hadn't meant to. But I did."

Taking a quick look his brother's way, Liam said, "In

twenty words or less, what's happened?"

Michael followed Liam's look, knew time was ticking, and decided to relieve the guilt he was feeling. "It's like this," he began.

Less than a minute after Michael began, he'd finished his tale and stalked out of the dining hut. Niall watched him go and Liam watched his brother.

Niall wore a look that was part anger, part pain, and if Liam didn't miss his guess, it was mostly pain. The anger was beginning to diminish.

"What's yer story, then?" he asked when Niall put the plates on the table. Seeing Niall's look of warning, though, he didn't pursue it. Liam knew his twin would eventually tell all, and he didn't have long to wait.

They were halfway through a meal that had lost all flavor when Niall finally spoke. "Michael's in love with Sine."

Liam nearly choked on his food. "What?"

"Ye heard me. Don't make me repeat it."

"Of course I heard ye, I just can't believe what ye're sayin'."

"It's true. He slept with her."

Liam had heard from Michael's own lips what went on but braced himself for the worst. He waited patiently for Niall to continue.

"The maids caught them and it was all over the island before Michael even got here for breakfast. He didn't deny it. Tried to, but I know him too well."

"Ye're sure he did…they did, that? When Michael told

it, he left out that little detail when he said they'd been found nude together, and I believed him. I guess he wanted me to fill in the blanks, only I didn't want to. Didn't want to admit to myself what everyone else was sayin'. I was hopin' it was a lie."

Niall shrugged. "No. No lie. He's done it to me before, long ago, only I thought we had an understandin' now. Guess not." He sat in silence, poking at the food on his plate without really eating. Trying to sound as if he couldn't care less, Niall continued in a different vein. "Give it time. Whoever is takin' photos will have sent them off. They'll be in the next tabloid, I'm sure of it."

Liam angrily pushed his plate away, aware of people gawking still, of the two of them looking like bookends despite the differences in their hairstyles. "Let's get out of here. I could use a drink," he snarled.

Niall let out a noise that was part laugh, part snort of derision. "Ye won't find anythin' worth drinkin' here," he said. "They've stuff, but not for the likes o' you and me."

"No bother," said Liam. "I brought some with me."

They left the dining hut and Niall held the door open for his brother, then watched as he carefully negotiated his way down the three wide, wooden stairs to the groomed walkway.

"Ye're doin' okay on those," he remarked as Liam step-thumped his way along the path.

"I won't win any races but I can get around," Liam replied sulkily. He couldn't wait to pull out that bottle of whiskey.

231

Chapter Seventeen

Michael lay on his bed, staring up at the ceiling at the rough-hewn timbers supporting it, and then let his imagination kick in, knowing that on top of that inner structure, outside, a thick layer of fronds gave it that special island appeal. He'd thought them a nice touch at first, like the island itself. A little paradise tucked away in a far corner of the ocean.

It was secluded, and yet that very seclusion had been a double-edged sword. It had provided the production with uninterrupted days and nights of filming, free of the usual hangers-on, paparazzi, and anyone else who just happened by. Sadly, it also allowed for the creation of a mini dictatorship, run completely at the whim of an offbeat director. One who, according to Tristan and Liam, should never have been here. How did he get here and why? How did this whole charade start?

He'd gone through the characters in the drama-within-the-drama, like a sideline to the film they were making. There had been undercurrents all along of something else happening, only he hadn't seen it coming, hadn't thought it was anything other than bad luck.

The bad luck had hit hard. Sine had been devastated. He'd seen a confident woman—someone who excelled at her craft, an artiste, a siren, a woman any man would be proud to have on his arm—crushed, broken. And underneath it all, he worried that she might do something stupid, like follow through with her sense of the dramatic and throw herself off the Cliffs of Mohr. She wouldn't be the first one ever to have done that, but he had faith that her sensibilities, which had seen her through a similar situation before, would prevail. No, he had to believe she'd be alright eventually. It was the pain she was enduring in the meantime that goaded his anger.

Where was she now, and why hadn't he stopped her from leaving?

Footsteps sounded outside and the quiet words, spoken in Irish, told him that Liam and Niall were walking by and he wondered if what he'd told Liam would make any difference. He had to think it would. Just had to.

Michael suspected that Niall was taking his brother to Sine's now vacant hut. Every other hut on the island was taken, and Michael was hoping that his three roommates wouldn't bother to show up for some time. He wasn't at all certain of the reception he'd get, whether they'd let him stay or remove him bodily from the hut. Perhaps they'd leave him be, since the real Liam had shown up?

He thought about what Liam had said, about suspecting that someone was purposely sabotaging the project, and thought he might know who it was. Sam had been the only other one that had worked on the motherboard with him. Who's to say that man couldn't have come back at another time and accessed Garry's email? If the man was half as clever as Michael thought, and Michaelhad been impressed with his knowledge and his ability to help, then it was all too possible that he could have been the one to send those photos off.

It bore looking into.

Sam, as if knowing he'd been on Michael's mind, entered the hut, glanced through the darkness over at Michael on the bed, and said a timid hello. Michael mumbled back, deciding the best course of action would be no action unless someone started something first.

Eventually, Sam broke the silence that seemed deafening. "It sounded pretty intense in there, what you guys were talking about before dinner. Locking everyone out was probably a good idea."

"Yeah," answered Michael, but didn't elaborate.

"So, what was the conclusion of all that?"

Michael shrugged. "Not for me to say. I'm just doing a job."

Sam pressed on. "So, if Liam has a twin, and that twin was acting as him…he said his twin is gay?"

Michael looked at the fella with his straight, dark hair

stuck out like a pin cushion, and made the decision to answer the question before it was asked. "Yes, he's gay. Yes, he's my partner. Yes, I'm gay. Anything else you'd like to know?"

Sam stood there, openmouthed and gawking. "I didn't mean to…"

"You didn't mean to what, be so nosey? Need to know everyone's affairs? It shouldn't matter what anyone's sexual designation is, but it seems to, at least on this island with this crowd. So let's just get it straight and leave it at that. If you don't want me in here, too bad. You can just relax because I don't look at every man out there as a potential partner. In fact, no one in this hut, or on this island, with the exception of Niall, interests me in the least. So get over yourself."

"It's cool, man, I was just wondering."

"Yeah, well, wonder no more." He lay on his bed at one end of the room while Sam went to his at the other, and tried to drift off to sleep. Since it was the end of the filming, and according to Liam's stories there was usually a cast party of some sort where everyone who had anything to do with the film got together and got wrecked, he and Sam might be the only two in the hut for a while. Getting wrecked sounded like a good idea. The only problem was that Michael had no interest in being wrecked with anyone here.

In his heart, he ached for Niall and wondered if Niall would be alone tonight. He needed to see him, needed to know, needed to fix things.

Eventually, the other two who shared the room entered and went straight to their beds. It was clear that they'd had enough of whatever they'd been drinking and would be snoring loudly, soon.

He wasn't wrong. Lying there in the pitch-dark room, he was wondering if their snoring would keep him awake, should he want to stay. No bother, he didn't. But what could he possibly say to Niall that would make Niall forgive him?

Until another thought entered his head.

He smiled to himself, a sly smile, and ensuring that everyone in the hut was asleep, he tiptoed out into the calm night, heading off to find Liam.

* * *

The mail boat dropped Sine and her bags off in Nassau and she soon settled herself into a four-star hotel. If she was leaving, she thought, she was going to enjoy the trip. Four stars was enough. Five-star, well, in her experience, they were just snobs.

The first thing she did was run a bath for herself in the tub, filling it full and using the entire container of bath salts provided to soften the water for her weather-roughened skin. Once she finished that, she crawled into the semi-soft, king-sized bed, hoping for a solid night's sleep before catching the first plane out in the morning. She had no desire to see anyone from the film set ever again, and that included Liam.

She choked up at the memory of his hands on her skin, his mouth on hers, but then had trouble distinguishing his touch from that of his brother. Niall wasn't the same kind of lover, although she'd never gone to bed with him. Yet her instincts were pretty solid when it came to the twins. Liam made love with a passion when he was with her, whereas Niall's kisses were anything but passionate. He faked it exceptionally well for the love scenes but she felt none of the connection that she had with Liam. Would she ever feel that way with someone ever again? She refused to think about Michael.

Swiping at the tear that tried to course its way down her cheek, she closed her eyes, and after a few more sniffs and swipes, finally gave herself over to sleep.

Two days later, she was finally home, finally back on Irish soil and wondering where to go from here. She picked up her bags and walked to the car rental counter. So far, no one noticed who she was, and if they had, hadn't paid any attention. She'd picked up the car, a little red compact, and made her way into the city, looking for a corner store that would have everything she needed. Lots of petrol stations had a convenience store, so when she found one, she pulled in and went inside.

Her confidence that she would be unrecognizable fled as soon as she paid for her few meager groceries at the counter. A woman had been gazing at the tabloids on display, put two and two together, and asked outright if she was the one in the photos. It wasn't just any photo. It was one of her and Michael in bed, Michael's hand on her breast.

Oh God, she thought, oh God, Liam.

It was hard to explain such a tan, especially on a redhead. Especially on a redhead with long, straight locks and a face that was unmistakeably familiar, even with her sunglasses on. Sine produced a quick smile and a quiet, "Excuse me," as she brushed past the woman who'd queried her, hoping that she could just book it out of there with no one being the wiser.

Flashes from cameras started popping in her face and she ran for the rental car, parked just down the street. She gained the car seconds before the small group of fans did, and threw her groceries inside, not caring that she'd likely bruised the apples and primed the fizzy soda cans. She was hoping they wouldn't burst, but in the meantime, she was in the car and pulling into traffic, getting away without being overly harassed. At least she hadn't had to answer any questions. She had moved too fast for them to catch her.

Fully provisioned for her journey to Galway, she intended to drive until she arrived, not caring for anything but the sanctity of her own four walls.

* * *

Niall showed Liam to the hut that Sine had used, noting the absence of anything that would have shown she was there. Liam walked in, checked the room, walked into the bathroom and out again, proclaiming it, in his words, "Fine."

He sat down on the edge of the bed and tested it for softness. "Hm, I guess it'll do. Pretty standard covers, though. Ye'd think they'd go for something a wee bit more exotic, like palm leaves and the like."

"From what I've heard and been told, this particular place is just getting started, which is why they were able to get it for the film. No one really knows about it yet and they wanted to make its first season a good one. Guess they'll have all kinds of bragging rights now," Niall said.

Liam was still studying the coverlet, fingering it and scrutinizing the pattern. "That B&B in Cahersiveen, the one we stayed at after Hank's weddin'. Ye don't suppose it looked like this, do ye?"

Niall stepped closer to Liam, leaned over to see what he was looking at so intently. "Could be. Well, maybe. I don't remember much about it. Michael and I were, uh, busy."

"Well, I was busy myself, but I recognized this pattern from a photo in a tabloid and thought someone had marked Sine and me at the B&B. But now I think, just perhaps, that photo was taken here."

"Here? But ye just got here," he said, rebutting his brother's remark.

"Y'eejit," scolded Liam, "not me. You. It had to have been you in the photo in that tabloid, not me."

Niall lifted his shoulders in a shrug and agreed. "Is that important?"

"Feckit, Niall but ye can be a brick when ye want to. Of course it's important. Leastwise, to me it is. Did ye ever have a scene, you and Sine, when ye were together in bed?"

Niall thought and then realized that Liam was right. "Yeah. It was to have taken place on board the ship, before they got shipwrecked. I think Sine said there was a problem with continuity so they just re-did the whole thing here."

Liam nodded. "Makes sense," he said. "If someone is sendin' photos out, it has to have come from here. And that someone has to have had access to the internet."

A knock sounded on the door, and Niall opened it. "Oh,

it's you," he said, seeing Michael on the other side of the door.

"Well, that tells me right away which one you are," Michael replied, stepping into the room.

"What's up?" asked Liam, thinking that Michael must have a good reason for seeking them out at this time of night.

"I've been thinking about the photos, and how they might have got off the island."

"Me too," said Liam, and Niall nodded. "So what's yer theory?"

"Whoever it is had to have internet access. I have a prime suspect in mind but it could be someone else or maybe he has an accomplice," suggested Michael.

"Ye mean like Felicia?" asked Niall, and it was Michael's turn to nod.

"Better yet, I've an idea how to flush them out. To prove it."

"Michael, the last time ye thought of a way to fix things, it didn't work out so well. Look where we are. I don't think this has done our relationship any favors," said Niall.

"I know, and I'm truly sorry, even if you don't believe me. But let me tell you what I think and if you don't like it, then we'll just forget it."

Liam and Niall exchanged glances.

"Fine," they said in unison, and the three sat down to strategize.

* * *

The following morning, Niall and Michael were still not seeing eye to eye. They'd each spent the night alone, neither willing to touch a spot too raw yet to prod.

With no filming left to do and the production staff reporting that the computerized electronics were magically working, both men found themselves at odds, and strangely enough, alone on the beach.

Michael glanced through furrowed brows at Niall before heading toward the rocky promontory overlooking the waves that crashed against the rocks and the small blowhole that was created when the water was high. The tide was out, the water low, but Michael didn't care. It was the solitude he craved just then.

Liam had taken himself off toward the other end of the island to investigate the villa. Feeling the need to be in his twin's company, and with a quick last look to where Michael had gone, Niall caught up with Liam, who, in any case, was not moving at any rate of speed.

"I'll come with ye," said Niall, hands in pockets, falling into step with his brother, watching their feet making footprints in the sand along with the indentations of Liam's crutches.

"Ah, so ye're comin' with me to see if the rumors about the lovely ladies at the villa are true?" Liam asked, hiding a grin because he knew his brother didn't care.

"Ye're goin' to see ladies? What of Sine?" Niall queried his brother as they made their way through the soft sand, only a few feet up from where the waves cascaded roughly onto the beach, depositing more sand, then taking it away again as it slid back to rejoin the ocean once more.

"Nothin' is for certain there."

"But, ye love her."

"I do. I also think she loves me but there's something I need to find out first. Dependin' on her answer...well, we'll see, I guess." Liam knew he loved Sine and wanted to explore that relationship more, but he also knew it was going to take time.

After they'd gone a good distance and the rock where Michael was sitting was out of sight, Liam stopped and looked at his brother. The silence stretched, the only sound came from the waves, crashing against the shore and then withdrawing again. Sunlight glinted off the cerulean tops of the ocean and Liam squinted through the glaring rays at his brother, meeting his eye.

"Go back, Niall. Make amends. Ye've too much invested in that relationship to see it all go south."

"He's cheated on me again," complained Niall. "Not only cheated but done it with yer woman," and he stressed "yer woman," to make it clear that he knew what was going on with Liam and Sine.

"Not mine. Not yet. But I appreciate the thought."

"It doesn't change the fact that he slept with her."

Liam couldn't disagree. "Did ye ever take into account how much whiskey they'd had?"

"Whiskey?"

"Irish whiskey," Liam clarified. "Good stuff, according to Michael. Not a twenty-Euro bottle, more like a fifty-Euro bottle."

Niall opened his eyes wide. "They drank it all? How are they still alive?"

Liam laughed because it was close to being true. "My understanding is that it wasn't a full bottle when Michael took it off by himself to get deadly drunk. And by the time he went to Sine's, just to talk mind, there hadn't been a whole lot left. But to someone like Sine, whose experience with whiskey is limited to say the least, a few good mouthfuls would be enough to put her over the edge. Remember, it's more than forty percent."

"I know, but he still slept with her. If he was that drunk, how the hell did he even..."

"Has he ever failed ye before?" Liam broke in, watching his brother's features, knowing Niall was getting close to forgiving Michael what Michael had done only out of love. Misguided, maybe, but with no intent to hurt anyone; quite the opposite.

"No. He's always been able to...ye know."

"I do, from what ye've let slip. So although he was raging, might even have had trouble standing at that point, he was still able to perform. And ye know he likes women, too. It's just who he is. So why not use such a talent to deflect ugly rumors from you, technically, me?"

Niall thought about it. Michael's words were, I did it for you, to protect you, protect her. "I suppose ye're right," he said, understanding dawning on him. "But they didn't really have to do it. Could have just faked it," he complained.

"Could have. I agree. Wish it were true. But think on it,

243

Niall. If ye've had that much and there's a nice body, hurtin' and needin' some cuddlin', what would ye do? Hm?"

They'd gone at least a kilometer up the beach; the villa was just an excuse to get away to talk, Liam knew. But Niall was done talking, and looking like he wanted to head back down the beach to see Michael.

"Look at it this way," grinned Liam. "By the time Michael puts our plan into play, ye might truly welcome him back into yer bed. It's been a while without, eh?"

"No. Well, not with Michael. Had Fee just the other night."

The statement came out so quickly and so matter-of-factly that Liam stumbled on his crutches and would have fallen if Niall hadn't caught him just then. "What the…?"

"Exactly," Niall said, straight-faced as if he were talking about the weather. "It wasn't so bad—at least, not as bad as I remember it as a teenager. Back then I was traumatized that it didn't make me feel any better than when I tossed off in the loo. It wasn't until I met Michael that sex really took on a different meaning for me."

Liam's desire to shake his brother senseless was suddenly very strong. If Niall had grown enough to bed Felicia, then he really had come a long way and should just get on with it.

"Niall, quit being an eejit and just go make amends. Don't let these arseholes win. If ye do, ye'll regret it for the rest of yer life."

Niall turned and cast his gaze down the way they'd come. Michael, they both knew, was likely waiting for him in the same spot on the rock they'd last seen him.

Hands deep in his pockets, kicking sand as he did as a child, Niall made his decision. "Right, then, I'm off," and strode quickly back down the length of beach they'd just traversed.

Liam watched Niall go and hung his head in laughter. How his brother had ever grown the nads to keep a relationship going was beyond him. Yet somehow, Niall and Michael seemed to work things out, through good and bad.

And would again, he was sure.

Chapter Eighteen

Michael was still on the rocky outcropping, staring at the sun falling farther from the sky. It was late afternoon, but here in the tropics, the sun set quickly; light one minute, dark the next. He felt Niall's presence rather than heard him, and half turned his head to note his approach from behind. He faced the ocean once again, hoping against hope that Niall wasn't here to tell him it was over for real. He didn't think he could take that.

The footfalls, ripe with the crunch of shell remnants and sand on the rocky surface, stopped, and Michael knew that Niall was right behind him.

"Are ye ready for tonight?" asked Niall, and Michael saw him from the corner of his eye, looking around the deserted outcropping, likely making sure they weren't overheard. It would have been difficult for anyone to overhear them anyway, what with the waves hurling themselves unbounded at the rocks. The crashing was at times almost deafening.

Michael nodded. "Yeah. It's my plan, so I guess I'm ready. You?"

Niall indicated with a grunt that he was. He'd crouched down, taken a stick, and was picking at something in a sand-filled cleft of the rock. Michael noticed and watched, neither one talking or feeling the need. This was how it used to be with them; they could be quiet together, enjoy being in each other's presence with no need for useless chatter.

He missed that time.

Niall kept chipping away and eventually worked the thing loose, a tiny shell, delicate and pearled, glistening with a myriad of colors like a rainbow in miniature. Lifting it to his lips, he blew on it, dislodging tiny particles of sand, then gently brushed the rest away with a lean, tanned fingertip. He placed it in the palm of his hand, flipped it over so the scalloped side was showing, rough and dull, cradled in his palm.

Michael watched, envying the shell against those lips and in those hands. Thoughts of what those hands, those lean fingers could do for him whetted Michael's appetite for something he was beginning to think was forever lost to him.

Niall's next words made him suspend that thought.

"I think we're like this shell," Niall said, stroking the back of the shell lightly as if it were alive. "On the outside, we're hard, crusty like, and we often don't shine much. But on the inside, we're delicate, we can be hurt, and like the creature of this shell, we can die, exposing our soft insides to the hateful world out there. Yet this shell, as delicate as it is, is still here. Its inside is still beautiful. Scarred, but beautiful.

"I guess what I'm trying to say, Michael, is that you are like this shell, still beautiful on the inside, even though ye've exposed yer soft side, let them see ye bleed. I have always

247

loved that about ye. That ye can take everything they throw at ye and still stand. Ye've always been someone I can count on that way, and I want ye back. Because the basic truth is that I love ye."

Michael looked away and stared at the sea, the ever-changing sea. Were he and Niall like that? Ever changing, loving one minute, estranged the next? He didn't know if he could take that, and for once, wanted the solidity of knowing that Niall was his for all time.

Yet he could crush the shell in Niall's hand between two fingers, just like he could crush their relationship. It wouldn't take much. A sideways glance, a rough comment or two. He could choose to destroy it just as easily as he could to repair it.

"You know I slept with Sine."

"I do. And any man that can drink that much and still perform deserves a medal." There was a hint of a smile in Niall's voice that Michael chose to ignore.

"I could love her."

"But ye don't. I could love her, too, but for a different reason. She's the woman my brother loves and there are qualities I see in her that I admire very much. So, in that respect, I do love her, too."

"No. You misunderstand. The morning after, when we were getting dressed, I told her I could love her."

"And what did she say?"

"That if she didn't love Liam so much, she'd be tempted to take me up on it."

"And that's it?" asked Niall, clearly wanting more.

"No," answered Michael. "I don't recall my exact words, but it was something to the effect that I couldn't manage two relationships at the same time because as much as I care about her, and I do, I also care about you, and don't want to live without you by my side." His voice began to choke up but he continued on. "Whatever I've done, Niall, I did it for love of you both. Not to hurt anyone and not to make a bad situation worse, although I may have done. I just thought that if Sine and I were seen together, if the maids knew we'd slept together, then it would deflect rumors from you, and I could at least protect you. Only I hadn't meant to actually sleep with her. My only defense is the whiskey. We got carried away; I got carried away," he corrected himself, "and for the hurt it caused you, to know I'd done that to you, I'm truly sorry."

Niall nodded, swallowed, the sound audible, and Michael knew he was feeling emotional too, although his face was turned away.

"Niall?"

Niall looked at him then, his lugubrious eyes a reflection of the cerulean sea beyond, and Michael was lost.

"C'mere to me," he said, and Niall edged closer, let Michael put his arms around him and met him, lips to lips, tongue to tongue. Michael ran his thumb lovingly across Niall's cheek, felt the bit of stubble there, and grinned through the kiss.

It would have been so easy to get it on, right then and there, but Michael recalled their planned tryst and knew

S. M. Cross

that very soon they could celebrate their reunion in a very comfortable bed.

* * *

On the edge of the jungle foliage, two sets of eyes watched the display on the rocks.

"That's disgusting," said one.

"Oh, I don't know," said the other, "could be kinda kinky."

"You interested? Why don't you join them later? I'll get a photo of all three of you."

"Two gay men and a woman," said Felicia, "Wouldn't that make headlines. Only, not me. I'm not in for those kinds of headlines. Too bad Sine took off so soon. We could have used her."

"There's only so much you can flog with someone like that. She's just not big enough news."

They retreated through the jungle, the fronds and dense foliage filling in behind them as they left.

* * *

"Have another drink," said Liam, handing his brother the bottle. "I think it's late and I'm for bed. That stroll up the beach took a bit more out of me than I'd planned." He gauged his brother, sitting next to Michael on the bed. They looked good together, he thought, although Niall was still hurting, the wound of Michael's infidelity still an open sore. It would heal, he was sure. Time would help and they'd be good as new if the look on Michael's face was anything to go by.

"You ready for later?" asked Niall in Irish, knowing

250

that he and his twin were the only ones who understood that ancient tongue. He handed the bottle off to Michael, who took a healthy swig and said nothing.

Liam nodded and answered in the same tongue. "I think I can get around on these okay. Might take me a while longer and I won't be quiet, but the paths are groomed and so long as I'm not too far away, I should be able to get a good shot at them."

Niall nodded and looked at Michael. "Okay?" was all he said, and Michael, who had picked up some words of Irish over time, seemed to understand what they were on about.

"All yours," came his simple reply as Liam stood and stretched.

"Ah, feckit," Liam said loudly in English. "Christ, any more of that stuff and I'll be weavin' my way in the wrong direction. It's that way, eh?" He was half out the door and, stumbling worse than he normally did, headed off in the wrong direction.

"Ah, no bother then," said Niall to Michael, somewhat louder than he needed to, "he'll eventually find his bed."

Michael came up to Niall where he stood at the door, the light from the room spilling out into the night. With one brown hand, he grasped Niall's chin, held it fast, and slanted his mouth across his lover's lips. Niall opened, took him in and feasted, the two of them performing their kiss by the light of the outside lamp before slowly moving inside, closing the door behind them, and ignoring the window with its shutters and louvers open to the night.

251

They didn't care that someone would come and take photos. They knew they could delete the most incriminating ones any time they wanted to, and so they didn't hesitate, didn't waste time in wondering if or when. Were only too eager to get each other naked and seal their bond.

"Wait," said Michael, when Niall would have slid his hands inside Michael's shorts and pushed them down.

Niall stopped, looked him in the eye, a brow crooked in question.

"I'll be nude for you," he whispered. "You don't have to show them what you have anymore. I'll do it. I'll take that ignominy for you."

"Ye don't get it Michael. I want ye. Now." He pushed Michael's shorts past the globes of his arse and they dropped to the floor where Michael lifted a tanned leg and kicked them off.

Michael's hand found Niall's rump inside his shorts and pulled him closer, moving his fingers to massage the firm cheeks of his arse. Niall moaned his pleasure.

"Leave yours on for now. I'll give ye what ye want. Just don't undress yet," Michael whispered in his ear.

He felt Niall's hand engulf him, stroke him.

"God, Michael, why'd ye do it?" Niall said in between mouthfuls of Michael's tongue.

"I told ye. I did it for love," came the reply, and the words slid out jumbled but Niall understood.

"It could have gone worse than it did, y'eejit," he croaked out. Michael was doing wonderful things to him.

252

"Liam will make it right with her, you'll see," he answered, moving his hand to come between them.

Niall didn't need help that way. He couldn't remember being so hard, so needy. "I need ye now, Michael, I want ye now."

"Are you sure? I mean, I need you to be sure."

Niall understood. There was being caught in the act and then there was really being caught in the act. He had no intention of allowing anyone to see him with Michael quite that way.

Instead, he grabbed Michael's arse, shoved his lad against Michael's washboard of a stomach, and pressed hard against the fabric of his shorts, rubbed himself into it. "Oh, God, I could almost have ye, just like this," he gritted out between clenched teeth.

A flash illuminated the night outside and Liam's voice rang loud and clear. "Caught ye red-handed."

Neither Michael nor Niall wasted any time and cleared the door in two strides. In another two they were at the window where Felicia and Sam were standing, mouths gaping open at the two men, Michael still unclothed.

Michael, bold as brass and proud of his body-builder's stature, simply walked over to Sam and held out his hand. "The camera. Now."

Sam dropped it to the pathway and ground the heel of his running shoe into it, glaring in defiance at Michael.

Michael only laughed. "You think that's going to stop me from retrieving evidence? I guess I should explain. Niall

253

and I are, well, we're the geniuses that work for Europe's top software company. We designed the software that is in that phone. I can tell you how to retrieve lost data. I can tell you how to do almost anything with a computer. And that motherboard was not really the frustrating job I made it appear. But I couldn't very well look the genius or we'd never have caught you in the act."

From behind, they heard Garry clearing his throat and Niall turned to Michael, saying, "I'll get your clothes."

"Garry set this up," Felicia tried to defend herself but Liam wasn't buying it.

"Garry isn't smart enough to set this up but he is dumb enough to play yer patsy," commented Liam.

"I resent that," Garry exclaimed.

"No, Garry, to coin a phrase, you resemble that."

"I came here to warn you guys, to tell you what these two were up to. That's why I'm here."

"And just how would ye be knowin' all that, hm?" Liam could hardly wait for the explanation.

"He was in on it, too," said Sam. "He found out I knew a little about computers so I was able to keep Michael on track and out of any email system, make sure he didn't go where he shouldn't."

"I knew you were clever," said Michael, having donned shorts and his t-shirt and looking respectable once again.

"That's true," sighed Garry. "Although the plan wasn't mine." He pointed a look directly at Felicia, who blushed and stammered as she tried to worm her way out of the accusation.

"Never mind," said Liam. "I did some checking earlier today. Everyone thought I'd shambled up yon beach, and for a while I did. But the goin' was tough and, well, I found myself close to the tent where all the gear is, and most folks were off enjoying lunch or the beach or whatever. Point is, they weren't there and you were, weren't ye, Fee? You were sending stuff off, I heard ye chuckling with young Sam here. Also heard ye talkin' about wreckin' the production, givin' it a bad name, and layin' it on Sine, to bury her even deeper."

Felicia straightened up, thrust out her manufactured breasts and, chin held high, said, "You can't prove any of that."

Liam had pulled out his mobile phone, the one he'd taken their photo with just as they'd taken the one of Niall and Michael. "Okay, just a minute, it'll only take a moment to find it. Ah, here it is, right on the front in this little box." He punched in a code, flipped across to where he wanted to be, and hit the button. The sound of Felicia's voice in conversation with Sam's was unmistakeable.

Niall was impressed. "Who the hell taught ye that one?" he grinned.

"Kevin at the phone store. He's deadly with a phone, that one."

"So he is," answered Niall, laughing, and then, "Well, I guess that's it for now. No one will be goin' anywhere for a bit, I expect."

"Well, maybe not right away, but we should expect the authorities at some point. Once I got that recording, I knew I had these two dead to rights and it won't take much to prove Garry's part in it all," said Liam, pocketing his phone. "So, since I was on my way to the villa, I thought to hobble the rest of the way, use their phone or radio or whatever they had, and guess what? They were comin' out to see us, and a couple of lovelier young ladies ye'll never meet. Took me to the villa, and guess who was there?" He didn't wait long, just a quick glance at the vacant faces told him they didn't know. "Tristan. Seems he's known them for years. We had good craic then!"

"Is that why it took ye so long to get back? And here I thought ye missed dinner."

"Ah, no, dear brother, after spending a lovely afternoon there, they provided Tristan and me with a good meal, then brought me back to a place where I could walk without anyone knowin' what I'd been up to."

The unmistakeable sound of a dune buggy bounded along the beach, and very soon, Tristan made his way to where the group was standing.

"Hello, ladies," called Liam, waving at the two women as they started to turn their vehicle back down the strip of sand toward the villa.

Niall cocked a brow at his brother. "Ye weren't jokin'. They really are a couple of lovely ladies."

"They are. And we all owe them a debt of thanks."

"You got that right," said Tristan, moving in to join them. "Care to bring me up to date?"

Everyone began talking at once but Tristan was having none of it. "How about we let Liam do the talking, hm?"

256

He gave Liam the nod and stood quietly by, assessing each player with unforgiving eyes.

"Right, then," said Liam, eyeing Niall and Michael with the look of an attending parent. To Felicia, Garry, and Sam, he only shook his head, and taking a deep breath, told Tristan what had gone on.

Nodding, Tristan elaborated what he knew. "I knew of the setup because Liam told me about it. I just didn't get back here in time to witness it, which is just as well because I was worried I might come too early and ruin it. However," he held up his hands when the guilty ones opened their mouths to argue, "since none of us are going anywhere for the next couple of days, I have a proposition for everyone. Follow me to the dining hut."

They did just that, Felicia, Garry, and Sam following Tristan into the hut, looking around for support from anyone else who might happen by. None did, and as they arrived at the hut, Liam noted it was Felicia who seemed the most worried, glancing about her as if she had an escape route planned and could pull it off.

Once inside, Tristan flicked on the lights and once again the door was locked against any who should travel their way. It was unlikely, late as it was.

When everyone was seated, Tristan faced them, a leader not to be toyed with. "I had heard of the problem Sine faced back in the States, but chose to ignore it. I don't deal in rumors or innuendoes. And since nothing actually occurred that could be construed as a criminal act, I set it aside. She was and is the best person for the role she portrayed. That brings us to the bullshit that has gone on here.

"Sam," the young grip looked up at Tristan, shame and fear resting uneasily on his features. "You hid a great talent. Had you confessed to having such computer skills, I would easily have sought to keep you. As it is, you will be returned home and will never, if I have any say in it, work in the film industry again. At least not on my side of the pond." Tristan's broad accent seemed to get heavier the more he spoke. "Furthermore, you have a lot of explaining to do about how Percy got on the no-fly list."

"I didn't mean it," began Sam, but Tristan shut him up with a raised hand, palm out.

"Don't even go there, Sam. While I have no proof at the moment, I'm sure the authorities will be able to track your work and prove otherwise. Just your telling me that you didn't mean to put him there expresses your guilt in doing so. Oh, and did I forget to say this whole session is being recorded? No one gets to say it didn't happen."

Sam hung his head and fiddled with a paper napkin, rolling it around between his fingers, fraying it, the actions of a nervous, guilty man.

"Garry." Garry wore a belligerent, defiant expression, whether to intimidate or profess bravery was yet to be seen. Tristan continued, "You were basically innocent of the goings on in this charade. You didn't plan it; you were only brought in on it. However, rather than calling a spade a spade, you went along with it, intentionally condoning the perpetrations of wrongdoing on a very talented actress, one who is not here to defend herself. You could have had the edge into legitimate filmmaking, had you played your cards right. The stuff in the can is good, regardless of the fact that you were in on the scheme to ruin a young actress. And while I don't like the substitutions you made or the rewrites that occurred, I think I can make it work. I believe it will bump Sine's status from supporting actress to co-lead."

A gasp from the group made Tristan look at the guiltiest of all. "Felicia."

Felicia, her face a study in conflicting emotions, stood tall, as if her stature would protect her from Tristan's words. She flung her dark red hair behind her, hair that was tinted darker than it really was. The ends were beginning to show the telltale signs of fading from the sun, dried and broken, much like she was.

Liam thought of Sine's dark locks, of the silkiness when he ran the strands through his fingers. God, he wished she were here!

"You can't put her name on the marquee above mine. It's in the contract," she spat.

"True. But there is nothing to say that I can't offer her more than you were paid, and spin it for the tabloids."

Felicia's mouth dropped open but no argument ensued. After all, Tristan had not reduced the amount he was going to pay her, nor was he going to deny her top billing.

Tristan carried on, not done with his critique of the situation. "So, Felicia. We know you engineered this whole thing, once you knew Sine was to be on the film, too. You couldn't do anything in Ireland, but from some of the things that occurred in the States, I'm wondering now if they weren't related to all this. Without going into detail, let's just say I'm going to have them investigated.

"As for your agreement with Jeffrey Harris, I think you might want a lawyer. Once he hears of this operation falling through, he's not going to want anything to do with you. I'll make sure he knows all about it."

"But you can't do that," Felicia began.

"Just watch me," said Tristan, a gleaming look of wile in his brown eyes.

"What about him," she pointed at Niall. "He was acting without a card. The union will have your head for that."

Tristan laughed. "Well, they would, except that he has a card."

"I do?" asked Niall, confused.

"Yeah, of course ye do," said Liam. "Sine got ye one before ye left Ireland. Ye're all paid up, so ye can keep on actin' if ye've a mind to."

Niall shook his head emphatically. "No thanks. I think I've lived in yer shoes long enough. I much prefer workin' with computers to people."

Tristan gauged the brothers and hid a smile. "One more thing, and then I think we're done here. No one, I repeat, no one, will talk to anyone about this once we're off this island. If I hear so much as a whisper, I will personally track down whoever it was and throw the book at them; and believe me, I have proof enough. I'm being very generous right now. Don't piss me off."

He gave the nod and Liam unlocked the door, opening it wide to the tropical night. Felicia was the first to leave, followed by Garry and Sam. It seemed each one knew that they'd gotten off easy, and remained quiet.

That left Liam, Niall, and Michael.

"I'm goin' to turn in. It's been a helluva day," said Liam. "I was hopin' to get off the island early to follow Sine, but looks like I'm stuck here with the rest of ye."

"Sorry, Liam." Sympathy was written in Tristan's eyes and the corner of his mouth was turned up in a smile. "Did you know, they have a heli-pad at the villa. We can order one up for you tomorrow if that'll be soon enough?"

Liam nodded, his face lighting up. "I'll make sure my bags are packed," he said, as he went out into the night.

Niall and Michael were about to follow when Tristan stopped them. "I believe you two were promised something."

They both halted at Tristan's words, looked at each other and then back at the producer.

"I've talked to the ladies at the villa. They'd like to extend an invitation to you lads."

Exchanging looks with Michael, Niall asked the obvious. "Why would they be interested in us?"

Tristan grinned. "Because they're lesbians. They understand you." If they'd seen a ghost, their mouths couldn't have dropped farther, thought Tristan. "Why don't you go gather your things. You'll have a lovely stay on a private island for the next two weeks. The ladies are only too happy to show you about to the places you haven't yet seen, and to help you enjoy the amenities of their private beach, their yacht, and, oh yes, they have a small craft they use so you can go parasailing if you want. Will that do?"

The two men were speechless. "Yeah," said Niall, taking a quick look at Michael before repeating his acceptance, "yeah, that's grand, that is."

"Good, because they'll be coming for you first thing in the morning. Now, if you'll excuse me, I have to get back to the villa myself. I'll be leaving with Liam in the morning. Seems there's a few things I need to do and put in place before anyone leaves this island." He stopped at the door and turned out the lights, letting darkness engulf the hut.

Niall and Michael watched him go, standing on the steps, letting their eyes adjust to the night around them. Then, hand in hand, they walked back to Niall's hut and closed the door.

"Where were we?" asked Michael, moving in close to Niall's heat.

"I think ye had yer hand on me arse and I really wanted ye, like."

Michael nodded. "Fine. You first."

"Drop yer drawers," came out of the midnight black room, lit only by the moon that was now high in the sky.

"I thought you'd never ask," whispered Michael, his voice a warm shiver in Niall's ear.

"Not askin'. Tellin'." His hands roamed the length of Michael's spine, kneading the strong muscles of his torso.

"Ooh, someone's getting bossy."

"Get used to it."

The deep throaty chuckle rumbled softly, then soon turned to moans of pleasure from lips locked together and tongues entwined.

"Is that what you want?"

"Yeah," breathed Niall.

"And this?"

"Oh, yeah, more of that."

"I've got you now." Michael kissed Niall's ear, sending delicious sensations down his spine to pierce his nads, their bodies moving in sync.

"Ah, Michael…"

Chapter Nineteen

L iam arrived back in Ireland, determined to chase after Sine without really knowing where she had gone. They'd been given return tickets to Cork, so it made sense that she'd go home to Ireland, rather than home to Chicago.

But what if she'd moved on? How would he ever find her? She had relatives scattered around the country in little pockets but he doubted very much that she would take refuge with them. She would have to tell them it had happened again and face yet another round of questions, reserved judgments, and taciturn opinions. She wouldn't know what had happened those last few days after she left. There had been no way to tell her. She was either purposely not answering her mobile, or it was turned off. In any case, Liam hadn't been able to contact her.

He picked up a rental car at Cork Airport and drove to his mam's home in Inishannon, to bring her up to date on the goings on. The news was met with cynicism.

"I don't understand it, Liam," his mam said. "It's all hogwash to me and they ought to throw the book at those three. But when it comes to Sine, and if ye love her as ye say,

264

then don't let anyone stop ye, not even her. As for Niall and Michael, there's naught for ye to do there, they'll work it out themselves."

His sister, Ciara, the one with beyond worldly knowledge, had given him a clue as to where Sine might be.

"It's clearly a bridge, Liam. I just don't know where. But it's small, an old one, the area very wild. I'm sure ye know it."

"I'm sure I do, too, if it's where I think it is. Wild, ye say?"

She nodded. "Yeah, like time stopped a couple of hundred years ago. Maybe longer."

"Did ye see a road?"

"Well, ye neddy, if there's a bridge, there's a road, don't ye think?"

He chuckled and she giggled.

"Christ, Liam, ye can be such a brick at times," but the look in her eye said that what she felt for her brother was genuine love.

"I get it from Niall," he grinned, and she winked an emerald eye back at him.

"But there's one thing ye need to know," she said, just when he turned to leave. "She's in pain," Ciara said.

"What? She's hurt?"

"Not physically, but in here," she said, laying her hand familiarly on her brother's heart. "And you are, too."

He couldn't meet Ciara's piercing green gaze and not believe her. She had pegged him completely, and that had been enough to spur him on.

As he drove toward the Black Valley, he recalled the tabloids he'd seen before leaving for the Bahamas. They had unbelievable photos, at least, Liam had thought so. He usually didn't pay attention to the rags. So many lives were shattered because of them, but at the time, he hadn't known the details. It wasn't until a few days ago that his niece had finally got up the gumption to tell him what she saw in the magazine he'd grabbed from her that day. "It's not you in the photo with Sine," she'd said, likely shaking in her boots at making him listen to her, "it's Uncle Niall. Look, there's part of his birthmark."

He'd looked closer, and sure enough, it was behind his right ear, barely visible.

"The photo could have been flipped," he'd said, not wanting to be proven wrong by a teenager.

"I don't think so," she argued. "See, there looks to be the mark on his ear where he once had that earring but it got infected and left a small scar."

Taking the paper from her hand, he'd scrutinized it even closer and had to admit she was right. So if that was Niall…

He'd had to wait until he got to the island to know the full story on that one, the similarities in the patterns on the bedcovers notwithstanding. The cast of players in the island drama, nonetheless, read much like a soap opera.

The culprits were caught, and that was good news. For the rest…well, he'd have to wait and see.

His accident hadn't helped matters. But even if he'd been

on the island, the technical problems would have undoubtedly meant the doom of that part of the production.

Niall had grown from the experience, thought Liam, slowing the car to take the sharp turn off the main road that would eventually lead to the valley. He'd thought it would have been his brother to suffer the most; Niall, who was such a hermit at heart, and having been out of his comfort zone for far too long. Instead, it had been Sine—worn out, demoralized, and ready to break—who paid the highest price.

Learning that Michael had taken Sine to bed was not what he had ever wanted to hear, and for a while all he wanted to do was to take Michael out back and use him as a punching bag. But that wouldn't solve anything. He blamed Michael completely; Michael, who loved women almost as much as he loved men. At that moment, Liam hated him; hated him for what he'd done to Niall. And to Sine. Forgiveness came hard but he knew he would eventually come around, for Niall's sake, and Sine's, too. He didn't know how Sine felt about herself since then but he could imagine. No wonder she wanted to hide.

For himself, he didn't care. She'd be his. After all, he'd been able to put the pieces together of what had really gone on between Michael and Sine, only Sine hadn't been there for him to comfort. She'd left, heartbroken and ashamed, going home to lick her wounds.

But this day would change everything. He knew it in his bones, his gut. His heart.

Every day for the last week, he'd gone to the bridge in

the Black Valley and waited inside his parked car, hoping for a sight. It had occurred to him that Ciara could be wrong, although she almost never was. His sister had a gift, an amazing ability to see into the future. Not that she could predict the future; far from it. She could only relay what images she was given, either through dreams or visions. So although it had crossed his mind that Sine might not show up if she saw him there first, he went anyway. Because, on that day, when steady rain poured from cloud to ground with a fury, he was certain he'd find her. He just had that feeling.

He spied his quarry on the bridge far ahead, through a rain-streaked windscreen with wipers that couldn't keep up with the deluge. He didn't know what made her want to come to the valley today, as desolate with its wild beauty as it could be, but maybe that was what she craved just then. Desolation. You could turn your back on whatever looked lovely and be faced with nothing but the rugged hand of nature. It would be like her, to seek out the isolation of the mountains and hide. For all she was a familiar face on the silver screen, she was an introvert underneath, someone who bled easily when pricked. Her acting ability was such that she was able to hide it, until she couldn't. It was as simple as that. And once the damn burst, she had to flee, to hide until she'd licked her wounds clean before she could face anyone again. It had taken her two years, the last time it happened, to go back to the craft she loved. But to do it, she'd had to leave her home country and start fresh somewhere else where she wasn't as well known.

Only to have it happen all over again. Only worse. They'd

not only dredged up the story from the past, they'd tried to duplicate the results of her past within the current production.

It had nearly worked. If he hadn't shown up when he did…he didn't finish the thought. He wanted to tell her now that it hadn't been her fault, that she was just an innocent victim, but he needed to hear something from her first.

She was standing on the old stone bridge, just as Ciara said she would be, hands stuffed in the pockets of her jacket, enduring a blustery, rainy day with no one about. Tourists didn't mind a lot of the weather idiosyncrasies about Ireland, but almost none of them liked the wind and the rain combined. And here it was, blowing fiercely and raining like all the furies of hell had been loosed in the valley, with no one about for miles.

Except the two of them.

Sine was drenched. Completely sodden, and she didn't seem to care. Her copper tresses were black with rain, plastered to her jacket like the long seaweed washed up and abandoned on the Garrettstown Beach near his grandparents' home. And even though the jacket looked waterproof, unless it was a sou'wester, Liam was sure it would be wet all the way through. She must be freezing.

He got out of the car, wrestling with crutches and the bulky plastic monstrosity that was his foot. He was lucky it was his left foot because it meant he could still drive. He'd rented an automatic car since he couldn't manage a manual shift and it galled him to have to stoop so low. Automatic, indeed, he chuckled to himself. Sine would be able to drive

269

them home if she wanted to try. But with his luck, his feisty woman would take the keys and leave him to walk the distance back to Killarney alone. Now wouldn't that be grand!

The rain suddenly slowed but was still coming down in scattered pockets, still gusty with wind, but not to the extent it had been a moment ago. Sine stood, her back to him, watching some ducks that seemed happy for the break from the storm and came out to paddle in the water beneath the bridge.

She still hadn't moved, although she must have heard the car stop and the door open and close. He was only steps away when she said, "How's your foot?"

Well, as far as openings went, he could deal with it. "Fine, but I didn't come here to talk about my foot."

"Why are you here, then? I didn't ask you to come."

"No. I came because I needed to hear from you how things really went. There's a lot that's unclear to me and I need to understand it all before…"

"Before what? Before you pass judgment on me? Sorry, I've heard that line before, try another one."

Her gaze hadn't left the pond so Liam manoeuvered himself up to the stone wall and leaned against it, relieving himself for the moment of carrying crutches. "Sine, look at me."

"Why? So you can tell me what a filthy, fucking slut I am? I told you, I've heard it all before. Nothing new there."

Liam knew this wouldn't be easy. She was too proud, too hurt to let him get close.

"I'm not the enemy here, Sine. I'm the man who loves you, or don't ye know that?"

"Love me? You?" She whirled on him, her hazel eyes glassy with tears. "Don't you dare tell me such lies. You believed the rumors about me. I'm not proud of what happened with Michael, but it did. It just happened. And none of this would have happened at all if you hadn't broken your stupid foot!"

"Yes. It's my fault. I broke my foot. And then instead of calling up the company and telling them what happened, ye thought we could just put Niall in there and all would be well. We know how well that turned out, don't we?"

"Don't lay all the blame on me. I had every hope it would work just as much as you did. You went along with it. You thought it would be fine. You said so!"

He leaned against the wall, glanced at a duck that had dipped its head into the rippled waters of the pool. Other ducks were beginning to leave the shelter of the bridge and join their companion in the icy water. A faint odour from the pond blew across his nostrils and he sniffed and rubbed the smell away with the back of his hand. "I want to know what happened, from your perspective. I'm not looking to place blame, to say who's at fault. I just want to know."

"Why? So you can ease your conscience?"

He deserved that. Underneath it all, it was exactly what he was thinking. "No," he lied. "I mean…I want to hear your side of it. Hearing that you and Michael slept together isn't what's bothering me. I mean, I care, just, well, it's just…"

The silence stretched. She wasn't going to make this easy on him.

A flurry of action in the pond, the sound of splashing and a couple of quacks helped to refocus his thoughts. He watched the two offenders swim away, shaking tails and resettling their feathers as they went.

He cleared his throat and started again. "You said that the rumors were true."

That got her attention. "What rumors?"

"What do ye mean, 'what rumors?' Ye know very well what I'm talkin' about."

"Rumors? About you? You mean in bed?" She wore a curious look, her forehead creased between her sculpted brows, her kissable lips scrunched off to the side as if nothing was making sense.

"Yeah. Those rumors. I want to know what it's all about."

She was perplexed, if her expression was anything to go by. "It was just something I'd heard. You know, rumors."

"So what was I then, at the B&B, at that time? Was it just a game?" It was time for truth, he knew, but his guts churned, fearful of what she might say.

"Game? No, I…you…we both wanted it. At least I thought we did. I mean, I came out of the bathroom and you grabbed my arm and one thing led to another."

"Ye didn't set me up, like I've heard? Ye didn't plan a tell-all to the tabloids as has been reported?"

"What?"

"Ye heard me. It's all over the feckin' tabloids, with photos!"

Her shoulders hunched under her sodden coat and she

clenched her fists as if to punch something. "Don't you see, you eejit!" she screamed at him, mimicking exactly what he would have said. "That was probably a scene from the film with Niall. How the hell else could they get a photo of you and me in that stupid B&B?"

He crossed his arms in front of his chest, leaned against the rock wall of the bridge, and thought a moment. She was unknowingly backing up what Emily had tried to tell him and what he had learned on the island. But his feelings went deep with this woman. She made him insecure where he never had been before, and until he knew what he suspected, that she loved him, he couldn't believe what everyone had tried to tell him.

"I don't know. But they had an article in there about you and me, about the rumor being true. The very words ye said to me that mornin'. So what am I to ye? Just a plaything?"

"Liam, no. You were never just a plaything to me. Never. I…"

"I haven't a good reputation anymore, ye know that? It's sordid, not at all nice. Says I use women and discard them like dirt."

"Well it never came from me," she defended.

"It's a quote from you, for Christ's sake," he challenged.

"Since when do you listen to tabloids? The only rumor I knew about you was that you never left a woman wanting. You always made sure she enjoyed her time with you. That's it. That's all I heard."

"So ye went to bed with me for the sake of findin' out

273

about my so-called reputation?" he accused her.

She was aghast, her mouth opened in anger. "I don't care about your fucking reputation," she glared at him, eyes blazing with unabashed fury. "It was never about that, and if that's what you think of me, then you can go to hell!"

"Well, what was I supposed to think?" he retorted. "Ye said it that morning at the B&B. Ye said that the rumors were true. How else am I to know what that means, other than ye couldn't wait to see if they were true? Christ, I loved givin' ye pleasure and that's what ye threw at me." He was angry too. Angry that she should see him only as a notch on a tally-stick of lovers, each competing for top spot. "So how did I do? Eh? Did I win the prize?"

She turned away from him, and he thought maybe she was crying. It tore at his soul.

"Go away. Just fucking go away."

"I would. But I want answers, too."

She whirled on him, looking so tired of it all. "I only ever wanted to love and be loved for me. I never wanted sordid stories to be circulated. I'm not the person in those stories."

"And ye think I want to be known only for what I can give ye in bed? There's more to me than that."

"I know that! I never said there wasn't. But if you think that I'm the one who's pinned that label on you, you're crazy. I only wanted you for you. I only wanted you to hold me, to treat me like you loved me, to make me feel like I was the most important woman on the planet in your eyes. I only ever wanted you because, for some god-awful reason, I found myself in love with you and was hoping that, just maybe, you'd feel the same. And if you can't understand that, then there's nothing to talk about." She made to walk past him, as if to leave and never turn back.

He was going to let her go. He'd had enough, been through enough to last a lifetime. He just wanted the quiet, peaceful countryside to enfold him as it used to do when he was a child. He'd leave home to his siblings and strike out across fields and hills, hiding in the forest, taking in the solitude of nature around him. Let it heal him. In that way, he and Niall were alike. When the pressures of everyday living encroached on sanity, they headed to the forest, just like Brandon headed to the sea.

But there was no forest here. No cover of trees to take shelter in. Only the rocky landscape, the moss and furze, the ducks and the sheep. And he couldn't walk. Could only hobble over to the car, get in, and drive away.

But he wasn't finished yet.

He grabbed at her arm as she made to move past, her need to go back up the road and out of the valley just as strong as his need to keep her by him.

She struggled but he held on, making her stop and face him. He took in her countenance, eyes filled with the tears that he knew were there, indistinguishable from the rain that had begun again.

He wasn't done with her yet. "That time ye came to Henry's house, when I was just home from the hospital. Did it mean nothin' to ye? Did ye not know I had promised to be true to ye? It's why I wanted ye to call me every day. I know how hard it is to call in to a film set, so I gave ye the freedom to call and tell me about yer day. Only ye never called and I didn't know how to reach ye."

"I couldn't call out. There was no cell service. And I got it mixed up. I thought you were going to call me."

"I couldn't. I was supposed to be on the set with ye."

"You don't have to tell me that. You and Niall are very different underneath." She shrugged out of his grasp. "It tore Niall up pretending to be you. Not just the acting part, the non-acting part, having to be you twenty-four seven. And then Felicia kept wanting to fuck him and Michael wanted time with him and I was putting pressure on him to be you. He nearly went crazy, took to hiding out just so he could get an uninterrupted good night's sleep. I think he used to go up to the villa and crawl into their pool house after hours. There were a few nights when he didn't make it back to his bungalow."

"Why didn't Garry step in?"

"Hey, we're all over twenty-one. He wasn't about to get involved in anything outside of the film. All he ever said was that we could do what we liked off set, just as long as we got our work done while we were on. And he stuck to that. People just kind of ran wild off the set, though. It was awful."

It was Liam's turn to feel awful. Hearing from her own lips what he'd learned firsthand from the others put it all into perspective.

The rain was pelting down again, threatening to flood the

car out of its spot at the roadside. He had no hat, nothing but his jacket pulled up around his ears. "Will ye at least come into the car with me? We can finish our conversation, maybe dry off a bit. It's feckin' cold out here."

"I don't care if it's cold. I don't fucking care about anything anymore. Why don't you just leave me be? Go somewhere else if you're cold." She was crying openly now, couldn't contain her feelings any longer.

Frustration grabbed at his nads like hands clutching, squeezing. He felt fingers of stress streak up his back and did the only thing he could that would make her see reason. He grabbed her upper arms and put his mouth to hers, roughly, not giving her a chance to withdraw.

Sine struggled, tried to pull away, and then gave in, her body turning soft in his hands. His grip lessened, he put his arms around her and as the rain poured down, held her to him, and kissed her deeply. Her arms came up behind him, fingers running through hair that had since grown, somewhat longer and thicker than the closely shorn look he'd needed for the film.

She yielded to him, let him in, and he took what she gave.

"This'll never do," he said, slowly relinquishing her mouth.

Her hazel eyes blinked through the rain cascading down her forehead. "Huh?"

"We need to go somewhere to get dry, so I can warm ye, proper, like."

"Does that mean what I think it does?" she asked.

His answer was to grin.

She was smiling as they walked slowly to the car, her hand on Liam's arm as he manoeuvered the crutches. "Liam?" she said, and to his muttered acknowledgement came her response. "Don't read any more tabloids, okay?"

He stopped at the car and turned to her, pulling her into his arms, breathing one word against her mouth as his tongue plundered hers, "Deal."

Chapter Twenty

It couldn't be a double wedding," Liam explained to Hank on the phone. "There's no way for Michael and Niall to be married proper like in Ireland."

"They could come here, where it's legal," said Hank. "I've a place in town with a spare room and there's the cabin up in the mountains. We can hire a minister or whatever they want, hold their ceremony here, or both yours and theirs. Together. Think on it."

"I will. But I think Sine's family is lookin' forward to a visit to Ireland."

"Okay, here's an idea then…what if ye were married here and then we all went back to Ireland for a grand celebration? We could commandeer the castle again. I don't think anyone would care, especially not if we opened it up to the villagers. After all, the castle has that mood about it."

"Ciara did mention something about a medieval fair, although ye know her; she says some things out of the blue and no one has any idea what she's on about until another piece of the puzzle falls into place. Maybe this is what she meant?" The more Liam thought about it, the more he liked the idea. People from the area would love to have a gathering, especially if paid for by someone else with free food and drink.

"Hank Mulligan, ye've got a grandiose scheme thought up, but it may just work. I'll put it to them and let ye know."

* * *

The mountains of British Columbia were indeed the best place to be, what with the large acreage available to them where Hank's old place had burned down. The pad where the lovely little cottage had stood was now vacant, the ground still being prepped for a new build, one they were hoping to begin next spring after the melt and after the birth of their first child.

Laura's cabin, three miles away toward town, was now the last stop on the road as far as public access went. It meant that both weddings could be held worry-free of interlopers, paparazzi, and anyone else who thought they could get a sneak peek at the ceremonies to be held. Rumors had circulated about a wedding taking place up the mountain but no one seemed to know any details. Nothing had been leaked about who it was; and in any event, while Liam was a household name in Ireland, he hadn't quite made the jump to North America yet, although now that he was marrying Sine, that status stood to change. It seemed that Tristan had no difficulty upping Sine's status in the film. Her performance genuinely trumped Felicia's and offers had begun to pour in.

Too focused on the wedding to think of doing another film right away, both Sine and Liam had decided on at least a six-month hiatus from working in order to settle into their new lives together.

The gathering was small, a family-only event, one in which Henry, Siobhan, and Emily were part of, as well as Liam's mam, Ciara, Brandon, and both Sine's and Michael's parents. They had purposely not invited anyone else.

Michael's parents seemed thrilled to be there, she, a doe-eyed, shapely woman with the darker skin she passed along to her son; he, a blond Englishman of medium height, striking in his features, with broad cheekbones and clear blue eyes. Michael seemed to have inherited few physical attributes from his father other than that man's stature.

They were all looking forward to the celebrations yet to come in Ireland, which were sure to be grand indeed! And as the two couples stood side by side, no one could ever doubt the love between them. The looks passed back and forth. Their differences and fears behind them, they now stood, shoulder to shoulder, listening to the minister, who was only too happy to officiate at such a double ceremony as this. She was a lovely lady with light, flowing hair streaked with white, cascading down the gold-and-white robe of her office. Her voice rang clearly through the warm summer air as she had them repeat the vows they had written to each other. The only flaw in the entire ceremony was when she turned to Michael and Niall and said, "You may now kiss the bri...er, husband."

The family had broken out in laughter and applause, and Niall's complexion suddenly took on a rosy glow. Michael, as usual, hadn't cared, but took the chin of the man he loved in both hands, brought their lips together, and gave everyone what they were hoping for: a kiss to seal their troth.

Sine and Liam did the same, grateful they were second-rate when it came to entertainment that day.

* * *

Later, after dinner that night in Hank and Laura's new house in town, Liam was asked to bring the family up-to-date on the outcome of the investigation. Standing on a well-bandaged foot, still recovering from his break, he began.

"First of all, before I get into things, I want to thank the other three members of the wedding party for their participation in a covert operation that could have gone terribly wrong, and almost did. Niall," he turned to his brother, raised the champagne flute to recognize him, "I have to tell ye, as much as ye may have had trouble bein' me, I had it just as bad bein' you and puttin' up with all those feckin' jokes about arse-bandits."

He received a great round of applause combined with laughter and ribald comments. "And Michael, thank God for you." They all knew that without Michael's help they might never have caught the three as they did.

"So here's the rundown for the rest of ye's, but before I begin, ye need to know how proud I am of these three, of the shite they put up with and the sacrifices they made on account of my own stupidity, especially my lovely wife, Sine. Ye'll never again have to endure such harassment and pain. I promise." He hadn't taken his eyes off her and was pleased to see she was still smiling. Perhaps it was the light glistening in her eyes but he knew how much she'd put up with for his sake and how much she loved him. Tonight he'd make her realize just how much he loved her.

"So, on to our feckin' story." Like any great orator, Liam wasn't afraid to color his words when the mood struck. "First off, there's Garry. Turns out that Garry, poor bastard, was an opportunist who got more than he'd bargained for. He just wanted to play in the big leagues and so when Percy Farquharson was unable to make it, due to suddenly finding himself on a no-fly list, Felicia suggested Garry."

"How did he end up on a no-fly list?" asked Henry. "Don't ye have to do somethin' bad to have that happen?"

"Ah, just wait, big brother, I'll get to that. Back to Felicia, though. Ye see, once Percy was banned from flying, at least until the investigation into that little gem cleared him, they were out a director. Our man in Ireland was already on another project and the company was scrambling. They didn't want the project to blow up just because of the tropical scenes being lost. So up steps Felicia and gives her personal recommendation, which at the eleventh hour was enough for the producers. They'd been caught with their arses bared and no help for it, had no backup plan. Directors just don't fall out of the sky, don't ye know, and Garry does, or rather, did," he amended, "have some credibility. But what no one knew at the time," he paused a moment for dramatic effect, "was Felicia's relationship with Jeffrey Harris, the lead actor who had been responsible for Sine's downfall."

"What?" exclaimed Sine, nearly choking on her sip of champagne.

S. M. Cross

"That's right, my sweet. While the actual liaison between Felicia and Mr. Harris did not come about until later, she figured he was as good a catch as any. Although God knows what she saw in him. I mean, he's nothin' like me, eh?" The smirks and rumbles of laughter came as he expected they would. Jeffrey Harris may have been a bastard but he was a damned good-looking one!

Liam continued. "So between the two of them, they decided to get even. Ye see, they reasoned it would make him feel vindicated and she would get rid of her major competition."

"I'm not her major competition, though," said Sine, her delicate brows furrowed in thought.

"Well, many others would disagree with your assessment of your own worth." He took a sip of his own champagne, clearly warming to his story. "Now, remember Sam, Michael's techie friend?" Everyone nodded and Liam continued. "This is where yer question about the no-fly list comes in, Henry."

Henry leaned back in his chair, relaxed and waiting for the story to continue, his arm lightly resting across Siobhan's shoulders.

Taking a rather large gulp of champagne, Liam suddenly choked on it, coughing to clear his throat of the bubbles that seemed to catch. "Ah, feckit, is there any whiskey? I don't think I can take this stuff anymore," he joked, still coughing, and someone passed him the bottle of whiskey they'd brought from Ireland.

A glass was poured and he took a sip, eyes closed, feeling

284

it slip down his throat and sighing his pleasure at the taste.

"Liam, get on with it, we aren't getting' any younger," prodded Henry.

Liam cleared his throat roughly, looked like he wanted to down the entire glass first but remembered his audience just in time. "Right then. So. Sam? Well, it turned out Sam was a techie who had aspirations in the movie business and a little bit of experience on that end. He had a whole lot more experience on the tech end of it though, makin' his livin' as it was, helpin' movie stars such as Felicia with their computer issues. She talked to her friend Garry and convinced him to hire Sam. Sam, of course, jumped at the chance to work on a movie that Felicia was to star in. Between you and me, I think Felicia had a thing with Sam, too, but that's neither here nor there."

Taking another appreciative sip of his whiskey, he looked down at his foot, freed of its shoe and happily so. It had begun to ache at the confinement during the ceremony, so as soon as they got in the door, he'd gladly taken both shoes off in favor of stocking feet.

"And then there's me," he said, and wriggled his toes in a delighted manner. It was getting less painful each day to walk on it and he was hopeful that soon he'd be running on it with no looking back.

"And what about ye, ye plonker?" jeered Niall. He and Michael were sitting together, fingers entwined, fingering the rings on each other's hands. Liam was suddenly struck that it looked so natural and he turned a smile at what he saw into one of personal embarrassment.

"Me and my foot. It was the perfect storm, so to speak. Had I been on the island from the first, it might be a different story, although I'd be the first to admit that my presence would not have been enough. It was really Michael who saved the day."

Cries of "Here, here!" and much table banging were heard throughout the room, and Michael bowed his head, acknowledging everyone's thanks with a wide grin.

When the crowded room quieted again, Liam's voice took on a somber note. "Perhaps my accident was meant to be. And I really do have a lot to thank Sine for, especially when she paid the highest price of all for the mess that occurred." He became serious then, and his audience hushed as if they, too, picked up the change in mood.

"Ye know, I thought it would have been Niall that would suffer the most. I mean, let's face it, Niall, ye're such a feckin' hermit at heart and ye were out of yer comfort zone for far too long. But no, it was my Sine, worn out, demoralized, and ready to break." He bent down, kissed her lips, and wiped at the tear before it could fall. She smiled up at him and he couldn't see anything but the love he felt for her reflected in her eyes.

Straightening, he continued. "The whole sordid mess came to a head when Tristan and I arrived. I think the only thing that kept people at bay until then was the fact that they thought Niall was me. I got a real awakening. Ye see, as an actor, I have all this power to sway the masses. I can sell underwear to people who don't want it and look like eejits in it. I can make them buy things they don't need, but hey, I have it, I say it's good, so people want it. I wear a black shirt in a film and suddenly it's the rage, everyone wants a black shirt, just like that one. It made me wonder what kind of power I had that could sway people so easily, and yet allow the ones I loved to be so damaged by my own folly. If I hadn't climbed that feckin' hill…" His voice trailed off but the room was still quiet. He wasn't finished. He swallowed past the choked feeling in his throat, downed the rest of his whiskey.

"Nothin' can change the past, and we can only go forward. Ye know, Sine, when I saw ye on the set that final day, ye were ready to break. But ye didn't. Ye finished, and ye won my heart. Ye'd already done that, but seeing ye then clinched it for me. I knew then that I would make it better for ye, to demand the respect for ye that ye deserved from others, because ye were too tired of fightin' to fight any more. And I will never let that happen to ye again, my love. I swear to you, I won't."

He pulled her to stand, took her in his arms and proved to everyone just how serious he was about protecting her. With his arms about her, he dipped her to the applause of the gathering, and held her there while he kissed her senseless.

He had Sine's trust, and relished the feeling it brought about when she gave herself completely into his embrace.

* * *

The celebration at the castle where Hank and Laura had sealed their vows was aglow with strings of lights and a real party atmosphere, so very like the medieval fairs of old.

287

Tables had been set up with food and drink and some of the local craftspeople had brought their wares to show off and sell to any who were interested.

Laura took Hank's hand and led him to one such table where a woman was showing off the Irish lace she was tatting. "Isn't it gorgeous?" she said to Hank, fingering the beautiful work with one hand, the other resting on her bulging baby belly. "We could do up some curtains, or edge the bassinette with this," she said.

"And what if it's a boy?" asked Hank, bemused. "I don't know if he'll appreciate being edged in lace, Irish or not."

The woman who was tatting smiled at the two, hiding whatever she was thinking behind dancing blue eyes.

"Well, I think we should, anyway. Just in case. It could be a girl, you know."

"Fifty-fifty chance, I'd say," joked Hank, and then decided to cave in to his wife's wishes. He was going to lose anyway, he knew.

Siobhan and Henry were strolling through the throng of folks, looking for the twins, who were clearly enjoying themselves. They found Niall and Michael, off in a corner, being a part of the celebration but keeping mostly to themselves. It was Niall wanting it that way more than Michael, they knew, but for an introvert, Niall had come out of himself somewhat since doubling as Liam, and was holding his own. Still, you couldn't change someone's innate nature overnight.

They finally found Liam, surrounded, as usual, by an

entourage of young women, who hadn't seemed to care that it was his wedding they were celebrating. Liam was laughing and joking, but for once refused to sign autographs, stating he was here for a good time, not for work. Sine was off chatting with her own entourage of young men and some women, too, all curious to see the woman the tabloids had been full of.

Liam didn't seem to have much trouble extricating himself from the knot of people about him, and as he approached his new wife, the crowd suddenly stepped out of the way. He took her hand, brought it to his lips possessively, and drew her close to him. Her answer was to smile up at him, reach for the kiss that was headed her way and Liam's soft words meant for her ears alone.

"Care to come watch the dancing with me, my love?"

The strains of music from the combined skills of musicians came floating across the late afternoon breeze. The high-pitched sound of the tin whistle could be heard above the accordion, and the strumming of more than one guitar filled in the background. The bodhran could be a solo instrument the way it set the beat and tone as young dancers in costume performed merry steps while others stood around watching. The revelers were all moving in that direction and it wasn't until they got close that they could see Emily amongst the dancers, joining in, although not in costume.

"It's a fine tradition," said Hank to Laura, as they stood and watched his niece dance with abandon; it was obvious she knew the steps well. Behind her, Brandon had joined the musicians, and even without the aid of a microphone, his guitar work and his voice rang pure and strong with the lyrics to the tune.

Sine and Liam had followed the crowd, and as they all gathered about to watch the display, she turned her gaze to her handsome husband, amazed as she always was that he was hers, and hers alone. "I was thinking that it's almost time to go. You know, we have some work to do to catch up to Hank and Laura," she said, eyeing Laura's baby bump.

A confused expression knit Liam's brows together until he realized what she meant. "Are ye sure? Ye don't want to wait a bit? What if the perfect leading lady role comes up?"

"I think we can deal with that if it happens. Right now, I just want to be with you."

"Ah, that's grand to hear because ye know, you are my leadin' lady. Always have been. Always will be."

"C'mere to me." She pulled her husband's head down for a deep, sensual kiss. A kiss that promised more before the night was through.

Ciara watched the two and grinned. "Ah, here we go again," she sighed happily.

Her mam stood beside her and watched, a smile bringing out the dimples in her cheeks. "They make a lovely couple," she said, obviously proud of her son and his new wife. "But what do ye think of Michael and Niall?"

"They'll have a family, too. But not for a while."

"I'd ask how ye know but I won't be daft. I'll just believe ye."

They laughed and turned into the crowd. There was

someone Ciara had been interested in at Hank and Laura's wedding and he was here now. "I'll see ye later, Mam," said Ciara, heading in the young man's direction.

Kathleen nodded and spied young Emily, now finished dancing and looking like she was headed for the refreshment table. She'd helped herself to a mug of stout when Kathleen caught up to her.

"And just what is that ye have in yer hand?"

Emily looked at the mug she was holding, a guilty look on her face.

"Come on, 'fess up."

"Ah, Gran, it's naught but a bit of stout."

"Ye're fifteen, not fifty. Put it down."

From behind them came Henry's voice. "Hand it over. I'll take care of it for ye."

"Ye won't," said another voice, and all three turned to see Siobhan sidle up to join them. "We'll hand it over to one of yer brothers," she said to Henry, and then took two cans of cola and handed one to Emily and one to Henry. "There, that'll quench yer thirst just as well."

Liam had noticed the group and chuckled as he and Sine walked by. "I think now's a good time to leave, don't you?"

Sine agreed. "Time to go make babies," she grinned.

It appeared Niall and Michael were also getting ready to go, standing and gathering their jackets against the incoming breeze. Ciara, who had been heading in Mam's direction with her new beau, looked up at the sky and sighed in displeasure. "A storm's comin'."

The young man beside her looked up and disagreed. "Looks like a fine evening to me," he remarked, his Danish accent almost undetectable.

"Oh, the evenin' will be fine. I'm not talkin' about the weather."

Her mam overheard her and turned to face her. "And what do ye mean by that?" She knew from past experience that Ciara never mentioned anything lightly.

In this instance, Ciara only shrugged. "Not sure yet, and don't know when or who, but there's a storm comin' for certain."

At that moment, Brandon joined them and took the mug from his mam's hands. "I thank ye for thinkin' of me," he joked, and downed the contents in one go. "Entertainin' is thirsty work," he exclaimed and then disappeared with boundless energy into the crowd once again.

Ciara's expression suddenly cleared as she watched him go.

"Brandon," she said, shaking her head in disbelief. "Oh, Brandon."

THE END

Keep reading for a sneak peek at the third intallment of the O'Farrell Legacy series, *Brandon: Bad Boy of Kinsale*.

Brandon: Bad Boy of Kinsale

Book Three of the
O'Farrell Legacy Series

Chapter One

Brandon O'Farrell awoke to the sounds of the sea birds crying their high pitched 'eee-eee' outside the window, and a brisk breeze blowing across his face, the scent of salt heavy in the air of Kinsale's harbour. Other sensations, a warm body hugging his back, while he in turn had his arm about a warm body spooned into him in front. It left him feeling hot but for the breeze through the gauzy curtains over windows cranked wide open. His eyes opened slowly to the bright, summer dawn.

Events of the night before came rushing back as he lay in limbo between sleeping and waking. It had been a marvelous ménage à trois. He viewed the blonde head tucked under his chin, saw the dark strands mingled with the blondc; a brief acknowledgement that she'd coloured her hair. Nevertheless, she was lovely; she'd been perfect, her breasts so firm with nipples hard and nubbed, and smooth skin, nearly as soft as a baby's over a bum ripe for caressing.

And in between her legs, her juices had coated him, smoothed his way. He was hard again, just remembering. Did he have another rubber? It was a brief thought, and then gone as the body behind him stirred and he felt a kiss pressed to his neck behind his ear. The stubble from the man's chin rasped against his skin. Is that what Niall liked?

Niall, his younger brother, one of a pair of mirror twins. Liam, the first twin, an actor, out-going and into the women; Niall, a techie as nerdy and reserved as they came, and gay. Niall had, Brandon knew, a very good-looking boyfriend. Michael had showed up at his half-brother's wedding last year, and he wondered, briefly, what men saw in other men, until the hand behind him cupped his nads and rolled them through his fingers like dice in a game.

The massage of his nads had him mellow out. Still flaming from the drink last night, he was half in a dream as his mind wandered back to his family. They were all living in Inishannon once upon a time, except for Henry, who lived in Killarney with Siobhan and young Emily. But now everyone, except for Ciara, the youngest, had left home.

Brandon, himself, had recently located to Kinsale, in County Cork, south of Inishannon and on the coast. He'd rented a room at a local hotel for the summer because flats were few and far between and it was too hard to sneak a different woman every night into a B&B. They usually frowned on that sort of thing. So he'd settled on the hotel, loved it for its amenities and didn't mind paying the outrageous sum they were asking. He was getting a good wage, after all.

He loved Kinsale, a picturesque little town with a lovely marina, perfect for sailboats, fishing boats and a few yachts. A port too small to accommodate the big cruise ships that docked further up the coast in Cobh, and thankfully so. Tourists flocked to Kinsale in the summer months and the likes of Brandon entertained them. He hadn't started out to do that, to play host to a bunch of gawkers but he'd found out quickly that they paid well, especially if they liked you.

And Brandon was someone they liked. No, they loved him. Especially the two in bed with him. The two, the man and a woman, had been in a tour group he'd taken around yesterday, and they'd soon made their desires known. It had begun over a racy song Brandon had sung, his old guitar humming with renewed vigor as he accompanied himself to the obvious pleasure of all. The couple had come up while he was packing his instrument away and began asking questions. Questions that led to…

Well, he knew where they were headed before they got there. She was pretty, curvaceous; he was handsome, very masculine looking but with an affectation that spoke volumes. He was so very obviously an arse bandit.

"How did you two end up travelling together?" Brandon had asked, curious.

"We both wanted to travel through Ireland," explained the woman in her foreign accent, which Brandon thought was possibly Dutch, "and decided it was much cheaper for us to travel together. Neither one of us had a partner, so, it made sense, ja?"

Brandon wasn't convinced that was the whole story but it was okay by him if that's what they wanted. Each to their own, his mam would say.

He felt the masculine hand move from his nads, the fingers splayed out in a caress that reached for that part of him that had hardened while the man had caressed his clackers. Brandon stretched, reluctant to let the woman he was spooned around go, but it felt so good to have a large hand on his flute. Especially one that was doing such grand things to him. He'd drawn a line last night, though. No fella was going to kick in his back doors without a fight.

The woman before him stirred and turned to face him. Immediately she put her lips to his, invaded his mouth with her tongue and began fondling his flat, male nipples with vigour. Between the man on his lad and the woman on his mouth and chest, Brandon was nearly beside himself. She grasped his hand and placed it on her crotch in silent instruction. Brandon was no fool and sliding a finger inside her, found her wet and willing. He was so hard. He wanted her but didn't have a rubber ready. No matter, between the erotic vision of the man on his lad and the scent of the woman's juices, it might not matter that he wasn't inside her.

His breath was coming in gasps. His climax was imminent. And then stars exploded inside his head.

* * *

Brandon woke to a headache that had him retching. Furthermore, he was a mess. And alone. The couple was nowhere to be seen.

296

The room was spinning wildly, made worse when he closed his eyes, and gripping the sheets in shaky fists, recognized in some corner of his brain that he was dealing with a concussion. The next thought that came to him was the two who'd been with him were not your usual tourists and as soon as he was able, he was going to check his pants to see if his wallet was still there. It wouldn't surprise him if he'd been robbed as well but until the room stood still, or at least slowed, he wasn't about to get out of bed.

Bed. It was not such a comfortable place at the moment. The room reeked like a toilet and one look through blurred vision told him a bigger story. Bodily fluids were smeared on the sheets, dark and red.

Blood?

His first instinct was to check his head. The goose egg sized bump had bled, but not profusely, and only on the pillow. That meant that perhaps it wasn't his blood.

That was just manky, thinking of whose it might have been and furthermore, why. Pushing himself to a sitting position, he squinted through the brightness of day coming through the two large windows with their multiple panes, and struggled to focus.

The room had been ransacked. Whatever they were looking for was now likely gone, although he didn't have anything here beyond some clothing, his wallet and his guitar.

Tripping on the crumpled sheets as he attempted to climb out of bed, he landed hard on the floor, just missing the side table with his forehead. "Just grand," he muttered to himself, and laid there with his cheek on the floor until the room slowed. "Just feckin' grand."

Resisting the urge to sleep again, he pushed himself upright, and with a hand on the bed for support, stood slowly until fully upright to survey the room. The once orderly space was anything but. The guitar he'd played on last night, now hung by its strings on the back of a chair. In pieces. Two large pieces in fact, and several smaller splinters which were scattered in a wide area. The thirty-six-inch television on the built-in desk had been the instrument's undoing. Bearing unmistakable signs of damage, he doubted the TV would still work.

His guitar, though. He had loved that guitar. It hadn't been new when he got it but it had a tone that spoke to him. A sadness crept over him at the thought of never hearing it again.

His gaze searched the built-in where he'd laid his car keys the night before. Nothing. The wardrobe was also emptied of any contents that had been inside, namely articles of clothing, now lying on the floor. Scanning the area through eyes blurred in pain, he found nothing that resembled car keys. Or his wallet, he amended, as he picked up his pants and checked the pockets in vain.

There was no hope for it. He couldn't let this one brush by as he had last year with the two girls. No, make that three. He'd forgotten about the one who'd come knocking on his door in the wee hours of the morning. That had been a bit messy, what with her caterwauling and carrying on and then trying to get her own piece of him by hauling the second girl from his embrace, just when he had been about to get a mouthful of nipple.

That poor girl had lost a fistful of hair fighting off her attacker but her friend wasn't about to be left out of the fray and came to her rescue. They ganged up on the interloper and before Brandon could figure it all out, had her out the door. A quick call to hotel security had taken care of the mess in short order, with one of the girls hiding in the washroom to defend the propriety of their position. Couples, after all, were a common occurrence in hotels. Not so much a ménage à trois.

This, however, could not be explained by simply playing the injured party. Hotel security wasn't going to like this one little bit and the Gardai would be called in, no questions about that. And once the shades were called, well, his mam would be there, followed quickly by his older brother, Henry.

Henry would know exactly what had happened, and for that, Brandon felt ill. His big brother, who had taken over after their da had been killed in a roll-over when Henry was fourteen and himself, just ten, leaving the twins, Liam and Niall, then eight, and Ciara, their youngest sibling and the only girl, four, to be brought up by a mother who worked odd hours as a nurse at the big hospital in Cork, and a brother who was just into his teens.

No, Henry would not be pleased and if Brandon didn't get a beating from Henry, he'd be surprised. That's how it was. If you got in trouble for fighting at school, you wouldn't get sympathy at home, you'd get another beating. And you likely would have deserved it, too.

Reluctantly, Brandon admitted to himself that he deserved this. He'd ventured into something that was too deep, even for him. Not only had he been taken advantage of, robbed and beaten, but now, after thinking about it, he'd have to wonder if the two had some disease? He'd been careful. He'd used rubbers last night. But then he remembered something about this morning, just before blacking out. And if that memory was correct…no, he'd blacked out just when it was getting interesting.

He glanced down at himself, at his flute hanging limp between his legs. Christ, he needed to get cleaned up!

The evidence of last night's antics was all throughout the bed sheets. He made a mental note to clean up as much as he could before he called housekeeping. Yet the question of the other man's physical health stole over Brandon like an icy chill. In one night of utterly depraved sex, might he now himself be in danger of carrying a filthy disease?

He rubbed his head where it was throbbing and felt the great lump there, the matted blood in his hair. Had the woman bashed him on the head with something? He glanced at the telephone on the bedside table. It was crooked, as if someone had thrown it down, not caring how it landed.

"Aw, fooooook!" He wanted to hit something but his head hurt too much to move. Add to that the worry that he'd had probably been the recipient of unprotected sex. That thought lay on him like a death sentence as he tried to dismiss it from his mind. No sense worrying over that until he knew if he had something.

In the meantime, there was the matter of his car, confirmed stolen if the empty spot in the parking lot out front said anything, and his missing wallet. He couldn't get away without calling the Shades and reporting both the theft of the car and his wallet. He could try and claim the hotel room was broken into but he had a sinking feeling it wouldn't wash.

First things first. He needed to get clean, so going into the bathroom to step into the shower, he stopped dead in his tracks at the scene before him. Smeared along the mirror over the sink and the clear glass walls of the shower stall were obscenities, written in lipstick, the very shade the woman had worn last night. Christ, he didn't even know their names!

Standing naked in the bathroom, he began to shake, and recognized he was in shock. At least, he figured so, as much as his brain could think just then.

Grabbing the sink for support, he waited until the wave of nausea and dizziness left him. Somewhere, in the deep recesses of his mind, he knew he needed help; this was much more than he could manage on his own. Worse yet, he had pain, low down in his gut, and he couldn't think straight.

In his entire life since the death of his father, Brandon had one person besides his mam he could count on, and that was Big Brother Henry. So before he showered, before he passed out again from shock, fear and injury, he went to the hotel phone and placed the call. No sense looking for his cell phone. He already knew it was gone.

Henry resisted the urge to throw his phone out the window. Of all the idiotic, lame-assed things his brother could have done, Brandon had proved himself to be real bollocks. If Henry didn't care so much about their mam or grandparents, he would have called the Gardai himself. As it was, he said he'd get there as soon as possible but Kinsale wasn't quite next door. It was going to take him the better part of two hours to get there, although with his knowledge of the backroads, he might be able to shorten it a bit. In the meantime, Brandon had been instructed to put a 'do not disturb' sign on the door and clean himself up.

And then Brandon had told him about the stolen car. That did it. This wasn't something that could be hushed up and swept under the carpet. They'd need to involve the shades.

"Are ye sure the car's been jammered?" Henry had asked him.

"Of course I'm sure. I parked it where I could see it from my room and it's not there. Ye can't miss a yellow car in a sea of white," he'd exclaimed.

"Yellow? Yer not talkin' of Grandda's car are ye? The yellow Mini?"

There had been a very pregnant pause on the other end of the line and then the voice quietly saying, "The very same."

"Dickbrain!" exclaimed Henry, "That car has been in the family since God was a teenager. How could ye let this happen?"

"Well it's not like I planned it, is it now! It was safe where

302

I left it, only I hadn't thought it would be taken like it was."

Henry had to give him that. They all loved that little car; had all learned to drive behind its wheel, everyone, from Henry on down to Ciara. It was a forty-year old car that his grandda had bought when new; when he had loved the colour yellow and thought everything he owned should be yellow. Well, mused Henry, it wouldn't be hard to identify it. He'd never seen another car anywhere, quite that shade. It was like a lemon on wheels without the connotation that lemons and cars usually had when put together. That little car could do anything.

And now it was gone. Hopefully, it could be recovered and still in one piece.

He finally got off the phone with his brother and resisted the urge to flatten something. He'd love to flatten his brother but figured he was likely already in a bad way. As he climbed into his car to make the trek to Kinsale, he dialed his wife, Siobhan, to tell her the news, thanking the fact that he'd had Niall install a hand's free calling system for him in the vehicle.

"He did what?" Her voice was not as shocked as it was tired. They were all tired of Brandon's antics. He'd been in trouble since the day he was born but without Henry knowing anything else about the situation, only that whomever Brandon had slept with last night had clocked him a good one and stolen him blind, he couldn't yet fully express his opinion.

"I don't know everything yet although I expect we'll find

303

out soon enough."

"So you're heading there now?"

"I am," he said as he pulled through the roundabout on the way to Cork. "It's sorry I am that I likely won't be at Emily's birthday supper tonight. I doubt I'll be back in time. I'll make it up to her when I get back," he offered.

Emily, his half-sister's daughter. Em's mother, Meara, had died of a drug overdose and Henry's mam had adopted her. There had been no other family. But as she'd been in Henry's care when Meara died, Henry said he'd raise her, and his busy mom, a nurse and mid-wife with on-call hours, day and night, agreed. Emily had become as dear to him as if she were his own and he truly hated not being there for her birthday. Feckit, but his brother was a gligeen!

"Let me know when ye get there," said Siobhan, and then, "drive carefully. I know you're pissed. So am I. But I love ye, so take it easy like, eh?"

"Right then. Love ye, too," said Henry as he signed off. He suddenly felt every one of his thirty-eight years.

END OF EXCERPT

Brandon: Bad Boy of Kinsale is the third installment of the O'Farrell Legacy series and is now available.

www.smcross.net

ABOUT THE AUTHOR

The daughter of an Air Force family, and therefore an extensive world traveler, Ms. Cross has been writing since the age of fifteen, creating stories around the places she has lived and visited. After writing an editorial column for a newspaper for fifteen years, she is now retired and living in Canada's north with her children, grandchildren and an assortment of cats and dogs.

BOOKS BY THE AUTHOR

The O'Farrell Legacy Series:
Mulligan's Dream
Double Take
Brandon: Bad Boy of Kinsale
A Winter Sky
C'Mere to Me

a chroi	(uh kree) my heart
a mhac	(uh wak) my son
a stor	(uh shtor - like 'store' with an 'h added) my treasure
An bpósfaidh tú mé?	(on bohs-ee thoo may) Will you marry me?
banjaxed	broken, usually irreparable
bean sidhe	banshee – In Irish folklore, the Bean Sidhe (woman of the hills) is a spirit or fairy who presages a death by wailing.
black stuff	Guinness
bowsie	thug, scumbag, wife-beater
box	vagina
boyo	boy, lad
cáilin	(colleen) girl
chipper	a place for burgers or fish 'n chips
chubbed	erection
Claddagh	a design on a ring, of two hands clasping a crowned heart between them
clot-heid	(clot-hade) cloth head - another word for idiot, more Scottish than Irish but used all the same
cop on	smarten up, leave off, settle down, etc.
craic	(crack) fun
eejit	idiot
fáilte	(FAHL-cheh) welcome - also the National Tourism Development

306

	Authority
fella	your guy, partner/husband/ boyfriend
flange/fanny	women's genitals
flute	penis
gabh transna ort fhéin	(gave tras orth hayn) go fuck yourself - literal - 'go sideways on yourself'
Garda/Gardai	police, also called shades
Gligeen	stupid person
gobsmacked	surprised
gonch	underwear
Gráim thú	(ghraw hoo) I love you
grá mo chroi	(yraw muh kree) Love of my heart
hoer	(Dutch) whore
horned up	horny
Is tú mo ghrá	(Is too moh Greah - the eah like in "yeah") I love you
jammered	stolen
jarveys	men who drive the jaunting cars
kip	sleep
lack	girlfriend
lad	penis
langer	multiple meanings – in the books it is sometimes used as a term for penis, as are 'lad' and 'flute'
loo	toilet
manky	dirty, flithy, disgusting
mo cáilin	(muh colleen) – my girl
mo chroi	(muh kree) my heart
mo chuisle	(muh kishla) my pulse
mo dheartháir	(Muh ghrih-hawr) my brother
moggie	cat
nads/clackers	gonads; balls

neddy   idiot, fool
Oiche mhaith agus codladh sámh (EE-hyeh
WY(h) ogg-uss KOLL-oo SAA-oo) good night
                 and sleep well
pennyboy   menial worker
plonker   country bumpkin, slow on the
                 uptake
póg mo thóin'   (pogue muh hone) kiss my ass
poot   (Dutch) homosexual man
ráicleach/raaklochk (rack lock)   slut
shandy   beer mixed with another drink -
                 lemonade, ginger ale, etc.
skank   untrustworthy, low-life criminal
                 type
sláinte   (slawnt-ye) health
sláinte mhaith   (slawnt-ye wa) good health
Striapach   whore
Tá tú go h-álainn.(TAW too guh HAW-linn)
                 you are beautiful
Táim I ngrá leat (TAW-im ing graw let)
                 I'm in love with you
thick   extremely stupid ('brick' is also
                 used)
wankers/gormless   idiots